Too Charming

Too Charming

Kathryn Freeman

Where heroes are like chocolate – irresistible!

Copyright © 2013

Penrose   Drive, Camberley, Surrey GU15 2AR, UK
                        www.choc-lit.com

A CIP catalogue record for this book is available
from the British Library

ISBN 978-1-78189-234-3

Printed and bound by
Clays Limited, Bungay, Suffolk NR35 1ED

To my men. My sons, who put up with their mother's weird desire to write about romance. And my husband, who didn't laugh too loudly when I said I wanted to give up work and write. He told me to go for it.

This book is your fault!

Acknowledgements

This book started with my parents, who always told me I could do anything I put my mind to. Thank you Mum (and Dad, because I know you're still watching over me).

Special thanks also to Helen and Maureen – two wonderful bosses who supported my crazy ambition to write romantic fiction.

Encouragement from friends and family has helped to keep me going. To my work colleagues from Stockley Park, Bagshot, Zurich and North America, David and Jayne, Charlotte, Michele, Priti, Sonia and Gill, my other Mum and Dad, my lovely Northern relies from Fleetwood – thank you all for your incredible support.

Too Charming would not have been the book it is today without the insightful advice from the Romantic Novelists' Association New Writers' Scheme, the guidance of my wonderful editor or the help of Jane, Emma and Caroline who were kind enough to plough through an early draft.

Finally, *Too Charming* would not have been published were it not for Choc Lit and their Tasting Panel. A heartfelt thank you to Georgina W, Stephanie B, Christine Mc, Lucy M, Elke N, Liz R, Caroline P and Jane T for giving me this opportunity.

You enabled my dream to come true.

Chapter One

At the sight of the tall, dark, handsome man climbing off the running machine, Megan's heart sank. Not, perhaps, the most usual of female reactions. Then again, there was nothing usual, or normal, about her reaction to Scott Armstrong. He made her nervous, pure and simple. It was hard for her to admit that. As a woman fast approaching thirty, she had enough experience dealing with members of the opposite sex to remain unflustered in the presence of one. Except, it seemed, when it came to Scott Armstrong.

Megan glanced at her watch and heaved out a sigh, knowing she'd cocked up her timings again. Scott visited the gym religiously between 6 a.m. and 7 a.m. every morning. It was the reason she'd stopped going so early. Until the last few days, that was, when she seemed to have suffered temporary amnesia. It was said that sleep deprivation caused the brain to turn to mush, and she must be living proof. It was time she got a better grip on that work–life balance everyone kept harping on about. Perhaps someone could persuade the criminals to have a couple of weeks off so she could catch up.

With a rising sense of alarm she studied the man now strolling confidently towards her. A man she was more used to encountering inside the Crown Court. He was attractive, certainly. Okay, strictly speaking she guessed *attractive* didn't do him justice. He was strikingly handsome. Steel-grey eyes, an athletic body, dark silky hair and cheekbones so sharp a woman could cut her finger on them should she want to trace them. Most of the time, Megan didn't. While, objectively, she could appreciate his beauty, she preferred her men a little more grounded and, well, ordinary. It wasn't that she had a type, just that she knew what she *didn't* like. And that included wildly attractive men who were used to simply crooking their finger and for the women to come running.

'Are you stalking me, DS Taylor?' His voice was deep and faintly amused. The voice of a man who was maddeningly sure of himself.

'The only place I'll be stalking you, Scott Armstrong, is in your dreams.' Her reply wasn't bad, she thought. Cool and uninterested.

Unperturbed, he smiled, the edges of his eyes crinkling. It was a sexy look. Damn, he was sexy. But he knew it, she reminded herself. 'Always, Detective Sergeant,' he replied smoothly. 'You're always in my dreams.'

Subtly he shifted his body so it was blocking her way. His action caused an immediate spike in her heart rate – and her irritation levels. Surely she knew better than to let such a move unsettle her? After all, in her line of work she frequently came across men who tried to intimidate. Men who thought they could use their superior height and power to unnerve and get their way. Then again, those men didn't usually have bodies reminiscent of a Greek God, or a face that could have graced the cover of GQ magazine. 'Your dream sounds more like a nightmare to me,' she replied with a casualness she wasn't quite feeling at that moment. 'Are you going to take your sweaty body out of my way, or do I have to report you for harassment?'

Again he smiled. It was a perfect smile. Almost too perfect. Fleetingly, it had Megan wondering if he practiced it in front of the mirror, but she dismissed the thought as unnecessarily cruel. Just because he was startlingly handsome, it didn't make him vain, though in her experience it did increase the odds.

'I think, secretly, you're here to ogle my legs,' Scott remarked in that deep, gravelly voice of his as he at last moved to let her pass.

From another man's lips those words might have amused her, but from Scott, she simply couldn't be certain he was joking. Deliberately, she raked her gaze down the legs in question. As they were long, lean and muscular, it wasn't a hardship. 'I've seen better legs on a camel.'

A grin split his face, notching up his attractive-rating even further. 'Lucky camel.'

Then, mimicking her action, he flicked a slow gaze over her legs. Though the desire to turn and run was almost unbearable, she held her ground. Her legs were good. Okay, make that goodish. Either way, she was more comfortable when they were under wraps.

'You, on the other hand,' he continued in his soft, deep, voice, 'have the legs of a graceful gazelle.'

A deep blush scalded her cheeks and she huffed out a breath. So much for her show of indifference. Still, it was a good time to remind herself that words came too easily to men like Scott. It was superficial flattery, nothing more, and she had a pretty good idea where he could shove it. 'Look, if we've finished with the zoology, I've got a workout to complete before my daughter wakes up.' The thought of six-year-old Sally, still tucked up in bed at the home they shared with her parents, helped calm her racing pulse.

Nodding, he took the towel from around his neck and wiped the beading sweat from his brow. Megan caught herself watching the play of his strong biceps as he moved the towel back and forth, and hastily looked back up at his face.

'Well, I'll see you in court.' He paused, looking back at her. 'I take it you'll be there this morning?'

'Oh yes. I'll be there to see Stuart Matthews put away in prison for a long, long time. Where he belongs. Where he should have been sent two years ago.' She was still pissed that Scott, acting as Matthews' defence barrister, had managed to get the weasel off on a technicality the last time he'd faced a jury. If he'd been found guilty and put away then, as he damn well should have been, he wouldn't have gone on to rob the four post offices he was being tried for that day. Instead he'd have been behind bars and the post office staff would have had a normal, though in all likelihood pretty dull, day in the office. At least one where they wouldn't have had to suffer a sawn-off shotgun shoved in their faces.

Scott simply shrugged, clearly unimpressed with her rant. 'We'll see. Loser buys the drinks, eh?'

Megan didn't bother to reply.

Scott watched as Megan strode away from him, head held high, her delicious bottom moving sensuously from side to side as she walked towards the step machine. He was damned if he knew what it was about Detective Sergeant Megan Taylor that always fired him up. Perhaps it was her no-nonsense, ballsy approach to life. The fact that she always gave as good as she got. Many times, he had to concede, she gave better. Her face wasn't bad, either. Generally he preferred blondes, but her short, pixie-like dark hair and flashing blue eyes weren't to be sneezed at. Then there was her body. Again, he'd put himself down as more of a voluptuous curves man, but her petite, slim, boyish figure definitely caught his attention.

As she climbed on to the machine she glanced his way and caught him staring. With a haughty glare she cut him dead. Smothering a laugh, Scott turned away and ambled towards the weights. That was it, in a nutshell. What really made him hot under the collar was Megan's attitude. The lady was most definitely a challenge. Maybe he really was as arrogant as she'd frequently told him, but it was a fact that women generally fawned over him. He didn't kid himself it was because of who he was. No, they were only interested in what they saw. The slick, well-paid barrister. The good-looking man. Underneath all that? Suffice to say that if they knew something of the emotional baggage he carried around with him, they probably wouldn't be so keen to get him into bed. Still, it suited Scott. He wasn't interested in long-term relationships. He preferred the ease of a quick affair. New, passionate, exciting. Moving on before things got stale.

Scott finished his workout with his usual 2k on the rowing machine, making it in just under seven minutes. A personal best. Feeling ridiculously pleased with himself, he headed off to the changing room and the rewards of a hot shower. As he let the steaming jets pummel his body, he wondered absently if his improved performance was down to the fact that he was getting fitter, or if it perhaps had something to do with the very occasional glances Megan had shot him when she thought he wasn't looking. He was a man, after all, and as every man knew, there was nothing like the attention of a hot woman to spur him into action.

After toweling off and dragging on some clean jogging bottoms and a fresh T-shirt, he headed out to his car, glancing at his watch. Still only 7.30 a.m. The early morning gym session was a killer, but getting exercise out of the way and still having plenty of time before court went a long way towards making the pain worthwhile. Opening the boot of the sports car, he unconsciously ran his hands across the sleek, shiny bodywork. She really was a work of art. Well worth the crippling loss from his bank account. After dumping the sports bag into the laughably small boot – definitely not the car for a family man – he eased into the driver seat and started the engine, grinning like a fool at the resulting roar.

Maneuvering out of the car park, Scott began to focus his mind on the day ahead. First a trip home to change, then off to court. A place he seemed to spend most of his life, in between occasional visits to chambers and fleeting hours of sleep. Today he had a pretty strong feeling he was going to be on the losing side. It wasn't something he particularly enjoyed, but it was hard to argue against evidence when it was so damning. Of course he'd play his part in court, give his client the best defence he could, but on this occasion it looked like the police had done their job. No doubt Mr Matthews would be looking at a pretty lengthy spell in jail after today.

And Scott would owe sexy DS Taylor a drink. There were worse ways to console himself after losing a case.

He was often asked how he felt about defending cases like this, where the evidence was so strongly supportive of guilt. To Scott, it wasn't an issue. A man was innocent until proven guilty. Period. His job was to make sure the prosecution team could prove that guilt with solid, tamper-proof evidence. As he saw it, he was the last line of defence. The last chance to highlight any holes in the evidence, to pick out flaws in the witness statements. He wasn't interested in convicting the guilty. He wanted to make sure the innocent didn't lose their freedom. And sometimes they did, as Scott knew only too well.

'We find the accused, Stuart Matthews, guilty as charged.'

On hearing the jury's verdict, Megan felt a warm buzz of satisfaction. This was what the job was all about. Putting away the bad guys. All the hours she'd spent on the case, gathering the evidence, interviewing the witnesses. It was finally worth it. One less villain on the streets. One less person to cause harm to others.

Gathering her things together, Megan congratulated the prosecutor on a job well done and immediately went to phone Ann. A colleague and close friend, Ann had worked with her on the Matthews case and would no doubt be anxiously pacing her office, waiting for the verdict.

'Well hallelujah!' Ann greeted the news with a deep sigh of relief. 'Of course, he should have been pronounced guilty two years ago.'

'Don't remind me.'

'Still, at least the sexy but slippery Armstrong couldn't work his Houdini act a second time. You got your man, Megan. We should have a drink to celebrate after the dance class this week. What do you think?'

'If you're buying, I think I agree.' After ending the call,

Megan walked out of court with a warm glow of contentment. This had all the makings of a great day.

'Congratulations, DS Taylor, I believe I owe you a drink.'

At the sound of Scott's deep, rich voice, Megan bit back a rueful smile. It appeared drinks were like buses. She'd not been invited for one for ages, but now she was flooded with invitations. This one, though, she was going to pass on. 'Thanks, but no thanks.'

That should have been the end of it, but once more she found him blocking her way, just as he had at the gym that morning. The cocky grin was still in place, too, though it was pretty much all that remained of the man she'd traded insults with earlier. The workout gear was gone, replaced with a sharp charcoal suit, though worn with the same nonchalant swagger as his shorts and training vest. His dark hair, hidden in court under a barrister wig, was now uncovered and slightly rumpled. It should have looked untidy. How typical that it gave him a rakish air instead.

As if aware of her thoughts, he threaded his hand through the thick waves and laughed softly at her succinct refusal. 'You wouldn't be scared by any chance?'

Because she was, she ignored his question and went on the attack. 'Chatting me up is just a giant joke to you, isn't it?'

For a brief moment he looked confused. 'Why do you say that?'

'I'm hardly your type.' He was hardly her type, either. Men as good looking as him didn't stick with women like her. At least not in the long run.

He raised a dark eyebrow. 'So I have a type now, do I? That's news to me.'

'I'm pretty certain single mothers or police detectives don't fall under your usual target profile. Just as defence lawyers don't come under mine.'

In her opinion they were a necessary evil, similar to smear tests and dental appointments. Unavoidable, but it didn't mean she had to like them. In fact when she thought of the hours of manpower that went into getting a criminal to court, only to have a barrister like Scott let them wriggle off the hook, it was another reason not to like the man.

With his amused grey eyes calmly fixed on hers, he reached out a finger and carelessly stroked her cheek. 'You're trying to use logic to understand something that defies logic. One of these days, Megan, you'll forget to think and just go with your instincts. Then you'll find out how incredible it could be between us.'

At his touch, shivers of awareness rippled through her. Quickly she stepped back. 'Don't count on it,' she replied stiffly, fleeing down the steps, away from him. When she'd reached what she deemed was a safe distance, she paused and glanced back over her shoulder. He was still watching her. On a whim, she spun round to face him.

'How can you do what you do?' she asked, genuinely puzzled.

He looked nonplussed. 'What, law?'

'No, defend scum like you did today, even though you know damn well they're as guilty as hell.'

Scott gave a nonchalant shrug. 'Everyone is entitled to a defence.'

'I know, but how do you sleep at night when you win a case you know you shouldn't? When you free a criminal who should be locked away?'

'It's simple. If the police do their job properly, the bad men get locked up.' There was a thread of irritation in his usually smooth voice.

'Not always,' she returned sharply. 'Sometimes a clever lawyer can get in the way of true justice.'

'Yeah and sometimes a clever lawyer can stop an innocent man from going down for a crime he didn't commit,' he retorted equally sharply.

His brief flare of emotion surprised her, but it disappeared as quickly as it had arrived. In its place was the cool, slightly mocking expression she was used to. 'Much as I'm enjoying this little conversation, I'm afraid I've got to go.' Once more he turned on his smile as he made his way down towards her. 'We'll take a rain check on the drink then? Better get it in quick though. Next time, no doubt, it will be you doing the buying, to congratulate me.'

Before her infuriated brain could think of a suitable reply, he was off, striding past her, a tall, broad-shouldered man wearing an expensively tailored suit and a cloak of staggering self-assurance.

Chapter Two

The phone on Scott's cluttered desk sprang to life, the ring interrupting his train of thought. He swore under his breath. Hadn't he asked the clerk to hold all calls this morning? Wading through great hulking textbooks of case law was bad enough without the disruption of the damn phone.

'Yes, Penny,' he barked unthinkingly into the receiver. Silence hit him, forcing him to restock and take a deep, controlling breath. He'd worked with Penny long enough now to know she was reliable, uncomplaining and highly efficient. Also to know that he couldn't manage without her. He started again. 'Sorry, what I meant to say was, how can I help?'

He heard the smile in her voice. 'I know you asked not to be disturbed, but I've got Nancy on the line, anxious to speak to you about a new case. I thought you wouldn't mind being disturbed for her.'

Acknowledging that he needed to add wise to Penny's list of attributes, Scott settled back in his beloved antique brown leather chair – he hated modern office furniture with a vengeance – and waited for the call to come through. Nancy was a solicitor, former lover, great friend and now, increasingly, the source of many of his clients. Someone he was, indeed, happy to be disturbed for. 'Nancy. How the devil are you?'

'All the better for speaking to you.'

He could picture her sitting in her office, blonde hair tied up in a prim bun, tortoiseshell glasses on the tip of her nose. They'd met while he was training for the Bar. Ten years older than him, she'd taught him many things, not all of them to do with law. Thankfully, when they'd parted ways as lovers, they'd managed to remain friends. 'What's this about a new case coming my way?' he asked, looking wistfully at the diving brochure on his desk. One of these days he *was* going to take that holiday.

'You're going to love this one, Scott. It's just up your street. The client is Kevin Rogers, currently remanded in police custody, accused of raping a prostitute.' He grimaced. 'I'll love this why, exactly?'

'Because Kevin claims the police are trying to stitch him up. He's had a few previous run-ins with them, once over a similar incident. On that occasion the victim changed her story before it came to court. Now, miraculously, another victim has come to light. Kevin swears blind it was consensual.'

Scott sighed and ran a hand through his hair. God, he needed a haircut. As well as a holiday. Not necessarily in that order. He knew why Nancy wanted him to take this case, or indeed any case to do with alleged miscarriages of justice by the police. It was fast becoming his specialty. 'Okay, let me talk to him.' He flicked through his diary. Maybe one day he would have a week with nothing more on than a round of golf. Maybe one day he could become a fat-cat lawyer, something he'd heard existed but was damned if he'd ever witnessed. 'Frankly, the best time for me is probably this lunchtime. Today is a good day. Otherwise we're looking at the end of the month.'

'Lunchtime works for me. He's still being held at the station. I'll see you there. Shall we say noon?' There was a pause as he imagined her typing the appointment into her electronic calendar. 'How busy are your evenings then, Mr Hotshot Barrister? Too busy to share a meal with an old friend?'

Instinctively Scott started to sigh, a reaction unlikely to go down well with the person on the other end of the phone, so he quickly tried to smother it. The trouble was, he had a nagging feeling that friendship wasn't all Nancy had in mind. Lately, ever since she'd split from her last boyfriend, she'd been a little too flirtatious for his liking. He might have been interested once, but that had been a long time ago and he had no intention of going there again. Mind you, that didn't mean he couldn't take her out to dinner, he reasoned. He just had to make the ground rules clear. Besides, the amount of cases she was putting his way, she was practically paying his salary. 'I'm never too busy for you,' he replied smoothly, playing the part she expected of him. 'By the way, who is the detective in charge of the Rogers case?'

'It's not Megan Taylor, if that's what you're angling for.'

Caught red handed, Scott could do nothing but laugh. Nancy certainly had the measure of him. 'Guilty as charged. I'll see you down at the station shortly.'

As he put down the phone, Scott tried to ignore the nagging sense of disappointment at the knowledge that he wouldn't be sparring against the sexy Detective Sergeant on this one. Not that he was surprised. He had a sense that Megan was a police officer who did things properly, by the book. One who was honest to the core and would never be seen misusing her power. Officers like that did exist. In fact, the vast majority of the police force were decent people trying to do a very difficult job. He knew that, just as he knew that it was past experience that soured his view, making him more than a touch cynical. It stood him in good stead when he was defending his clients. Alas, it didn't help in his relations with the police in general, or a hot-looking DS in particular.

Megan was walking through the doors of the station and into the welcome fresh air when her mobile rang. Absently she answered it, her mind more focused on the steaming cup of real coffee she was about to get her hands on than the person on the other end of the phone. Proper coffee was something she'd spent the morning dreaming about as she'd sipped at the dark sludge from the station vending machines. Seconds after taking the call, however, Megan was sitting on the station steps in shock, her legs too unsteady to support her, all thoughts of coffee banished from her mind. With trembling hands she clutched the phone closer to her ear. 'Sorry Dad, speak up. I can't hear you properly. Did you say Mum's fallen down the stairs?'

'Yes, dear, we're at the hospital now.' Before she could picture the worst, her Dad's calm, soothing voice continued. 'They say we haven't to worry, she'll be fine, she's just a bit shaken up. They're checking to see whether she's broken anything.'

'Oh God, poor Mum.' Shutting her eyes, Megan held a hand to her forehead and tried not to picture her mother lying in a crumpled heap at the bottom of the stairs. 'Are you sure she's okay?'

'I'm sure, Meg. She's more embarrassed than anything. You know your mother. She hates to be a burden to anyone.' He cleared his throat. 'She also hates to let you down, but really, I'm not sure we can look after Sally this afternoon. I mean I could leave your mother and pick Sally up but …'

'Don't be ridiculous, Dad,' Megan interrupted quickly. 'You need to stay at the hospital. I'll take care of Sally. You concentrate on looking after Mum.'

After saying their goodbyes, Megan slipped the phone into her pocket and took a deep, shuddering breath. Then she buried her head in her hands, fighting to recover her control. For a minute there, when she'd first heard about the fall … God, she'd thought that was it. That her mother was gone.

Dazed, she tried to get up, but her body was still weak with shock and relief. Sagging back on to the steps she decided to give herself another minute or two before going back inside. The call had shaken her more than she wanted to admit. A harsh reminder not only of how much she loved her parents, but of how much she relied on them.

'Problem?'

Her heart, racing with adrenaline a few moments ago,

sank like a stone in her chest. She wasn't up to another round with Scott Armstrong, not when her defences were down. Raising her head she found his tall, dark figure looming over her, blocking out the sunlight. Steel-grey eyes, usually full of mockery, looked at her with what seemed to be genuine concern. Still, she shook her head. 'No problem.'

His eyes narrowed. 'You're telling me it's your usual practice to sit on the steps of the station with a face as white as a sheet, trembling?'

'Of course it isn't,' she snapped back. It was pure instinct, but still, she was ashamed of her harsh tone. For once Scott was trying to be nice. The least she could do was be civil in return. 'Sorry. My dad's just phoned to say Mum's fallen down the stairs. He's taken her to hospital.'

'Ouch. Is she okay?'

'Yes, apparently she'll be fine, though they're checking to see if she's broken anything.' She took in a deep breath. 'You must think I'm crazy to react like this over a simple fall, it's just that ...' she trailed off. How could she explain to someone as shallow as him what an important role her parents played in her life?

'You've just started to realise they're not young any more.'

His perception took her by surprise. As did the quiet understanding she saw in his eyes. 'Well, yes, I guess I have. They're more than just parents to me. They're my rocks. I live with them. They look after my daughter while I'm at work. Without them ... shit!' She suddenly remembered Sally.

Again he looked at her, waiting for her to elaborate, but she was already preoccupied looking through her mobile phonebook. 'Anything I can help with?'

Once more she shook her head. 'No, thanks.' He was still staring at her, clearly waiting for an explanation. She decided there was no harm in giving him one. 'My parents were going to look after Sally for me this afternoon because I've got to be in court. It's typical that today, of all days, the school is finishing early. Now I'll need to find someone else to look after her.' Glancing down at her watch she swore again, only this time under her breath. 'In just over an hour.' Quickly she got to her feet. 'Excuse me. I've got a lot of phone calls to make.'

'What about Sally's father?'

Megan laughed, though there was nothing remotely funny about that question. 'What father?'

The corner of Scott's lips twitched upwards. 'Well, I'm sure I remember from biology lessons that to make a baby there needs to be an egg and a sperm.'

'Yeah, that part was easy enough,' she acknowledged sourly. 'It was the bit after that he couldn't cope with.' She was about to leave it at that, but realised it sounded bitter and ungracious. 'Sally doesn't have a father, at least not in the usual sense of the word. He's no longer in our lives.'

'That must be hard on you.'

And wasn't that the truth. But she'd had her parents to help, and Sally was easily the best thing that had ever happened to her, so not all that hard, really.

'Look, I can shuffle things around and pick Sally up, if it helps.' The words shot out of Scott's mouth before he had a chance to sanction them. It was only when they were out there, hanging between them, that he wondered where on earth they'd come from. Looking after her kid. Was he nuts? Then again, he thought as he looked at those gorgeous legs peeking out from her skirt, playing the Sir Galahad card wasn't a bad idea. It was bound to get him that little bit closer towards what he wanted. Him and her in bed together. Naked. Actually, he didn't even need the bed part.

Feeling pretty pleased with himself, he glanced over at her, only to find she was gaping at him in open-mouthed astonishment.

'Pick my daughter up?' she repeated slowly, incredulity

dripping off every word. 'You've got to be joking. Aside from the fact that we're always at loggerheads, have you even got any experience with children?'

Okay, maybe she had a point there, but he was damned if he was going to back down now. 'I used to be one,' he countered.

'Umm, in case it's slipped your notice, Sally's a girl.'

Another good point, but Scott was losing interest now. Sure, there might have been an ulterior motive to his offer, but if she didn't trust him to look after her kid for a few hours then she could inconvenience someone else for the afternoon. 'Well, the offer stands.' He shrugged, hoping to convey indifference. 'It's up to you.'

Megan hesitated. She'd known Scott for over a year now and though they were hardly best buddies – on occasions it felt more like mortal enemies – he was a highly respected barrister. At times a very annoying one, true, but one she knew she could trust.

But trusting him to keep her daughter safe was one thing. Letting him meet that very precious part of her life was another. Glancing sideways she caught him casually studying her, the slight smirk indicating he knew where her thoughts were going. Even as her mind circled round the concept, she realised it didn't actually matter what she thought of Scott. The man was a stranger to her daughter. Sally might be a confident little girl, but Megan wasn't so sure she'd be happy to spend the afternoon with a man she didn't know. Even if he was a friend of her mother's. Which, of course, he wasn't. 'Thanks, but I'll give the afterschool club a call. Hopefully they'll have a place for her.'

'Suit yourself.'

Before she had a chance to say anything further, he'd turned his back on her and was striding down the steps. She was left with a view of his rapidly retreating back and an odd impression that she'd upset him. Of course that was highly unlikely. Much more likely was the fact that he was, right now, laughing with relief at his close escape.

Ten minutes and several phone calls later, Megan anxiously looked down at her watch. The afterschool club was apparently full, Ann was tied up with work, the mother of Sally's best friend was off for a long weekend and Megan was fast running out of options. She could just about manage to collect Sally; she wasn't actually due to give evidence in court until around 3 p.m., though the prosecution team wanted her in earlier so she could go through her statement. Then what was she going to do with her?

Barely believing she was doing it, Megan climbed into her car and drove the few miles to the local law chambers where Scott worked. If she had to grovel, she told herself as she parked next to a snazzy sports car, it was best to do it in person. With the countdown to the end of the school day ticking in her head, she dashed over to the impressive old building and rang the bell. Mercifully, when she told the answering clerk who she wanted to see, she was buzzed through. It meant that Scott was still in his chambers. It didn't necessarily mean he would want to see her, or that his offer still stood.

Though she'd been in the chambers before, she couldn't help but be impressed by them all over again. What must it be like to work out of this beautiful Georgian building, rather than the seventies police station where she spent her days? Here the decor was simple and elegant. It spoke of discreet wealth and sophisticated taste. In the police station the decor was functional and drab. It spoke of poor funding and hard-nosed officers.

'DS Taylor.'

Megan assumed the lady sitting at the desk in the reception area must be the clerk. Middle-aged, slightly portly and very smartly dressed, she looked highly efficient. Not, Megan thought with a small smile to herself, Scott's idea of his ideal clerk. That was probably someone younger, blonder, with pneumatic bosoms and a plunging cleavage. She doubted this lady flashed her cleavage at anyone. Not even her husband.

'I wasn't aware you had an appointment?'

'Err, no, I don't actually,' Megan stumbled over her words. God, she hated asking for favours. Especially when she knew she would probably live to regret it. 'But I was hoping Scott would be able to see me anyway?'

The lady nodded, though not a single hair on her immaculate head moved. 'I'm sure he will. He's in his office. I'll just ring and let him know you're here.'

'If you don't mind, can I just go through?' Megan didn't want to take the risk that Scott would fob her off through the clerk.

'Sure, go right ahead. His office is the first on the left.'

As Megan crossed the expensive wine-red carpet, she was annoyed to find her pulse racing erratically. For the first time in her many encounters with Scott, she felt firmly on the back foot. A fact that made her even more uncomfortable than usual. Taking in a deep breath, she knocked on his door.

'Come in.' Scott's deep voice resonated through the woodwork.

Sitting at a large, old-fashioned desk, Scott didn't immediately look up when she entered, so Megan stood in the doorway and took the opportunity to study his surroundings. And him. The room was traditionally furnished, with solid antique furniture and warm red walls. Scott had taken off his jacket but was still wearing his white court shirt, though the top buttons were open and the collar carelessly discarded on a nearby chair. Cufflinks had also been abandoned and his shirt sleeves were rolled up to reveal tanned and muscular forearms.

Ignoring the prickle of awareness, she cleared her throat. 'Sorry to disturb you.'

Scott looked up with a start. Clearly she was the very last person he'd expected. 'Detective,' he drawled, pushing back against his chair. 'To what do I owe this honour?'

'I was wondering.' She looked down to find with horror that she was wringing her hands. For goodness sake, just ask him and be done with it. 'Does your offer to look after Sally still stand?'

Scott smiled to himself. Ah, so that's what she was after. No wonder she was looking so anxious. Still damnably hot, but anxious nonetheless. 'Pretty desperate now, huh?' he asked, knowing full well that if she'd had to come back to him, every one of her usual fallback options must have failed. He had absolutely no doubt he was at the very bottom of her *only in dire emergencies, if every other person I know can't help out* list.

He watched as she opened her mouth, clearly about to protest. Then she shut it again and shifted awkwardly. 'As a matter of fact, yes.'

A slow grin slid across his face. 'Well, it seems I finally have you right where I want you, DS Taylor.'

'Oh? Where, exactly, is that?'

'In need of my help. Prepared to agree to anything in order to get it.'

Megan stared back in astonishment. 'Don't tell me the offer to look after Sally was just part of your plan to get me into bed?' Her tone was scathing, her look withering. Then she shook her head, as if she had trouble believing he'd actually said what he had. That made two of them, Scott thought glumly. 'Well, I tell you what. Forget it.' She turned and headed for the door.

'What about Sally?' Scott asked, in between cursing himself and his big mouth. Sometimes he took this cocky git persona too far.

'I'll manage.'

Exhaling in frustration he reached behind her to the handle, stopping her from opening the door. 'If you'll just calm down for a minute, Megan.'

'I am calm,' she bit back, turning to face him. 'Now, if you don't mind, I have a daughter to pick up.'

Feeling like the lowlife she thought him to be, he stepped immediately away. 'Look, I didn't mean anything by my earlier remark. It was a stupid joke.' He knew his voice carried a hint of desperation, but that's how he felt. 'If you still need my help, I'm happy to give it.'

'And what do you expect in return?'

He closed his eyes briefly. 'I repeat. It was a joke,' he replied heavily, moving away and thrusting his hands into his trouser pockets. 'I expect nothing in return,' he continued flatly. 'Absolutely nothing, not even your thanks.'

Megan studied him, struggling to decide whether she should leave Sally in his care. 'Well of course you'll have my thanks,' she replied carefully. 'I'd be really grateful, it's just …'

'You won't be grateful enough to buy me a drink. Yeah, I get it.' He stalked back to his desk and grabbed his jacket. 'Come on then. Let's go and collect your daughter.'

Following him back through the chambers, acutely aware of his rigid shoulders and battling to keep up with his punishingly long strides, Megan found herself wondering if maybe Scott Armstrong wasn't quite as thick skinned as she'd originally thought. What he'd said had been unbelievably crass, but right now he had all the bearings of a man who'd just been mortally offended.

Chapter Three

Driving through the busy traffic towards the school, Megan kept glancing sideways at Scott. The closer she got, the more she started to doubt her sanity – and her instincts as a mother. Could she really leave Scott, a man she might trust – but barely liked – in charge of her *daughter*? Sure, Sally wouldn't come to any harm with him, but what was she going to think, being bundled off with someone she'd never met before? As she pulled into the school car park, Megan made up her mind. She was going to tell him thanks, but no thanks. She'd take Sally with her to court. Take her chances on finding a spare office and a kind court official.

'Having second thoughts?'

Scott raked her with his cool, sardonic gaze. Damn the man. He knew bloody well what she'd been thinking and now, in order to back out, she'd have to admit he was right. Call her pathetic, but that really galled.

As they climbed out of the car, she was saved an immediate reply by the appearance of Sally. As always, just seeing her daughter was enough to lift her heart. One sock up, one down, her blouse hanging out of her skirt, half her dark hair falling out of the plaits she'd painstakingly put together this morning. No, not the smartest pupil in the school, but she'd defy anyone to say she wasn't the most gorgeous.

'Mum.' Clearly expecting to see her grandparents, Sally dashed over to her and flung her arms around her neck. 'Why are you here?'

Scott watched the interaction between mother and daughter with interest. Sally looked so much like a tiny version of her mother – it was incredible. Whoever the father was, he clearly featured as little in the genetic makeup of his child as he did in her life. The dark hair, big blue eyes and dimpled smile were all there, only in miniature. Scott would bet his bottom dollar that outside work Megan was probably as untidy as hell, just like it appeared her daughter was.

'Grandma's had a little accident.' Megan was saying, bending down to Sally's height. 'She'll be fine but she and Grandad can't look after you today.'

Sally nodded, taking it all in. 'So what's going to happen to me? Will you come home?'

'Well ...'

'Your Mum has got to answer some questions in court today.' Scott bent down so he, too, was eye level with Sally. 'I'm Scott, a friend of your mum. Pleased to meet you.' Unsure how he should greet a kid, he stuck with adult rules and held out his hand.

Sally frowned and glanced up at her mother.

'I think he's expecting you to shake his hand, Sally,' Megan replied dryly. 'It's what grownups do when they meet each other.'

Smiling shyly, Sally put her small hand in his and shook.

'The thing is,' Scott continued. 'We wondered, while your mum's in court, if you wouldn't mind looking after me for a bit. You know, maybe take me to the park? Make sure I don't get into trouble. That sort of thing.' Sally giggled. 'You don't need looking after.'

'I might do when I get to the park. It's been a long time since I've been on a slide.'

Listening to Scott, Megan found her mouth opening and closing like a goldfish. Where was the awkwardness she'd expected from him? It seemed the bachelor barrister had a surprisingly good rapport with children. At least if her grinning daughter was anything to go by.

'Okay. I'll look after you at the park.'

At Sally's happy agreement, Scott shot Megan a look laced with barefaced triumph. It left her with a strong desire to scream, something he obviously guessed, from the amusement that danced in his eyes. But as she silently fumed next to him, she knew she was powerless to do anything other than accept the situation. Sally had just happily agreed to go to the park with him. It was exactly what Megan herself had wanted half an hour ago. So why did it now feel as if she'd seized defeat from the jaws of victory?

'Well, if you're sure ...' she began, but even as she said the words, Scott and Sally were walking back towards the car, chatting away as if they'd known each other for years. Megan made a mental note: have a word with Sally about being won over so quickly by handsome and charming boys.

A short while later, Scott glanced down at his temporary charge as she watched her mother disappear through the court doors. Outwardly at least, she didn't seem too concerned. It was he who was anxiously twitching his fingers, wracking his brain for something to say. Megan's earlier words came floating back to him. He didn't have any experience of dealing with children. Scarily true. As an only child, he didn't have nieces or nephews to practice the finer points of childcare on. In fact, he couldn't remember the last time he'd actually spoken to a child, since he'd been one himself. Then he looked again at Sally. She was six years old, for goodness sake. How difficult could it be?

'Did you have a good morning at school?' he tried as they walked away from the court.

She nodded her head. 'I suppose it was good – for school.'

That made him laugh. 'What would be a good morning if you weren't at school?'

A slight frown formed across her face while she carefully considered his question. 'Watching cartoons, eating pancakes and taking Dizzy for a walk.'

'Dizzy?'

'My dog. She's black and white and Mum says she hasn't got all her marbles. That means she's a bit crazy.'

'Ahh.' Eyeing up a break in the traffic, he was about to dash across the road before he realised his responsibilities. Instead he sedately walked the several yards to the zebra crossing. 'And what would make a good afternoon when you're not at school?'

This time Sally grinned, her dimples coming out in full force. 'Eating ice cream and going to the park.'

Laughing, he helped her cross the road. 'Well, Princess Sally, today your wish is my command.'

She giggled again and he couldn't help but think how refreshing it was that at least one of the female Taylors laughed at his jokes.

It had been decades since Scott had been to a children's park, but it quickly became apparent that in those intervening years the swings and slides had shrunk and were now too small for him. Undaunted he managed a go on the mini-assault course, leaving Sally in stitches as he attempted to balance on the two-foot-high tightrope.

'No, you do it like this, silly,' she told him, and proceeded to nip across the rope with all the poise of a ballerina. Totally at odds with her rather dishevelled appearance.

He threw his hands up in mock despair. 'Okay, you win. Are you ready for a sit down yet?' He was panting, which was crazy. He worked out religiously, for crying out loud, but for some reason he couldn't keep up with a kid on the playground.

As they ambled towards the café, Sally happily chattering away, his mind swung back to Megan. If he managed to fight his way through that prickly exterior of hers, would she be as talkative as her daughter? He wasn't sure if the thought intrigued or terrified him, but he was determined to find out. He understood why she was fighting the attraction, which any fool could see was blazing between them. No woman wanted to be thought of as easy. But surely it was only a matter of time before Megan started listening to her body, instead of her head? As a patient man, he was prepared to give her that time. He figured she'd be worth the wait.

They found themselves a seat in the little café. Red and white checked plastic table covers, wooden chairs and walls covered with bright posters. It was more cosy than chic, and a long way from his usual hang out. Its one redeeming quality was that it was right opposite the court should anything go disastrously wrong.

'What are you going to have?' Scott asked Sally.

'Chocolate ice cream with chocolate sprinkles,' came the immediate reply. There was a small hesitation, and then a quickly added, 'Please.'

Scott relayed her request to the pretty young waitress, and was adding a black coffee for himself when he thought: damn it. When was the last time he'd enjoyed an ice cream? 'And make that two chocolate ice creams.'

'Both with sprinkles?' The waitress was eyeing him with undisguised amusement.

Feeling slightly embarrassed, Scott nodded. 'Why the heck not.' Today was clearly a day for tripping down memory lane to his childhood. Not that he wanted to go too far down that particular path.

'You're funny,' Sally told him, watching him with her vivid blue eyes.

He was about to ask her if that was funny as in he made her laugh, or funny as in odd, but decided against it on the grounds that he might not like the answer.

'Do you work with my mummy?' Sally asked as the waitress returned, placing their ice creams in front of them.

As Scott considered how best to reply, the waitress caught his eye and held it for longer than was strictly polite, her message quite clear. After nodding his thanks, Scott turned his attention back to Sally, surprised to find that talking to the little girl held more interest than flirting with the waitress. 'No, I don't work with your mum, not really,' he answered honestly, trying to gauge how much a child might understand of the legal system. Probably as much as the average man on the street. In other words, not a lot. 'She's a police woman. She catches the people who break the law. Some of those people then go to court where a judge and a group of people called a jury decide if there is enough evidence to prove that they did what the police say they did. If they agree there is enough proof, the judge decides how to punish them. Sometimes by putting them in prison.' Her bright eyes were still looking at him with enough focus to indicate she understood what he was saying. 'I'm a lawyer, specialising in defence. It's my job to question the evidence the police have. To put the other side to the story. To show the jury there could be another explanation for what happened. That way, when they are making up their minds whether the person is guilty or not, they do it with all the facts.'

'Is that where Mummy is now? In the court with the judge?'

'Yes, that's right. She's telling the judge and the jury what she saw. Giving evidence.'

'Will she be finished soon?'

He looked at his watch, wondering how long it would take a six year old to eat an ice cream. Probably not long enough. 'It's hard to say. These things don't always run to a strict time.' A hint of worry crept into her face. 'But I'm sure she'll be with you as soon as she can.'

Seemingly satisfied with his answer, Sally tucked back into her ice cream. He couldn't help but smile at the mess she was making, with melted chocolate dripping from the spoon on to the table, and over most of her face. 'I thought you were meant to eat ice cream through your mouth, not absorb it through your skin.'

Giggling again, she stuck out a chocolate-coated tongue at him and tried to rub at her face.

'Here, let me do that.' Taking hold of a serviette he tried to dab at her mouth. 'You know, this is really a job for mums.'

'What about dads? Can they wipe faces?'

He finished wiping her clean and leant back in his chair, using the time to consider his reply. He had to admit that the simple question had him momentarily flummoxed, not a feeling he was used to. 'I'm not sure,' he replied cautiously. 'I've never been one so I don't really know.'

'I don't know either. I don't have a dad.'

Okay, so how was he supposed to deal with that one?

'My friends all have a dad,' Sally continued, saving him the trouble, 'but they don't seem to do much. They go out to work mainly.'

'Yes, that's what dads do, I guess,' he agreed, his brain desperately trying to find another, less stressful, topic.

'My mum has to work because I don't have a dad.'

'Well, a lot of mums work anyway, even if there is a dad.' He figured Megan would be pleased with his answer to that one.

'I guess they do.' Sally looked solemnly into his eyes. 'When I get older I'm going to work so Mum doesn't have to.'

Oh, crikey. At the sincerity of her words, and the sentiment behind them, he felt his chest tighten. Hastily he grabbed for his coffee and took a sip. 'What job do you want to do?' he asked, moving the conversation on to safer ground.

She licked the final remnants of ice cream off her spoon. 'I want to catch the bad people, like Mum does.' Then she cocked her head to one side and considered him. 'Or maybe I'll be a lawyer, like you.'

He almost choked on the coffee. So much for safer ground. Talking to kids was like walking across a tightrope. Just when you thought you'd got your balance, a gust of wind came along and knocked you off. 'I'm not so sure your mother would approve of you becoming a lawyer,' he muttered under his breath, gulping down the rest of his drink.

'Why not?'

Utterly charmed by her, he struggled to hold back his

laughter. There was no doubt about it, she was damned good with the questions. In fact, she had all the hallmarks of an excellent lawyer. 'Perhaps you should ask your mum that,' he replied evasively, then swiftly changed the subject. Again. 'So, what do you want to do now? We can go over to the court and wait on the steps, or stay here and have another drink.' He eyed her speculatively. 'Maybe if we ask the waitress nicely, she'll find us some paper and we can do some drawing.'

'Will Mum know where we are?'

He nodded. 'Yes, she told me she'd come here when she was finished.'

'I want to stay and draw then.' She pushed out her bottom lip. 'I'm not very good though.'

'Well, that's okay, I can teach you.'

'Really?'

The wide-eyed, interested look was back in her eyes, which was a blessed relief. 'Yes, really. I'm pretty good at drawing.'

'Mum says it's bad manners to tell people how good you are. To blow ... something, I can't remember.'

Laughing he called the waitress over. 'To blow your own trumpet.' He quickly ordered two soft drinks and some paper and pencils. 'Yes, that's true, but you tell your mum that when you're as good as I am, it's hard not to.'

Chapter Four

Megan hurried out of court as quickly as she could. Today the trial had run behind schedule. Of course it had. Why hurry things up, just because Sally was being looked after by a man her mother didn't like enough to go out with, but whom she'd just left in sole charge of her daughter? God knows what she'd been thinking. No doubt poor Sally would be bored out of her mind by now. That was the best-case scenario. Worst-case: she was having a tantrum and causing chaos. She even felt a smidgen of sympathy for Scott. Three hours was a long time to look after somebody else's child. Especially when you had no experience with the little treasures.

The straight skirt and high shoes she was wearing – an outfit she only ever suffered for court appearances – weren't exactly helping her progress towards the café where Scott had promised he'd be waiting. Visions of Sally with tears down her cheeks, and an exasperated Scott telling her to pull herself together, shot through her mind as Megan pushed open the door. That was supposing he was still with her, of course, and hadn't decided to dump her in favour of a woman more his own age. No, he might be a womaniser, but even he wouldn't have done that, she told herself firmly. Or would he? Beginning to feel the first clutches of anxiety, she scanned the busy café, looking for a tall, dark-haired man and his small companion. She picked out a young girl, her face looking down at the tabletop with rapt concentration, and almost skipped past her. Narrowing her gaze, she took a harder look. Could that really be Sally? And sitting opposite her, his face a mixture of pleasure and pride, was that actually Scott?

For a moment she stood, stunned. Then, breathing a huge sigh of relief, she meandered as casually as she could down to their table. 'Well, what have you two been up to?'

'Mum, look what I've drawn!' Sally was scrambling down from the table and thrusting several pieces of paper under her nose.

Taking hold of the precious works of art, Megan dutifully studied them. For once she was actually able to make out what her daughter had drawn. 'Hey, these are really good. Is that Dizzy?'

Smiling proudly, Sally nodded her head. 'Scott showed me how to draw a dog. You have to start with circles to get the right portions.'

'Proportions,' Scott interjected, leaning back against his chair and clasping his hands nonchalantly behind his head.

Megan glanced over at him, meeting his smug gaze. He had the look of a man who knew he'd been underestimated but had come out on top.

'That's right, pro-por-tions. Scott's a really good drawer, Mum. He says he's so good he's allowed to ...' She sucked in a breath and recited slowly, 'blow his own trumpet.'

'Did he now?' Once again Megan met Scott's eyes. The smugness slid away, replaced by a sizeable dose of embarrassment. He was trying to hide it, but he was definitely squirming.

'I might have exaggerated a little for comic effect,' he murmured. 'Then again, if you look at what we've drawn ...'

He gave her a crooked grin – one that didn't just light up his face, it reached his eyes and made them glitter. Chewing on her lip, she dragged her gaze away and back to Sally's drawings. She was not going to be charmed by the likes of Scott Armstrong, she reminded herself. She knew better than that. Still, she probably could afford to warm to him slightly. After all, he'd not just looked after her daughter all afternoon. He'd entertained her.

Sifting through all the drawings spread across the table, Megan caught herself grinning at the cartoon animals he'd captured so brilliantly. 'They're very good.'

He quirked an eyebrow at Sally and grinned. 'See, I told you.'

Finding his grin was making her want to smile back, Megan deliberately turned to her daughter. 'What else have you been up to?'

'We went to the park. Scott was too big for the swing, but he had a go on the balancing ropes.'

Again, Megan cast a quick look of surprise at Scott. The funny thing was, she could actually picture him, starched white shirt open at the collar, dark-grey suit crumpled, playing in a kid's park. Although every inch a man, there was still the hint of a boy about him when he smiled.

As she continued to quiz Sally about her afternoon, she became aware of Scott quietly settling the bill. 'Hey, I'll get that.'

He placed a hand on her arm, stopping her from delving into her handbag. 'I've got it.'

She shook her head. 'No, don't be silly. You've been looking after Sally all afternoon. The least I can do is settle this.'

Scott sighed. 'Megan, it's a couple of ice creams and some drinks. Leave it.'

'But I ...'

'You don't want to feel indebted to me, I get it.' He reached for the jacket that was on the back of his chair. 'You're not. I told you before. The slate is clean. Let me settle this.'

Before she had the chance to say anything further he moved towards the door, holding it open for them. Even offended, as he clearly was now, he didn't forget his manners. All part of the charm offensive, she guessed. Thanking him politely, she took hold of Sally's hand and walked with her towards her car. Scott's tall, broad figure strode out ahead of them, the stiff set of his shoulders telegraphing his displeasure. Well, if he wanted to be shirty with her, it was up to him. All she'd done was try and do the decent thing and pay. Clearly Scott was old school. A man who thought a woman's place was at home, ready to greet him after his hard day at work. No doubt she'd be wearing a silk négligée, even in the middle of winter. In Scott's world, allowing a woman to pay the bill probably diminished his manhood.

Scott thrust his hands into his pockets and kept walking. He didn't know why her insistence that she pay for the drinks had thrown him off so much. After all, he was used to her giving him the cold shoulder. But from the moment she'd believed he was going to use her gratitude as a way of getting her into bed, he'd taken offence. It was one thing pursuing someone he believed was attracted to him but didn't want to acknowledge it, and quite another going after a woman who clearly didn't rate him much.

When he reached the car park he turned around, more than ready to say goodbye and get back to the comfort of his normal routine. Children and their prickly mothers were far too complicated for him.

'Mum, can Scott come back to ours for tea?'

Sally was looking up at her mum with pleading eyes and Scott shook off his irritation for long enough to grin to himself. Well now detective sergeant. Let's see how you get out of that one.

'I, umm ...'

Megan flushed, clearly embarrassed. Mean-spirited git that he was, he enjoyed watching her discomfort. Not that it made her look unattractive. Far from it. The blush of red across her cheeks was achingly ... well, if he wasn't a testosterone-fuelled man, he'd go as far as to say it was sweet. Endearing. As were the blue eyes that, at that very moment, implored him to help her out.

Relieved to be in the driving seat once more, he shrugged. 'What? Can I help it if the girls love me? Young and old alike?'

'For Pete's sake.' Megan gave an exasperated snort. 'Sally, of course Scott is very welcome to come round for tea, but I'm afraid today isn't a good time. We need to go and visit

Grandma in hospital.' She glanced quickly over at Scott. 'Perhaps we can do it another time.'

'Sure,' he agreed lazily. 'Though I won't hold my breath.'

Megan glared at him briefly and then turned her attention to her daughter. 'Sally, why don't you get in the car? I need to talk to Scott for a minute.'

Megan waited until her daughter waved Scott goodbye and moved out of earshot before turning to look at him. He might be so maddening that he made her want to slap the smirk right off his face, but today he had also been very kind. 'Look, I really am very grateful for what you did this afternoon,' she began, feeling an uncomfortable rush of awareness as she looked into those calm grey eyes. 'You have no idea what it meant to me, knowing Sally was out with you rather than stuck in an office somewhere.'

'And you weren't worried about her welfare, with me?'

Once more he was giving her that lazy, amused look. 'Well, okay, yes, maybe I was a bit, but ...' She shook her head. 'Look, Scott, for once can't you just take what I'm saying in the spirit it's intended?'

He nodded. 'I can do that.' He started to walk to his car, but then stopped and turned back. 'And there's no need to be grateful. Your daughter was a joy. It's me who should be thanking you.'

She was still staring long after he'd walked away. Scott the arrogant charmer was easy to resist because frankly, for all his good looks, she didn't like him. This other Scott – the one who had helped her out today, the one who hadn't just watched her daughter, but had bothered to spend time engaging with her – he wasn't quite so easy to ignore.

When Megan caught sight of her mother sat up in the hospital bed later that day, her heart lurched in her chest. She looked so fragile, her face pale against the white sheets. Since when had her mum grown old? It just wasn't possible. But then the elderly lady in the bed caught sight of Sally. As her mouth turned up in a huge beam that lit up her face, Megan felt a surge of pure relief. Her mother's smile was still as strong as ever.

'What a lovely surprise,' she exclaimed, stretching out her hand, ready to give her granddaughter a hug. 'Two of my favourite people.'

Sally looked around. 'What about Grandad?'

The lady in the bed laughed. 'Don't worry, he's also one of my favourites. He's just gone to get himself a drink.'

Megan bent over and kissed her mother on her cheek. 'How are you, Mum?' she asked softly.

'I'll be a lot better tomorrow when they let me go home.' She glanced at her daughter and patted her hand. 'I'm fine, darling, really. Silly old fool that I am, I managed to twist my ankle when I fell. They're keeping me in as a precaution, that's all.' She looked over to her granddaughter. 'So who looked after you this afternoon, Sally?'

'Scott did,' Sally replied proudly, snuggling up to her grandmother on the bed. 'He took me to the park, bought me ice cream and taught me how to draw a dog like Dizzy.'

Megan didn't miss the quick, all-too-knowing look her mother darted at her. 'Scott is just someone I know from work, Mum,' she replied quickly. 'Don't start to read anything more into it.'

'He's a lawyer,' Sally announced. 'I told him I might want to be one when I grow up, but he said my mum wouldn't be very happy about that.' She looked over at Megan. 'Why not?'

Sitting on the end of the bed, with two pairs of eyes fixed firmly on hers, Megan silently cursed Scott. It seemed even from a distance he was capable of making her life difficult. 'Scott is a defence lawyer,' she tried to explain, knowing full well her mother was taking in her every word and gesture. 'There are some lawyers who work with the police to try and help put away the bad guys. Some, like Scott, are there to defend the person the police charge, making sure they aren't put in jail unless there is proof they took part in the crime.'

'So you and Scott aren't on the same side?'

Exactly, she wanted to reply, but stopped herself because, while it was how she felt, it wasn't entirely fair, or true, for that matter. 'Well, we don't work together, but we do both want to make sure justice is done and that the only people who are put in jail are the ones who deserve to be there. So I guess you could say we both have the same aim.' She could almost see Scott grinning at that carefully worded reply.

'Sally, sweetie, can you see Grandad?' Her mother pointed towards the entrance of the ward. 'Why don't you go and say hello?'

Megan watched her daughter skip towards her father and turned to the lady sitting up in bed. 'Clever move, Mum. You think I don't know you're about to interrogate me?'

Her mother chuckled. 'You leave your precious daughter in the hands of a man we've never heard of and you think you *won't* get an interrogation?'

Sighing, Megan stood up. 'Really, there isn't anything going on between Scott and me.'

'Would you like there to be?'

'No.' Her reply was firm and quick, but it gave her a little jolt to realise it wasn't entirely true. The man she'd had a glimpse of today – the one who could be lurking behind the glib lawyer with the self-assured good looks – had intrigued her. She'd never have believed Scott capable of patiently teaching a young girl how to draw, not if she hadn't seen it with her own eyes. Was it all just part of his charm offensive? First he'd demonstrate his soft side, then he'd start reeling her in? She wished she knew, wished she didn't feel like a fish on the end of his bait, flapping around trying not to get caught, but sensing that ultimately it was futile.

Her mother regarded her knowingly. 'It's about time you

started living a bit, Meg. Your father and I worry about you. A young, attractive woman like you shouldn't be coming home to her parents every night.'

'I don't. I come home to my daughter. And you know perfectly well I can't just go out on the town whenever the whim takes me, dating any man who takes my fancy. I've got Sally to consider.'

'Consider, yes,' her mother replied gently. 'Hide behind, no.'

Megan winced, but the arrival of her father and Sally saved her from having to reply. Just as well, because the conversation had all the hallmarks of turning into a full-scale argument: one she'd had with her mother several times over the last few years. Of course it was true Megan hadn't really dated, at least not seriously, since Luke had left her over three years ago. A few men had tried to get close to her, including those with a bizarre fetish for female cops. Probably imagining her using the handcuffs. Then there had been the other extreme. The men who, when they'd found out she was a cop, had been totally put off. Intimidated. No one had fitted into that healthy middle ground: finding her attractive for who she was, and respecting what she did.

The sad truth was that three years *was* a long time to be without a stable man in her life. A long time to be without the joy of being touched, kissed, caressed. Loved.

But it wasn't long enough to forget the heartbreak of discovering the loving was all one-sided. Something she wasn't in a rush to experience again.

Chapter Five

Scott had never been happier to reach Friday afternoon. The week had been a tough one. In between court appearances, he was having a hard time trying to put together a defence for his latest case, Kevin Rogers. Accused of raping a prostitute, Rogers was a belligerent man who Scott couldn't see any jury warming to. Especially the women. But beneath the aggressive manner, Scott had a strong feeling there was some truth in what the man was saying. It wasn't hard to understand why the police might, if Rogers was correct, have resorted to some shady practice in order get their suspect put away. Clearly he'd been in trouble in the past, and by all accounts wasn't exactly up for a man of the year award. Indeed, the prostitutes questioned had all declared he was rough, often hostile and rarely paid up. But being a mean bastard didn't automatically imply Rogers had committed rape. At least not in Scott's book. The man had been charged with a similar crime a few years back, but just before the case came to court the victim had withdrawn her statement. Though the feeling from the prosecution team had been that she'd been leant on, Rogers insisted it was the other way round. That the so-called victim had been told to cry rape, but at the last minute had backed down, scared of committing perjury. Now Rogers was claiming another false victim had been found. One who was, so far, sticking to her story.

'We need to talk to the woman involved in the previous case again,' Scott told Nancy as he gathered together the contents of the file they'd been working through. 'We need to find out who leant on her and why. Though we won't be able to use the information in court, it will at least give us some insight into what's going on.'

'Agreed. I'll set something up.' She sat back in her chair and crossed her elegant legs. 'So, any plans for this evening?'

Scott had to forcibly stop himself from laughing out loud. Christ, he'd do well to even get to Friday evening, never mind actually do something with it. He shook his head. 'I know, all work and no play makes Scott a dull boy, but no, my only plans are to finalise one of my cases for court on Monday.' Sounded simple. In truth, it would probably take him the most part of the weekend. One thing he was never accused of was being under-prepared for a case. It didn't matter if he had to work all night on it. He'd be ready to give his best come Monday morning.

'No time for a quick drink?'

She was looking at him expectantly, her body language indicating it wasn't just a drink she had in mind. Wearily Scott rubbed a hand across his shoulders, trying to iron out the knotted muscles. A night out with a willing woman was probably just what he needed. A few drinks, a few laughs and then back to his for some steamy sex. Yeah, he could really go for that. Sadly, much as he still liked Nancy, she was no longer what he had in mind when he thought of his perfect evening. Or sex. The woman he was thinking of was younger, slimmer, with short dark hair and huge blue eyes. A woman he hadn't seen since he'd looked after her daughter a few days ago. Irritatingly, he'd even found himself hanging round the gym slightly longer than usual, hoping to bump into her.

Shaking his head he gave Nancy an apologetic smile. 'Sorry, I'll have to give that a miss tonight. Some other time.'

Megan was standing in the chambers, right outside Scott's room, a split second away from turning round and walking straight out again. She would have done, had the clerk not been sitting by the only exit. The hand she'd raised, ready to knock, hesitated. She couldn't do this. Didn't even want to. It was her daughter who'd insisted they should invite Scott round. Megan knew Sally's ulterior motive was to spend more time with the man who'd taught her how to draw. What she wasn't sure on was her own motive in agreeing to invite him. Why hadn't she just said no?

As she stood outside debating with herself, the door suddenly opened and she came face-to-face with an attractive blonde woman. Older than herself, but with the type of classic beauty that didn't dim with age.

'Oh, sorry.' She stood back to let her past. 'It's DS Taylor, isn't it?'

Megan nodded, realising the other woman looked familiar.

'Nancy Whitehead. Solicitor. I've seen you round the police station and in court a few times, but I don't think we've ever formally been introduced.'

Megan took the hand that was offered. 'Nice to meet you, Nancy. I'm Megan.'

It was then that Scott appeared in the doorway. All six-foot-plus of him. Again he wore his white court shirt, opened sufficiently to show the tanned column of his neck. Finding the palms of her hand suddenly and annoyingly damp, Megan rubbed them discreetly on her trousers.

'DS Taylor.' He nodded towards her, casual, his face unreadable. 'What brings you here?'

No way. What she had to say to him was embarrassing enough, without the addition of an audience. One who was looking at her and Scott with undisguised interest. 'I, umm.' She nodded towards Nancy. 'Perhaps you should show your visitor out first.'

He gave her a cool, speculative look before turning back to Nancy and bending to give her a quick kiss on the cheek. 'See you next week.'

Nancy didn't immediately move. Instead she gazed at Megan a moment longer, her eyes positively swimming with speculation. Then she turned to give Scott a slow smile. 'Don't forget, if you get through your work, my offer tonight still stands.'

With a nod in Megan's direction, Nancy sashayed out of the office.

'Well, that was a warning shot across my bows, if ever I heard one,' Megan remarked dryly, her nostrils twitching from Nancy's perfume.

Scott grinned down at her. 'Do you need it?'

'Hardly.' She strode past him into his office, but when she turned she found he hadn't followed her. Instead he was leaning against the doorway, gazing at her with a look of amused disbelief. 'Look, let's get this quite clear. I have no romantic interest in you whatsoever.' And she hadn't. At least not in the cocky man who was looking at her now.

'And yet here you are, in my office, for the second time this week.'

Nonchalantly he shut door before moving back into the room. Megan told herself she was just being a woman when her attention was caught by the way his taut, muscular thigh stretched the material of his trousers as he perched on to the corner of his desk. 'I'm here at the request of my daughter, not myself,' she clarified quickly, shifting her gaze to above his waist. 'It seems you've made quite a conquest there.'

The smug grin changed to one of genuine warmth. 'Ditto.'

For a moment their eyes met. There were so many things she could find to dislike about him, but it was hard to ignore the obvious affection he had for her daughter. It was also hard to ignore the mesmerising glare of his smoky grey eyes. The way they tugged at her, drawing her in. 'Sally …' The name came out in a croak. She pulled her eyes away from his and coughed to clear the sudden tightness from her throat. 'My daughter wanted to know if you were free to come round for tea tomorrow.'

'I see.' He shifted off the desk, moving to stand directly in front of her. Slowly he raised his right hand and placed it gently on her chin, forcing her to look up at him. 'And her mother?'

The thumping of her heart went up a notch at the feel of his hands. At this close distance she could see that his eyes weren't just grey. There were flecks of blue and silver, too. And a pulsing, shimmering heat. 'Her mother is here, asking you.' Try as she might, she couldn't keep her voice steady. 'Isn't that enough?'

He studied her for a few seconds longer before moving round to the other side of his desk. She found herself pathetically grateful for the physical barrier between them. 'I guess I'm naturally interested to know whether this is purely tea with your daughter, or whether you'll be there, too.'

'I'll be there and my parents will be there.' She took some satisfaction in the startled look he gave her. 'I guess it won't be your average Saturday night out, so if you're not interested ...'

'I didn't say I wasn't. I'm just curious to know the ground rules, that's all.'

'It's quite simple. My daughter likes you. Any friend of hers is a friend of mine.' The corners of his lips twitched. 'Okay, I can live with that. For the time being.'

There he went again. Pushing for more just when she thought she'd put him firmly in his box. 'Friendship is all that's on offer. Take it or leave it.'

'Well, as you've put it so graciously, how can I possibly refuse?' he countered smoothly.

Knowing she was never going to win a verbal sparring match with him, she quit before one got started. 'Right then. We'll see you tomorrow around six.' She quickly gave him the address, anxious to get away from his searching, knowing eyes and her increasing awareness of him. Not as a pain in the arse lawyer, but as a man.

'Any particular dress code?'

'Casual.' She went to open the door. 'Oh and bring some pens. I think Sally has another art session in mind for you both.'

'And flowers?'

The boyish grin was back. The one she was beginning to

find disarming. She found her lips turning up in a responding smile. 'My mother would love some. Tulips are her favourite.' With that she quickly let herself out.

As the door clicked shut, Scott sank back into his chair and let out a deep breath. Well, that invitation was out of the blue all right. He mulled it over in his head, not quite sure how he felt about it. Seeing Megan again was a definite plus. Her daughter, too. But meeting the parents? That was something he avoided at all costs, even with the women he actually dated. Yet here he was, on the brink of meeting Megan's parents and they hadn't even shared a kiss. Still, he had a feeling she was warming to him. Or at least getting less cold. A meal, even with her family in tow, was certainly progress. If he kept things moving in that direction, surely it wouldn't be long before his dreams became reality and he'd have a naked Megan beneath him. Writhing in ecstasy.

'Well?'

Megan had hardly stepped foot in the house before her mother fixed her with a piercing look in the hallway. 'Well what? Did I have a good day? Not bad, as it happens. I had a couple of leads on a big murder case I'm involved in, and I'm halfway through clearing my in-tray. All in all, worthy of a small celebration, I think.'

'That's good to hear, darling, but you know perfectly well that wasn't what I was asking. Can we expect this mysterious Scott of yours for dinner tomorrow?'

'He isn't my Scott, but yes, he did say he would come.'

'Yippee!'

Megan hadn't been aware that Sally had snuck into the room. Reaching out her arms, she sighed with contentment as her daughter rushed into them.

'Is he really coming round tomorrow? Really and truly?'

'He said he would, so I guess he will.'

'Then I need to find all my pictures,' she said excitedly,

wriggling away from the arms she'd only been too happy to settle into a moment ago. 'He'll want to see what I've done.'

As she dashed off upstairs, Megan was left wondering if she'd done the right thing by giving in to her daughter's demands. What if the man didn't turn up? Or worse, turned up and didn't pay Sally any attention? She could only hope she hadn't set her daughter up for a harsh early lesson on the unreliable nature of the male species.

'This Scott must be pretty special to have inspired such adoration in Sally,' her mother remarked as she hobbled on crutches towards the kitchen.

'I think it's more the case that a six year old can't see past the flashing good looks and easy smile.'

'Hmm, good looks, eh?' Her mother mockingly patted her hair. 'Well, I'm looking forward to his visit even more now. I can't remember the last time we had a handsome young man within these four walls.'

There was a loud cough from the front room. 'Don't think I can't hear you,' her father muttered, making them both dissolve with laughter.

'Present company accepted, Stanley.' Her mother shuffled over to the sink and was about to start peeling the potatoes when Megan gently pushed her to one side.

'I'll do that. You go and sit down. Take the weight off that ankle.'

'I will if I can sit here and listen to you tell me something about the man we'll be welcoming into our house tomorrow.'

'My God, Mum, you're like a dog with a bone.'

'Yes, I am. And as any self-respecting dog will tell you, they won't let go of the bone until they're well and truly satisfied.'

Her eyes were twinkling with devilment and Megan had to laugh. 'Okay, okay. Where do you want me to start?' Taking the potatoes out of the bag, she set to work, concentrating on removing the skin from the potato and not her fingers. 'He's been working out of the local chambers for nearly two years now. I bump into him from time to time in court. Usually when he's trying to defend a man I know is guilty as hell.'

'Ah, I can see the tension straight away.'

'Yes, I'm sure you can.' And so would her father. He might be retired, but he was still very much a cop. 'Though his job isn't the only thing that annoys me about him. It's his whole demeanour. He's so damnably sure of himself. So certain that he only has to smile at a woman and she's putty in his hands.'

'Well, it seems to have worked with Sally,' her mother remarked.

'Only because she hasn't met anyone like him before.' She turned to look long and hard at her mother. 'I have, and I've still got the scars to prove it. Whatever you're thinking right now, don't. I'm not going down that route again.'

'It seems to me that you've decided not to go down any route, which is a crying shame.' Her mother reached out and took hold of Megan's hand. 'You've got a warm, loving heart my darling. It's wrong that you've let one mistake put you off men forever. You should be out there having fun, dating, finding your soul mate.'

Megan knew there was more than a grain of truth in what her mother was saying. It probably *was* time she dared to dip her toe back into the dating pool again. For a woman who prided herself on being able to stare down a knife-wielding thug, it seemed she turned into a giant wuss when it came to dating. But it was one thing getting back into it again, and quite another doing it with Scott Armstrong. He had 'danger, beware' written all over him in bold red letters.

Chapter Six

Scott unzipped his backpack and carefully placed the things he needed for the evening into it: a set of artist's pencils, two bottles of wine (one red, one white, as he didn't know the Taylors' preferences) and three bunches of flowers. The latter were the most problematic, but he went with the theory that it was the thought that counted, not the state of the actual flowers when they were received. After closing up the bag and donning his well-worn, black leather jacket, he left the house, shutting the front door firmly behind him. There she was, waiting for him. Gleaming in what was left of the evening sun, all wicked lines and screaming power. His Harley. To Scott, transport wasn't about getting from A to B. It was about living the moment. Sadly, the Harley wasn't entirely practical for day-to-day use. Travelling on it lost some of its appeal when he was forced to carry books, case files and a computer on his back: which was why he'd invested heavily in the sports car. To some, the car would be a luxury but to Scott, it was an absolute necessity. If he had to drive a car, it needed to be one whose engine he could actually feel throbbing when he put his foot down. But it was travelling on his bike in the evenings and weekends that he enjoyed the most. Sometimes he'd just set off and go, with no destination in mind, simply for the thrill of feeling the wind on his face. Being as one with his machine.

Knowing he was grinning like a damn schoolboy, he slipped on his helmet, swung a jean-clad leg over the powerful machine and gunned the engine. The evening might turn out to be a disaster, but what the heck, at least he would enjoy the drive there and back.

The house Megan lived in with her parents was a rambling old cottage, set on the edge of a leafy part of the town, about fifteen minutes away. At least by Harley time. Enjoying the satisfying crunch of tyre on gravel, he pulled on to the driveway and turned off the engine. Shaking off his helmet he noticed the small but immaculate front garden, the honeysuckle around the front door, and wondered who the gardener of the house was. Somehow he couldn't picture Megan on her hands and knees, weeding flower beds. Getting dirty, yes, but he imagined her more at ease chopping up firewood or mowing the lawn. There was definitely a hint of the tomboy about her. Something he was surprised to find himself appreciating more than the dainty, feminine style of most of the women he spent time with.

Megan was upstairs, pretending to herself that she wasn't obsessing about whether she looked okay, when she heard the deep throb of an engine coming up the road. It was about the right time, but surely that sounded more like a motorbike than a car? Poking her head out of the window, she felt the sudden race of her pulse when the powerful bike entered their drive and a familiar muscular figure climbed off. All she could think was: wow. She'd been prepared for his sleek sports car, the one that suited the image she wanted to have of Scott: smooth, polished, slick. She wasn't prepared for the sexy, slightly edgy man who climbed off the bike. A man she wasn't sure she knew at all. Especially when she watched him take off his rucksack and produce a small bunch of flowers for the little girl who opened the door to him. The beam of delight that crossed her face was so huge Megan had to swallow against the unexpected lump in her throat. Flowers for her and her mother she'd expected, as it fitted the man's stereotype. But to think of bringing some for Sally? He was either more cunning that she thought he was, or a whole lot nicer than she'd given him credit for.

Following a final check in the mirror, Megan smoothed down her wayward hair, took a deep breath and walked as casually as she could down the stairs. 'That's quite some machine you've got there,' she remarked as they met in the hallway.

He smiled at her, a hint of boyish pleasure vying with the usual cocky grin. Her already racing pulse hitched up another notch.

'Thanks. Are you a bike fan?'

She shrugged. 'I can't say I've had much experience with them. An old boyfriend used to drive one, but I ditched him before I ever got to ride on it.'

'I'd better not waste any time getting you on the back of mine, then.'

She was all set to argue that they weren't even going out, when he thrust a slightly crumpled, but undeniably pretty bunch of large daisies at her. The harsh words died on her lips. 'Thank you,' she found herself whispering instead. Ridiculous. Where was her cool indifference now? How was it that men only had to buy women flowers and they became tongue-tied and gooey-eyed? Or was she just ludicrously out of practice?

Aware that her parents were hovering behind her, staring with blatant curiosity, Megan stood aside and made the introductions.

'Mum, Dad, or should I say Dorothy and Stanley, this is Scott Armstrong. Barrister and occasional childminder.'

'Pleased to meet you, Scott.' Her mother smiled broadly at him. 'And call me Dotty, everyone else does.'

Megan rolled her eyes as she glanced at her mother. Seventy something years old and she was almost simpering. What was it with Scott and the opposite sex? Why did otherwise sensible women go weak at the knees when they met him? She watched as he took her mother's hand, kissed it and produced a bunch of tulips from behind his back. Oh, he was smooth all right. But surely her mother could see through that? Then she remembered her own reaction to the daisies and had to acknowledge she was every bit as bad.

Scott liked Megan's mother immediately. She had the same slight frame as her daughter and, he imagined, the same smile. Not that he'd actually ever had Megan's full, natural smile directed at him. Her father, however, was a different matter. Though he accepted the bottles of wine politely, Scott had a feeling he was going to have to try a lot harder to get him on side. He remembered hearing that he'd been a police detective, too. No doubt when it came to their opinion of defence lawyers it was like father, like daughter.

As he was thanking them graciously for the invitation to dinner, he felt a small hand tugging at his elbow and looked down to find Sally smiling shyly up at him.

'This is Dizzy,' she told him, holding up a motley looking dog with dark brown eyes and a lopsided face.

'Pleased to meet you, Dizzy,' he replied gravely, picking up a black paw and shaking it.

The dog looked nonplussed, but Sally laughed.

'Would you like to see the pictures I've drawn?' she asked, her voice slightly hesitant.

Out of the corner of his eye, Scott was aware of Megan watching, a tense look on her face.

'Absolutely.' Scott grinned at Sally. 'That's exactly why I've come. Why don't you bring them down here so we can all take a look?'

He was equally aware of Megan letting out a deep sigh of relief. What, had she really thought he'd ignore her daughter now he'd got his foot over the threshold? 'So, Scott, I understand from Sally that you're a dab hand at drawing,' Dotty mentioned as they sat in the warm, cosy living room a few minutes later, admiring Sally's artwork. 'Well, I ...'

'He's really good,' Sally interrupted. 'Good enough to blow ...'

'Thanks, Sally,' Scott cut in quickly. No way was he going to have that boast repeated again, and certainly not in front of Megan's parents.

'Where did you learn to draw?' This question came from Megan, who was watching him carefully, as if deciding whether to like him or not. Boy did she look good today. He wasn't sure whether he fancied her more in the casual skinny jeans and turquoise blue T-shirt she was wearing now, or the smart skirt and sexy heels she wore to court. Then again, the Lycra leggings she'd had on in the gym scored highly in his book, too.

With an effort he tore his gaze away from her and concentrated on the question. 'I didn't learn, as such. It's just something I did a lot of as a child.' Which was a time he didn't want to revisit. Not any part after the age of seven.

'Really?' Megan arched a perfect dark brow in surprise. 'I can't picture you as a boy, drawing. You seem more the outdoors type. Playing football. Chasing the girls.'

Refusing the offer of another drink from Stanley, Scott sat back on the armchair and forced himself to smile, pushing the bad memories firmly back where they belonged. In a padlocked box in a dim corner of his mind, never to be let out. 'I did quite a bit of football and girl chasing, too, but I liked to draw. It ...' he trailed off, irritated that he'd almost said what he'd been thinking: that doodling had been a welcome distraction; a comforting world of his own he could disappear into. 'The girls seemed to love it,' he said instead. It was at least partially true, as he'd later discovered.

'Are your parents still around?' Stanley asked, his eyes watchful. Scott found he could easily imagine what it must have been like to be questioned by Detective Taylor senior. Clinically methodical, picking apart answers like a micro-surgeon until he had the full picture.

Luckily, this was a question he'd expected. One he'd already worked out a reply for. 'My father died a while ago, but my mother's still alive. She lives with me from time to time, in between holidaying and visiting friends.' It sounded believable. Like she was having the time of her life. If only she was. If only he knew where the hell she'd disappeared off to this time. Or when she was going to bother coming back.

'How nice. Where is she now?'

Scott paused fractionally. 'No doubt somewhere warmer and sunnier than here.'

Megan was watching Scott as he answered her father's questions. He was an expert at not giving away information he didn't want others to know, but she was a detective, trained to look at body language; the slightest hint that the suspect was lying. There was something Scott was covering up. It irked her that she wanted to know what it was. Why did it matter that, as a clearly sporty person, he'd spent a lot of his childhood inside, drawing? Or that he didn't know where his mother was?

Her increasing interest in him worried her. It seemed the more she was getting to know him, the more he was starting to grow on her. That being said, she was a long way from being convinced that going out with Scott Armstrong was a good way to start dating again. It would be like a minnow taking swimming lessons from a shark.

With a small sigh, she rose from her chair and went to put the final touches of the meal together. Anything to distract her from thinking too much about dating Scott.

Not that he was going to make that easy, she thought wryly a little later as he gently pushed her mother back into her chair, telling her that she wasn't to clear up. He and Sally would do it. And yes, that was her daughter now carefully clearing the table, her face a picture of concentration as she carried each plate to the kitchen for Scott to load into the dishwasher. The same daughter who usually wasn't seen for dust when there were chores to be done.

'That's a Harley Sportster you've got there isn't it?' Her father asked as they all settled back in the sitting room to drink their coffee.

'Yep. The XR1200.'

'I bet it has the Evolution engine? You've got to love the sound of those engines.'

Scott was grinning like a proud father. 'The V-twin engines, angled to give it that distinctive throaty growl. It's why I bought the bike.' He took a sip of his coffee. 'Are you a bike fan then, Mr Taylor?'

'Used to be. There was a time when Dot and I would race around the countryside together.' He glanced over at Megan. 'Life before responsibility.'

'Not that you regret having me, eh, Dad?' Megan teased.

He chuckled. 'Not at all. Still, seeing that Harley of Scott's on the drive, makes me think back to those good old days.'

Megan shook her head in mock despair. 'I can't see what all the fuss is about, personally. It's just boys and their toys.'

Suddenly Scott levered his large frame out of the low armchair and walked towards her, holding out his hand.

'What?'

He grasped her by both hands and hauled her on to her feet. 'I'm about to show you what all the fuss is about.'

Momentarily dumbstruck, Megan felt herself pulled towards him, acutely aware of the warmth of the hands that enclosed hers. Hands that were strong and surprisingly calloused, not smooth as she'd expected.

'That's very kind, but you don't need to bother,' she protested when she'd finally found her voice. 'I'm not sure I really want to know.'

Ignoring her, he tugged her towards the door.

'I haven't got a helmet,' she heard herself muttering. As excuses went, it was probably pretty desperate because he was bound to have—He looked back and grinned. 'I've got a spare.'

As a last resort she glanced back at her parents, her eyes pleading. They simply smiled.

'Go on, darling,' her mother had the audacity to encourage. 'You'll enjoy it. I know I did.'

Before she could argue any further she was standing outside next to the machine itself. She eyed it curiously, prepared to admit that it did look kind of sexy. In a powerful, menacing way. Much like its owner right now.

'A few rules before we start,' Scott began as he reached for the spare helmet and planted himself in front of her. Very close. So close she could feel the warmth emanating off his big, solid body. 'First rule, you have to relax,' he continued as he lowered the spare helmet gently on to her head, flipping up the visor as he made sure of the fit.

She found herself staring straight at his chest, her eyes on a level with the V of his shirt. 'Like that's going to happen,' she mumbled, all too aware that her usually steady pulse was racing. And it wasn't in fear of the bike.

'I'll go slowly,' he replied, misunderstanding her concern, which was just as well. He was arrogant enough already. 'Rule number two, you have to mimic what I do. If I bend to the left, you bend to the left. If I bend to the right …'

'I go right. I've got it,' she interrupted.

His light eyes shone with suppressed laughter. The bugger was really enjoying this. 'Okay. Rule three is keep your arms around me at all times.' His lips twitched. 'I know you'll enjoy that rule. I certainly will.'

She let out a sigh of frustration. 'Look, can we just get this over and done with?'

Laughing he reached for his own helmet. 'Okay, gorgeous. I can see how keen you are to get your arms around me. Final rule. If you want me to stop for any reason, squeeze my shoulder.'

Megan felt like squeezing his shoulder right now. In fact she might not stop at the shoulder. She could find her hands moving up to his neck and squeezing that tightly, too. He infuriated her almost as much as he mesmerised her. As she watched, he climbed effortlessly on to the bike, then turned to her expectantly. All she could really see of his face were

52

his eyes, but it was enough to tell her he was smirking. Mimicking his action, she flung her leg over and shifted so she was close, but not touching. His shoulders loomed in front of her, stretching the black leather of his jacket. Biting her lip, she cautiously placed her arms lightly around his waist.

Scott revved the engine and Megan gulped. Jesus. The pulsing power beneath her legs. The warm, hard feel of Scott's body. Before she had a chance to worry about how sexy and intimate it all felt, he was accelerating off down the road.

Scott was in his element. Riding his bike, the wind on his face, Megan sitting behind him, her arms finally starting to relax around his waist. He wasn't stupid. He knew exactly why she hadn't wanted a go on the bike. It was the very reason he'd wanted to take her. By fair means or foul he'd decided he wanted to feel those toned arms of hers wrapped around him. All evening he'd been watching her, aware of her every move. She wasn't immune to him. He could see it in the way her eyes had drifted towards him every now again, immediately dropping his gaze when he'd met them. She clearly didn't want to be interested in him, but she was.

Pulling back into the Taylor's driveway, he brought the bike to a skidding stop, smiling to himself as Megan immediately snatched her arms away from his waist, and then leapt off the bike like a scalded cat. With calculated slowness he removed his helmet and casually dismounted.

'Well, what did you think?'

She ran a hand through her short, cropped hair, fluffing out the flattened strands. 'It was fine.'

'Fine?' He wasn't deceived by the lukewarm response. The bright blue of her eyes, the flush on her cheeks, all told him what she'd just experienced rated a little more than fine.

'Yes, fine,' she replied firmly, tucking the helmet away under the seat.

He took a deliberate step towards her, pleased to see a flash of wariness cross her face. It was better than indifference. 'Which bit of it was fine?' he asked softly. 'The part when you sat close to me? Or when you wrapped your arms around my waist? Synchronising your movements to mine?'

She swallowed. 'I, umm ...'

He forgot her parents were probably watching from the window. Forgot about everything but the deep blue of her eyes, the fullness of her lips. He bent and kissed her.

The power of surprise was clearly on his side. He didn't think she would have opened her mouth quite so readily for him otherwise. With no intention of relinquishing the head start he'd been given, he swooped, delighting in the taste of her. The feel of her. On a powerful surge of desire he put a hand to either side of her face and dove in deeper, wanting to lose himself in the aching sweetness he found there. He hadn't expected that. Her shyness. Gentleness. As he leaned in, moving her between the bike and his now full arousal, he felt her melt against him, her body relaxing into his. God she felt so unbelievably good. He knew he should pull away, not least because he couldn't afford to walk back into her parents' house with a raging hard on, but he was damned if he was going to give up this pleasure too quickly. Taking a hand from her face, he moved it to her hips, smoothing it over her deliciously taut bottom before tugging her towards him even further, desperate to feel her tight against him.

It was Megan who finally called a stop to it. Megan who moved her hands between them and pressed them on his chest, pushing him away.

They stood facing each other, their breathing shallow and ragged.

'Come out for a drink with me,' he demanded hoarsely, desire still flickering brightly in his eyes.

She shook her head. 'No.'

'Are you still in denial?'

'Don't be ridiculous.' Her reply was cool and steady but

when he reached for her wrist, and ran his thumb over her pulse, it was hammering away, ten to the dozen.

'Then prove it by coming out with me.'

Megan closed her eyes and he guessed she was mentally arguing with herself, pitting her instinctive physical attraction to him against her judgement of his character. In the end she gave up and laughed. 'Okay, very cute. As I'm too tired for your verbal gymnastics right now, I'll meet you for one drink.' He was powerless to stop the smug grin that slid across his face. Her eyes narrowed. 'That's all you're getting, Armstrong. One drink.'

'That's all I need,' he countered smoothly, taking her hand and walking her back towards the front door. She rolled her eyes, but it merely made him grin wider. Finally, she was softening towards him.

Chapter Seven

Monday night was dancing night. It had been for as many years as Megan could remember. Somewhere in her mid-teens she'd abandoned the tap shoes and ballet tutu, but she hadn't stopped dancing. Now, teetering on the edge of thirty, she was into jazz. It made her smile, exercised her body and gave her a chance to catch up with a good crowd of friends, most notably Ann.

'I've got aches in places I didn't know I could ache,' Ann grumbled as they found a spare table at the sports club bar and sat down for a well-earned drink. 'At one point, when we were doing all those straddle jumps, I thought my legs were actually going to fall off.'

'Hey, stop complaining. It keeps you fit.' Megan took a deep drink of her sparkling water and sat back against the chair, her body humming with the after effects of a thorough workout. An hour in the dance studio beat an hour in the gym any day. It was just a shame the classes were only once a week.

'Speaking of fit.' Ann raised an eyebrow and looked across at her. 'How did your date with the delicious Scott Armstrong go?'

Megan shook her head and gave her friend a warning stare. 'How many times do I have to tell you, it wasn't a date. It was a thank you. My parents and Sally were there, for heaven's sake.'

'And will you be seeing him again?'

About to take a drink, Megan put down her glass and sighed. 'Well, I did sort of find myself agreeing to meet him for a drink after work tomorrow.'

'Ah!' Ann's exclamation was one of self-righteous triumph.

'There is no "ah" about it. We've agreed terms. Friends only.'

'You mean you've stated the terms. I hardly see Scott agreeing to them. He looks like a man who goes after what he wants, and from the way I've seen him eye you up, what he wants from you isn't your friendship. Great as it may be.'

'He only wants me because I haven't immediately rolled onto my back and asked him to stroke my belly as soon as he's shown an interest.'

Ann burst out laughing. 'I have to admit, if his eyes had wandered in my direction, I might have found myself doing exactly that. And purring, too.'

Megan's eyes rounded in horror. 'God, please don't tell me you're another one of Scott's fan club? What does the guy do to create such a following?'

'What, you mean aside from being drop-dead gorgeous, with the body of an athlete and a smile that melts a woman's insides?' Ann shrugged her shoulders. 'I haven't a clue.'

Looking down at her glass, Megan wiped at the small beads of condensation clinging to the outside. 'That's all about what he looks like, Ann,' she replied quietly. 'Nothing about the man himself.'

Ann frowned. 'Why are you so against him, Megan?'

And why haven't I changed the subject? Megan berated herself. Now she was stuck with the impossible task of explaining her feelings about Scott to Ann, when she couldn't even explain them to herself. 'I guess he's everything I've told myself I should dislike in a man,' she replied with a sigh. 'He's a charmer, a smooth talker, very aware of his own good looks.' It sounded so simple. Except ... Except when he smiled at her, really smiled, not the cocky veneer of a smile but the boyish grin that made his eyes crinkle ... When he smiled at her like that, she went weak at the knees.

'I'll admit he has an almost breathtaking confidence about him,' Ann conceded. 'But frankly, that's all part of his appeal. Who wants quiet and shy when you can be swept off your feet by bold and dazzling?'

'Being swept off your feet isn't what it's cracked up to be,' Megan muttered, annoyed to find the bitterness creep into her voice. Three years later and she *still* couldn't think about that part of her life without feeling humiliation and pain.

Ann regarded her thoughtfully. 'You've never really talked about Sally's father. I presume that's who you're talking about when you mention being swept off your feet?'

Trying to lighten the mood, Megan cocked her head to one side. 'I should know better than to make an ambiguous statement to a fellow detective.'

'And now you're trying to change the subject.'

Megan glanced up to find Ann pinning her with the type of death stare she usually reserved for juvenile delinquents. Only a select few knew she wasn't nearly as stern as she sometimes appeared. 'It showed, huh?' She tried a smile, but Ann wasn't in the mood to be fobbed off. 'To be honest, there isn't much to tell.'

'Then why does it still hurt to talk about it?'

Megan couldn't help but laugh. 'Maybe because I'm such a total fool when it comes to matters of the heart?'

'Aren't we all?'

Deciding that Ann wasn't going to let the matter drop, Megan settled back against her chair. 'I met Luke when I was at school. He was my first boyfriend, my first love, my first everything.' Her friend nodded, encouraging her to continue. 'After school he went away to university and I stayed here and joined the police force, but at the end of each term he'd come back and we'd pick up where we left off. He was—'Megan closed her eyes and instantly recalled his face '—beautiful, I suppose is the word for it. Dazzling, as you'd call it. Blonde hair, eyes the colour of the sky on a sunny day. Girls flirted with him wherever we went, but for some strange reason he seemed to prefer me. I was too scared to question it, worried that if I did, I'd find a secret ulterior motive for him being with me. Instead, I just thanked my lucky stars that it was me who went home with him.'

'He should have been thanking *his* lucky stars,' Ann countered.

Megan smiled. 'That's one of the things I love about you, your blind loyalty.' Before Ann could interrupt, Megan held up her hand. 'It isn't false modesty. You didn't meet Luke. I know it's a bit of a cliché, but he really was breathtaking. Not just his looks, but his charisma, the way he could talk to you and make you feel so incredibly special. Like you were the only person he was interested in.' A humourless laugh shot out of her. 'Of course the truth was something else. When I surprised him by turning up to his university campus one evening, I quickly found out I wasn't the only one he was interested in.'

'Ouch.'

Even now, Megan could feel the utter desolation she'd experienced that evening. Not just because she'd knocked on his door to find him half dressed with a stunning, scantily clad woman hovering behind him – though that had sliced through her heart like a knife – but because all those dreams she'd been nurturing had suddenly blown up in her face.

'Yet you stood by him?'

Megan fought to control the emotions that even now were never far from the surface when she thought about that fateful night. 'Yes. I'd turned up to the campus scared but thrilled by the knowledge that I was pregnant. Of course it wasn't planned, but I knew I wanted the baby, the product of our love. God, I'd only known she existed inside me for three days, but already I loved her.' She bit her lip, her hands unconsciously playing with the drinks mat on the table. 'I decided I owed it to her to give him another chance.'

Ann reached across the table and briefly clasped her hand. 'I hate knowing this doesn't have a happy ending.'

Megan gave her a wobbly smile as she recalled the naive

twenty-two year old she'd been, filled with foolish notions of marrying the man she loved. 'Luke promised me the other woman was a mistake, one he wouldn't make again. He went on to finish his studies and we lived together for a few years, but the relationship had lost its sparkle. I loved him, but deep inside I couldn't trust him again.' Diving into her handbag, she pulled out a pack of tissues and wiped at the stupid tears that were creeping down her cheeks. Hadn't she cried enough over that man, for goodness' sake?

'How did it end?'

'Turns out I was right not to trust him. I didn't need to be a detective to realise he was having another affair.'

Ann winced in sympathy. 'So you threw him out?'

'I didn't have to. He positively ran out the door. He was young and ambitious.

'Being tied down by a family wasn't how he saw his life panning out.' She took a sip of her drink to ease the catch in her throat. 'He was also wildly good looking, so being tied to one woman didn't feature, either.'

'From the sounds of things, he was also irresponsible, selfish and immature. Don't make excuses for him, Megan.'

Had she been? Megan guessed she probably had. Even when she'd hated Luke, a part of her had still been in love with him, prepared to rationalise his behaviour rather than see him for what he'd been: weak and self-centred. 'You're right. There are no excuses. If I ever give away my heart again, it'll be to someone who's strong and steady. Not flashy and charming.' She would tell herself that over and over again, until she forgot what it felt like to have Scott's lips slide over hers. Forgot all about the way she'd melted against him.

Sat in his home office, bent over his computer, Scott felt nothing like the flashy charmer Megan believed him to be. What he felt like was a tired, overworked shell of a man who was starting to become disillusioned with his life. Sure, he still loved his job, but the hours of reading and preparation that went behind each case were taking their toll. He was a victim of his own success. The harder he worked, the better he was, the more in demand he became.

Giving his watch a cursory glance he sighed and stretched out his shoulders. Ten o'clock. He had maybe two more hours left in him, at most. First though, he needed more caffeine. As he padded downstairs to make himself another coffee, Scott reflected that the trouble with his life was that work *was* his life. Outside it, he had nothing. Sure he had a handful of friends he could socialise with, should he ever get the time, but that wasn't much to show for thirty-odd years. Splashing hot water into his mug, he wondered if his broodiness was just a product of not having a woman in his life at the moment. He was probably just horny. What had it been? Six months? Maybe more? Whatever, it was too long. He was a man who needed women, who enjoyed their company, both in and out of bed. It was fair to say that over the years, he'd enjoyed a lot of women. It wasn't that he was against a steady, long-term relationship, but more that he'd always gone for the simple, easy option. The woman who knew what she wanted and wasn't afraid of letting a man know it. That type of woman made for short-term fun, but not for anything long lasting.

Recently, however, he'd found himself becoming more selective. Turning down offers he'd have jumped at a year ago. He'd have liked to put it down to a more discerning, mature taste now he was creeping through his early thirties. But was that really it? Or was it that since he'd started to take an interest in Megan Taylor, all other women had failed to measure up? Though why the hell he was still knocking on that particular door he simply couldn't work out. With her cool, 'friends-only' attitude, she was so far removed from the usual women he dated, it was laughable.

With a deep sigh he thrust the steaming coffee mug on to his desk and settled back into his battered leather chair. He didn't have time to toy with thoughts of the sexy DS this evening, though if he played his cards right after their drink tomorrow, he might be toying with more than simply thoughts. A grin spread across his face as he turned his attention back to his screen. Within seconds it had been replaced with a frown.

Chapter Eight

The bar where Scott had chosen to meet was halfway between the police station and the chambers. Though Megan had been there a few times, generally she and her fellow detectives avoided the place. It was too trendy, too pretentious. Too full of smooth lawyer types: men like Scott.

'So, now you've got me here, what exactly do you want from me?' she asked as he brought the drinks to her table. Today he had on a bold, purple check shirt and purple tie, loosened at the collar. She wished she could tell him he wasn't able to carry it off. She couldn't.

He quirked an eyebrow at her question. 'I'm not sure the things that come immediately to mind are suitable for such a public place, but I'm game to discuss them if you are.'

Shaking her head she took a sip of lager and told herself to stop feeding him such obvious lines. 'I mean, what are we going to talk about?'

He considered her through narrowed eyes. 'We could start with what it is, exactly, you've got against me.'

'I thought we agreed to only one drink. What you're asking would need a whole evening.'

'Touché.' He raised his glass at her. 'Okay, let's just pick the top three items to start with.'

'Umm. Top three. Let me see.' She pretended to consider the question, adding them up on her fingers.

'Come on, don't hold back on me now. Saying what you think isn't usually a problem for you.'

She gave him a small smile. 'No, it isn't, is it?'

'Especially when it comes to what you think of me.'

At that moment his expression was neither cocky nor smug. It was guarded and tense. He clearly expected her to reel off a litany of his shortcomings. As if she really had that right to judge him. 'I don't have anything against you, Scott. I have an issue with the job you do, but not with you.'

'Why do I get the feeling that's not entirely true? That you're holding back on me?'

She took a drink and made herself answer honestly. 'Okay, the truth is, you unsettle me. Make me nervous.'

He looked so astonished, it was almost comical. 'No way.'

'It's true. I've met your type before, and it ended badly. I'm in no rush to repeat the experience.'

'My *type*?'

He was clearly unhappy with her use of the word, but she didn't know how else to put it. 'You're handsome and charming, Scott.'

'At last, she notices.'

A laugh burst out of her. 'Of course I noticed.' She hesitated, wondering how to phrase the rest.

'I sense a giant *but* hovering on your lips.'

Again, she found herself smiling. 'Okay then, *but*, in my experience, handsome and charming is a dangerous combination.'

'Dangerous how?'

She wasn't about to admit that it was dangerous to her heart – not to a man who probably never engaged his heart when it came to relationships with the opposite sex. 'Tell me, why are you so determined to get me out on a date?' she asked instead, desperately changing the subject. 'You can't really fancy me.'

'Why not?' His grey eyes were unflinching.

'Come on, I didn't have you down as cruel. Please don't make me spell it out.'

'Spell what out? How I find you incredibly attractive?'

She couldn't stop the flush that stole across her cheeks at his words, or the rapid flutter of her heart. 'That's just my point. You don't find me attractive, not really. It's just that your ego can't stand to be ignored. It's still trying to work out why I didn't immediately bat my eyelids and jump into bed with you, like every other female you've ever gone after.'

'That's simply not true,' he countered, thumping his beer glass down on the table in a rare show of frustration. 'I like you, Megan. I'm interested in getting to know you more …'

'So that you can tumble into bed with me and cross another conquest off your list, before moving on to the next woman?' Now she was being the cruel one, but somehow she couldn't stop the words from flowing. 'You think I don't know how it will end?'

'Psychic, are you now?' he replied cuttingly, his eyes glinting dangerously. 'You know that's a pretty damning character assassination.'

The coldness of his tone stopped her in her tracks. She was allowing her past experience to colour her judgement, which wasn't fair. The man in front of her wasn't heartless or callous. He was the same one who'd taught her daughter how to draw. Who'd brought them all flowers, only a few days ago. 'I'm sorry. It was wrong of me to say what I did. I didn't mean to insult you, it's just—'

'You have no interest in dating me,' he supplied for her. 'Tell me, Megan, you're nervous, but of what exactly? I know you feel the heat between us. You can't kiss me like you did the other night and then sit here and deny you feel anything.'

No, she couldn't. 'Of course I find you attractive. I suspect there isn't a woman alive who doesn't.'

'Here we go with another *but*.'

She acknowledged his attempt at humour with a lift of her lips. 'But I've learnt my lesson. There was a time, before Sally, that I was only too happy to hook up with a man like you. A man for whom charm and flattery were simply a way of life.'

'I take it you're talking about Sally's father.'

'Yes.' As she was prone to do when talking about something too personal, Megan fiddled, this time with the stem of her glass. 'He chased me, much as you're doing now. Foolishly,

I let him catch me. I believed him when he told me how gorgeous I was and how much he loved me. How I was the only woman for him.' Megan reflected sadly that this was the second time she'd dredged this sorry tale up in the space of a few days. It didn't hurt any less. 'I let him break my heart,' she finished simply.

'And now you think all men are the same?'

'Now I tread very warily when I come across handsome charmers like you.'

'Flattered and insulted in the same breath.' Shaking his head, he laughed harshly. 'So where does that leave us?'

If she had any sense, it would leave them as passing acquaintances at best. Hostile adversaries in the court room at worst. But despite everything she'd told him, and every warning bell going off in her head, Megan found she didn't want to walk away from this man. There was something about him, his company and his flattering pursuit of her, which made her feel gloriously alive. She hadn't felt like that for a very long time. 'It leaves us enjoying a drink. Between friends,' she finally replied.

'And if I want more?'

She ignored the pull of his deep, husky voice and the lure of his clear grey eyes. 'That's all that's on offer.'

Scott thought for a moment. 'Okay then, as my friend, why don't you come with me to the Law Society annual shindig on Friday? Think of it as a chance to put on a sparkly dress and admire me in a tux.'

Had he listened to a word she'd just said? Megan closed her eyes. When she looked up again, he was watching her expectantly. 'I have no desire to see you in a tux thanks, and I don't own a sparkly dress.'

'Now you're just being pedantic. Come on.' His grey eyes turned soft, his voice even more persuasive. 'There'll be hundreds of people there, so you'll be perfectly safe.'

'I'm more than capable of looking after myself.' The

moment she said the words, she knew she'd fallen into his trap. The one where she'd already imagined herself there.

He grinned. It was the grin of a man who'd been dealt a poor hand, only to find it looked like it might win him the game. 'Perfect. I'll pick you up at seven.'

So Friday night, still reeling from her total inability to refuse Scott, Megan found herself in a vast ballroom, surrounded by legal professionals dressed in their finery. From her vantage point on the first floor balcony, she stood and watched. It wasn't hard to pick out Scott, despite the fact that he was wearing the same black and white evening uniform as every other man down there. He was the one with the impossibly handsome face, the tall, imposing figure, the bold confidence. All of this was obvious not just from the way he carried himself, but from the way a crowd, or should that be a flock, of women had gathered around him.

'Lost your date?'

She turned to find an aging, balding, rotund man leering at her cleavage. 'No, just taking a break.' Deliberately she turned her back on him, hoping he'd get the message. Unfortunately, it meant she was back to staring at Scott again. Back to noticing the obscenely large entourage he'd managed to collect in the short space of time it had taken her to find the ladies.

'Great view you've got up here.' Her new friend obviously couldn't, or wouldn't read body language, because he'd now squeezed his way in next to her. 'Good place to line up your next conquest, eh?'

At that moment Scott tipped back his head and laughed at something one of his harem said.

And the man on the balcony sidled even closer to her. 'Who've you got your eye on then?'

His breath smelt of whiskey and his body radiated off so much heat it was like standing next to a furnace. A furnace that was still ogling her chest. It was so pathetic, she didn't know whether to laugh or cry. This was the type of man she was used to attracting: overbearing and dull. A man at polar opposites on the attraction scale to the one holding court below her.

'Nobody in particular,' she lied.

His eyes followed hers and landed on Scott. 'Is that him? The good looking cad with all the ladies buzzing round him?'

'He's the man I came with,' she replied stiffly, edging away. She wasn't going to hang around while he went on to point out the obvious differences between herself and Scott. The fact that Scott was down there, the centre of attention, while she was hiding away up here like the proverbial wallflower.

'How about a dance?' He waggled his eyebrows suggestively. 'Might make him jealous.'

Oh God. She had about as much chance of making Scott jealous as she did of making *Playboy* centrefold. 'Thanks, but I'd better not. We don't want to risk making a scene.'

At that moment Scott looked up. Eyes that were still crinkled with laughter searched and met hers. Held them for several heart-thumping moments before winking and turning his attention back to the blonde woman by his side.

'Better go and claim him then, love. Before she does.'

Though her heels hampered her escape somewhat, Megan positively raced back down the stairs. She told herself that her speed had more to do with escaping furnace man than doing as he'd suggested. But as she neared Scott, who was now dancing with the blonde woman, draped around him like a fashion accessory, she felt a stab of such irrational jealousy she knew she was lying to herself.

It was happening again, she thought with a shiver of fear as she walked back to their table. The seemingly irresistible pull towards a man who was, ultimately, going to break her heart.

Whilst waiting for Megan to come down from her perch on

the balcony, Scott had found himself accepting the offer to dance with the tall blonde lawyer who'd been stroking his ego for the last ten minutes. Why the hell not? Megan was only here under sufferance and was determined to keep their relationship platonic. Kathy, on the other hand, was clearly ready to jump into bed with him as soon as he said the word. And unlike Megan, the blonde laughed at his jokes, gushed over his work and generally made him feel invincible. Sadly, unlike Megan, she also failed to arouse any interest in him, despite her best endeavours. Endeavours that included sinuously rubbing her agreeably curvy body against his as they shimmied on the dance floor. It irritated the hell out of him that he was so unmoved by her. God, at this rate he was going to spend the rest of his life bloody celibate, only ever wanting the one woman he couldn't have.

With that diabolical thought in mind, he made his excuses to the now miffed blonde and strode back to the table, where Megan had finally decided to return.

'Come, dance with me.'

She stayed sitting, shaking her head. 'Please tell me you didn't drag me here to try and make me jealous,' she remarked, nodding over in the direction of Kathy who was watching them both from the side of the dance floor, her face like thunder.

He sighed. Surely she wasn't serious? 'That depends. Is it working?'

'Hardly.' She took a sip of her wine and glared back at him. 'In order to be jealous, I'd have to care.' Then she expelled a long, slow breath. 'Look, dance with other women if you want to. I'm really not bothered. But I am angry. I hate being played. I feel like this is all part of some big game you've got going.'

Scott reached out for her hand and dragged her to her feet. 'This is no game,' he told her quietly. 'You took your sweet time coming back from the ladies. I was asked to dance. It would have been churlish to refuse.' He studied her, his eyes taking in her lithe, toned body, tonight squeezed into a midnight-blue silk dress. 'If I'd known you wanted to dance with me so badly, I'd have come and found you.' Not allowing her any room for refusal, he led her towards the floor.

'I didn't say I wanted to dance,' she started to protest but he turned and placed a finger on her lips, silencing her.

'Sweet Megan, for once in your life, can't you shut that kissable mouth of yours, turn off that impressively smart brain and just go with your instincts?' He drew her stiff, unyielding body into his arms. 'Just let yourself feel,' he whispered huskily into her ear. 'Just feel.'

Right on cue, the music slowed to a seductive ballad and Megan felt herself doing exactly what he wanted her to do. She started to feel. It was intoxicating, being held in his arms, her senses swamped by the touch of his strong, hard body and the scent of his sexy aftershave. She hadn't liked seeing him dance with the busty blonde, hadn't liked the sharp stab of jealousy she'd felt at the sight of them together. God, what was she doing here?

'You don't dance like a cop,' he remarked after a few minutes, clearly surprised at the sure way she was following his steps.

She arched an eyebrow. 'Don't tell me, you were expecting me to dance flat-footed?'

'Something like that,' he agreed, trying to hide a grin.

'You, on the other hand, dance just like a lawyer.'

He raised a questioning eyebrow.

'Smooth and quick on your feet.'

'Somehow I don't think you mean that as a compliment.'

She didn't dispute it, merely smiled, and it left him feeling oddly out of sorts. Would she always see him as the slick lawyer first, the man a long way after? No doubt she believed his dancing skills were a product of some fancy private school, rather than a mother who'd loved to dance and had passed that joy on to her only child.

Determined that, for a few moments at least, he would get her to think of him as a man rather than a defence lawyer, he eased Megan even closer towards him. 'Did I tell you how stunning you look tonight?' he asked softly in her ear. 'And how much I want to run my hands over that silk-covered body of yours.'

To emphasise his point, he smoothed his right hand down her back and on to the curve of her buttocks. Deciding he liked the feel of that, a lot, he moved his left hand down to join it.

'Where I come from, that's called groping.'

He laughed, feeling a buzz of satisfaction when she didn't slap his hands away. Perhaps she didn't want to create a scene. Or perhaps she was enjoying being held as much as he was enjoying the holding. With that thought in mind, he gently squeezed her, bringing her hips snugly against his. Of course in doing so, it was hard to hide his obvious state of arousal.

'Jesus, Scott, what the hell?' She tried to pull away, looking up at him crossly when he wouldn't let her.

Totally unabashed, he grinned and kissed her gently on the mouth. 'Don't tell me you've never felt a man's arousal on the dance floor before.'

'Of course I have.' But the red blush that swept across her face told him the usually unflappable detective was feeling distinctly flustered. 'But we agreed, friends only.'

'Hey, you're the one who instigated that rule, not me,' he argued. 'I can't promise not to be aroused when I'm pressed against an attractive woman. It's a normal male reaction.'

'Does it happen with all the women you dance with then?'

'Fishing for compliments now?' he retorted, acutely aware of his lack of reaction to the attractive blonde lawyer earlier.

She blushed even more furiously. 'No.' Clearly embarrassed, she tried to wriggle out of his grasp, but Scott held on tight.

'Look, I can't help it if you turn me on, Megan. You know how attracted I am to you. I've made no secret of it.'

'But I don't understand,' she told him, shaking her head, looking almost painfully confused. 'Why me? When you could have any woman here in the blink of an eye, why bother with me?'

Those words coming from another person would have sounded artful and contrived, but the dark-haired woman looking up at him now was anything but. Her face conveyed genuine confusion.

'It's the challenge, isn't it?' she continued, eyes flaring with irritation. 'The thrill of the chase.'

Disappointment crashed through him. 'Come on, not this again. I can't deny there's some fun in the chase, but believe me, I would have found you just as attractive, and the situation a damn sight less frustrating, if you'd come to your senses and swooned in my arms on day one.'

'And if I'd done that, you'd now be dancing with someone else tonight.' Suddenly she broke away from his hold. 'Take me home.'

Without waiting for the song to end, she turned and strode off the dance floor. Scott watched her slim retreating figure with a mixture of disbelief and frustration. Disbelief that a woman he'd always thought of as confident had allowed her ex to undermine her so much: she now genuinely didn't realise how gorgeous she was. Frustration because she was so determined to always think the worst of him. It wasn't as if he deliberately set out to sleep with a woman and then dump her, just for the thrill of totting-up another conquest. It was more that in his experience, once the heat had dissipated, the relationship fizzled out.

With a deep sigh he followed after her. He wondered, as they trailed to the car, why couldn't he set his sights on a different woman? One less willing to judge him, and far more willing to sleep with him.

'Sally's father has really done a number on you,' he remarked evenly as he finally parked outside her house.

Megan turned to face him, her eyes looking luminous in the moonlight. 'He broke my heart, Scott. Do you even know what that feels like?'

He thought back to the relationships he'd had. Some had been more fun and had ended with more regret on his part. None of them had touched his heart. 'No,' he answered shortly.

Then she laughed, a bitter laugh that masked a great deal of hurt. 'Of course not. It's men like you that do the breaking.' She stepped out of the car and briefly looked back at him. 'What was the length of your longest relationship, Scott?'

He was aware of an uncomfortable flush crossing his face. 'I can't recall,' he replied stiffly.

'Okay, let's talk ballpark. Are we talking weeks, months or years?'

Shifting on his seat, he tried to think of a way out of this conversation. He couldn't. 'Weeks. But that's totally irrelevant.'

'Is it?' Carefully she shut the door. 'Thanks for an interesting evening.'

Watching her disappearing up the driveway Scott realised, with more than a touch of despair, why he had no interest in any other woman. Even angry with him, she was by far the most sexy, strong-minded and, damn it all, *fascinating* woman he'd ever met.

Chapter Nine

Scott figured he had nothing to lose by asking Megan out again. Either she'd laugh in his face, in which case he'd put the phone down and try again the following day, or she'd realise he wasn't going to give up and agree straight away, saving them both a lot of hassle.

'How about another drink?' he asked as soon as she answered.

He heard her sigh. It was a sound he was getting quite familiar with. 'Are you out of your mind? I'd have thought the last non-date we had was bad enough to put even you off.'

He winced at the emphasis on the *even*. So, it looked like she was going to choose the first, laugh-in-his-face, option. Well, he had the stomach for a long chase. 'As a matter of fact, I enjoyed our evening,' he asserted. 'Well, the bit before you walked out on me on the dance floor.'

'If I recall correctly, you forgot the ground rules.'

No, he hadn't forgotten them. He just wasn't prepared to play by them. 'A drink,' he repeated. 'You and me. Just friends.'

There was a gaping silence. He could almost hear her brain ticking over, wondering how to turn him down without giving him the opportunity to accuse her of being scared. 'This is ridiculous,' she finally replied. 'We don't even like each other all that much.'

'Hey, I like you. And it will only take one more drink to convince you that actually, even though I'm a lawyer, I'm quite likable, too.'

He couldn't be certain, but he had a feeling she was reluctantly smiling on the other end of the phone. 'Okay. One more drink. Absolutely no dancing or touching of any kind.'

'What if our fingers accidentally meet when I hand you your drink?'

'Then you might accidentally end up with it running down your shirt.'

He had no doubt she would do that, too. 'You strike a tough bargain, detective, but I guess if that's the best you can offer, I'll have to take it.'

A satisfied smile spread across his features as he put down the phone. On the face of it a drink-only date, which offered no opportunity for touching, wasn't a great achievement. But Scott knew there were some things in life that were important to approach slowly. When he put together a case he built it up carefully, starting from the bottom, rather than rushing straight for the jugular. Getting Megan to go out with him required a similar skill. Taking small steps, building a solid foundation. He'd kissed her once and experienced her instinctive response. She'd been like molten lava under his touch. He was quietly confident that at some point he'd get to sample that again. Until then, as long as he was seeing her, she would be thinking of him.

A few days after the ball, and just over a week after their first drink together, Megan found herself once more in the same bar, with the same man. She must be out of her tiny little mind. He pushed, she ran. That was the plan. So how come she was meeting him for another drink? It had to be because, no matter what she might say out loud, having a sexy man chase her, look at her with the smouldering intensity that Scott did, thrust all sensible thoughts out of her head. It was thrilling – scary as hell, but undeniably thrilling. So long as she kept her head and didn't start to believe she was anything more than a challenge to him, having the occasional drink together could be fun. Couldn't it?

He placed the ice-cold lagers on to the table and sat down opposite her once more. Somewhere between the bar and the table he'd taken off his tie and loosened his collar. He'd also run a hand through his dark hair, leaving it slightly dishevelled. It was as if he knew she preferred the more casual look on him. The one that had him looking less like a lawyer.

'How are things down at the station?' he asked as he took his first sip. 'Caught any bad guys recently?'

'A few. Let any off, recently?' She'd intended her reply to be a joke, but from the way his eyes immediately shuttered, she could see it hadn't been taken as one.

'We never did touch on that particular objection you had against me, did we?'

She held up her hand. 'I'm sorry. I was trying to make a clever reply, that's all. A poor attempt at witty banter. Please, forget I said it.'

Above his clear grey eyes, his brows knitted together. 'No, I don't think I can. You clearly have something against what I do and, I guess, looking at it from your point of view, I can see why. Equally, as a key player in the justice system, you can surely appreciate that it's vitally important that every accused person is entitled to defend themselves in court. What was it William Blackstone said? *It is better that ten guilty persons escape than that one innocent suffer.*'

She acknowledged the truth of his words with a small sigh. 'I can accept that, but I find it hard to understand how you can defend those you know perfectly well are just plain guilty.'

'I don't know they're guilty. I can assess the evidence against them, see how strong it is, but I don't know if they're guilty any more than you do.'

'Okay, okay, a clever use of words, but you know what I mean. There are some cases where it's blindingly obvious.'

'To you, maybe, but when I take on a case I always tell myself that the client is innocent. That way I ensure I do a proper job.' He cradled his hands around his glass. 'It's my job to make sure the jury see both sides to any argument, Megan. My ethical duty to point out any flaws in the prosecution case.' His face grew sober. Grim almost. 'People should lose their freedom only if there is really strong evidence to justify it. Not because of the whim of a dirty cop who wants to big up his number of collars.'

'Now wait a minute.' For a moment she'd been enjoying debating with him, pitting her wits against his, but now he'd gone too far. 'Is that what you think motivates us? Numbers?'

'No,' he replied quickly. 'Not all of you. Not even most of you. But some of you?' He looked her straight in the eye, his eyes like granite. Cool and hard. 'A very small minority of you, yes.'

There was something in the way he looked at her that told her he wasn't saying this to upset her. He was saying it because he genuinely believed it. 'Have you had experience of this?' she asked quietly.

'It happens.' Scott felt the familiar bile rise in his stomach and quickly moved to another topic. 'What motivates you, Megan? What made you want to become a detective?'

If she was surprised by the change of subject, she didn't show it. He'd come to realise that Megan wasn't often wrong-footed. 'The desire to do good. To follow in my father's footsteps.'

'Yeah, I heard your Dad was a police detective, too. That must've been tough, growing up with a father in the force.'

Her eyes flickered. 'It had its moments. Kids can be cruel sometimes.'

Didn't he know it? 'I'm guessing they only dared go so far. The thought of your father appearing on their doorstep must have put the fear of God into them.'

She smiled and his heart seemed to lift a little in his chest. 'He was pretty scary. Still is, sometimes.'

'I bet you can twist him around your little finger though, when you want to.'

Her face relaxed and she laughed. A soft, sexy sound that made more than his heart stir this time.

'I bet I can.' Glancing down at her watch she drained the rest of her pint. 'Well, it's been,' she searched for a word, 'interesting, but I've got to go. I have a daughter waiting to hear her bedtime story.'

Nodding he stood and went to ease back her chair. 'Why don't we have a meal next time? I'll pick you up. What time does Sally go to bed?'

'Err, around half seven, but—'

'Good. I'll come by just before that so I can say hello.'

She blew out a deep breath. 'Scott, I've already told you—'

'Where is the harm in a meal between friends?'

'Is that what we really are?' she asked, moving so she could study him with her cool blue eyes. 'Friends?'

'For the time being, yes.' Taking her elbow he led her through the thronging crowd of after-work drinkers and over to her car. Once there, he positioned his body so she was between him and the driver's door. 'Of course the more you get to know me,' he told her softly, his face inches from hers, 'the more you're going to fall for my not inconsiderable charm and outrageous good looks. Then you'll find you want nothing more than to get into bed with me.'

Before she had a chance to say anything, and her flashing eyes said she had plenty of retorts, he kissed her. It wasn't for as long as he'd have liked, but when her hands crept into his hair and pulled him even closer to her, he was pretty certain he'd made his point. That was when he drew back.

Opening the car door for her, he waited until she was settled into the driver's seat before giving her a final peck on the cheek. 'Until next time, Megan.'

The barefaced arrogance of the man, Megan repeatedly muttered to herself the next morning, as she attempted to break the back of her mounting paperwork. She still couldn't get Scott's parting words out of her head. Nor could she forget the way he'd kissed her. And her inflamed reaction to him. If that was how he kissed a friend, what on earth did he do to a lover? And why was part of her aching to find out?

'So, how was date number three?' Ann popped her head around the door. 'Or was it four? I forget, because I think you claim that the meal at your house shouldn't be counted as a date.'

'None of them were dates,' she muttered darkly. 'And if you want to hear the details, you need to come in. And close the door behind you.'

Ann's eyes lit up. 'Ooh, details that require privacy. Excellent.'

Laughing, Megan swivelled her chair round so she was facing her friend. 'The details don't require any privacy, but I do.'

After pulling the door firmly shut, Ann crossed her arms and gave Megan the look she gave anyone she was about to interrogate. 'Come on then, spill.'

'He kissed me again.'

Ann's eyes widened in shock. 'Again? Why didn't I hear about the first time?'

'Because it was nothing. It was when he came round to my parent's house.'

'You're telling me the man looks like a God, but can't kiss?'

Megan fiddled with the pen on her desk. 'Okay, maybe it was a lot more than nothing.'

Suddenly Ann grinned. 'I'd say, missy. Your bright red cheeks are rather giving that one away.'

Unconsciously Megan's hand went up to touch one of her, yes okay, distinctly warm cheeks. 'All right, I admit, the man can kiss. Really, totally-lose-yourself-in-the-moment, kiss. The first time, we'd just climbed off his bike and he kind of swooped. I forgot I wasn't meant to like him. Forgot my parents might be watching. Forgot everything.'

There was an explosion of laughter from the other side of the desk. 'Meg, honey, this has all the ingredients of a raunchy film. The bad-boy lawyer in his black leathers, sitting on his bike, snogging the uptight detective in front of her parents.'

'I'm not uptight.'

Ann cast an eye up and down Megan's admittedly sensible work shirt and dark trousers. 'So says the woman who's been out with the dashing lawyer four times, kissed him twice and still insists they're just friends.'

Megan let out a sigh of resignation. 'I'm being stupid, aren't I? It feels like I'm trying to push back this giant wave, but in reality it's going to roll over and suck me up anyway.'

'Being caught up in a wave doesn't have to be a scary experience, Meg,' Ann told her, reaching out to give her arm a quick squeeze. 'Not if you relax and give in to the thrill of it.'

Perhaps, Megan thought. But once you'd been churned up and spat out by a powerful wave, it was pretty hard to relax at the sight of another one relentlessly surging towards you.

Chapter Ten

Running a concerned hand over Sally's burning forehead, Megan shook her head. 'I'm going to phone Scott and cancel.'

But as she reached for the phone, her mother got there first, snatching it from her. 'Don't be silly. She's running a temperature, that's all. Your father and I are here to keep an eye on her. We'll phone you if there's any change. Besides, any minute now the paracetamol will start to kick in and she'll sleep it off.'

Megan was torn. Though she really didn't want to leave Sally, she knew perfectly well her daughter was in good hands. If she was honest, the real issue here wasn't Sally at all. It was her cowardly desire to find a legitimate way out of tonight. A genuine excuse to break off her date with Scott. For there was no denying that this time it *was* a date. Somehow he'd railroaded her into going out with him. Simply cancelling on him wasn't an option. It would look like she was running scared, and she wasn't. No way. Cool, steady, Megan Taylor wasn't terrified to death of the way her heart seemed to flutter at the mere mention of his name. Of course she wasn't. Still, cancelling their date because she didn't want to be away from her poorly daughter was surely a reasonable move.

'I'm fine, Mummy,' Sally piped up, her pale face smiling at her. 'You have to eat with Scott, like you said you would. A person should keep their promises.'

Patting her daughter's silky hair, Megan gave a rueful laugh. So much for her handy excuse. 'Okay, darling. But you need to promise me that you'll go straight to bed when you've said hello to him.'

Just then she heard the purr of a car engine, the crunch of gravel, and, a moment later, a knock on the door. *Here comes the devil*, she muttered to herself as she walked across the hallway to let him in, doing her best to ignore the scramble of her pulse and the thump of her heart against her ribs.

When she opened the door she immediately felt his eyes slowly assessing her, making no apology as he looked her up and down.

'You're a sight for sore eyes, DS Taylor,' he murmured, smiling as his eyes continued their slow rake over her body.

She wanted to be insulted. The way he was staring at her was impolite, to the say the least. It should have felt degrading. But as she registered the unmistakable heat in his eyes, the obvious appreciation, it was hard to take offense. Pretty hypocritical too, as she found her body melting in response. 'Come in for a minute,' she replied quickly, discreetly giving him a quick once-over as she moved to let him in. Dressed in a white shirt, dark navy blazer and faded jeans, he looked strikingly handsome. Far too handsome for her.

'Hey, Sally,' he exclaimed as his eyes found Megan's daughter. 'How are you doing, kid?'

'I've got a temperature, but I'm okay.'

He frowned and bent down to be on her level, running his hand over her forehead, just as Megan had done. 'You do feel a bit hot.' He turned to Megan. 'Are you sure you want to go out? We can take a rain check.'

There it was. An excuse handed to her on a silver plate. All she had to do now was agree she'd rather stay at home. So why was her tongue stuck firmly to the roof of her mouth?

'Nonsense.' Her mother came into the hallway, replying for her. 'Sally has her grandparents with her. She'll be fine. You two go out and enjoy yourselves.'

To his credit, Scott looked over to her for confirmation. She found herself nodding. So much for mother of the year.

Rummaging into the pocket of his jacket, Scott pulled out a large, expensive-looking tin of artists' crayons. 'Here you go, Sally. Something to practise with tomorrow, when you're feeling better.'

A faint flush of pleasure crept over her otherwise far too pale face. 'Cool. Thank you.'

'My pleasure.' Straightening up, Scott found Megan staring at him with an expression that was far from pleased. Whether that was to do with his gift, her daughter feeling unwell, or the prospect of an evening with him, he wasn't sure. 'Right then, we'll get on our way.' He bent to kiss Dot. 'We won't go far, and I'll have her back early, I promise.'

Tutting gently, Dot shook her head. 'Don't you let Megan fret. Sally will be just fine with us. You go and show her a good time.'

That made him chuckle. 'I will, Dot. You don't need to worry about that.'

He waited until they were in the car and driving towards the restaurant before he asked the question. 'Go on. Shoot. Tell me what's on your mind.'

Obviously surprised by his question, she glanced over at him. 'What do you mean?'

'Come on, Megan. Back there, in the hallway, you had a face like thunder. Something upset you and I have a feeling it was more than just worry about Sally.'

She turned and stared out of the front window. 'Buying my daughter presents to worm your way into my good books won't work, you know.'

He jerked a look at her, swore under his breath, and quickly pulled up by the side of the road. 'I think you'd better explain what you mean,' he ground out, trying to keep a lid on the temper now bubbling inside him. She didn't mean what he thought she did, did she?

Jutting her chin out and straightening her spine, she regarded him coolly. 'You know perfectly well what I mean, but I'll spell it out anyway, so there's no confusion. Getting into my daughter's good books won't automatically get you into my good books. It certainly won't get you into my bed.'

Filling the air with several choice profanities, he clenched the steering wheel. 'If you think, for one moment,' he told her in a voice that was as controlled as he could make it, 'that I'm trying to befriend your daughter for the sole purpose of getting you into bed, then we might as well turn round now and go back.'

Megan turned and studied him. Then she gave him a small nod. 'I just wanted to be sure. It wouldn't have been the first time a man has bought her presents and tried to charm her with a view of getting to me.'

His eyes narrowed. 'I've never had to resort to bribing a child in order to get a woman into my bed.'

She slid him a look and a small smile. 'No, I don't suppose you have.'

Her reply took some of the heat out of his anger, but he still felt insulted. Deep, down to the marrow, offended. 'And, just so we're clear, I won't be compared to any other bastards who've let you down before,' he continued with barely concealed annoyance. 'Yell at me if I cock up, sure, but don't simply assume that I'm going to, based on what other men have done before me.'

She nodded. 'Message received.'

They continued the rest of the journey in an uneasy silence. Not exactly the way Scott had imagined it in his head earlier. In fact when she'd opened the door to him, downright sexy in a midnight-blue satin shirt and skin-tight black jeans, he'd reckoned on having to interrupt the journey for an entirely different reason. A much more pleasurable one.

As he slickly manoeuvred into the car park and turned off the engine, Megan studied the man next to her. Tense, angry, brooding, he was clearly affronted. She broke the silence. 'I'm sorry, Scott. I've been thinking about how I worded it and, well, I could have been more tactful. And, anyway, Sally is a better judge of character than I am. She wouldn't have taken to you quite so quickly if she didn't think you were genuine.'

He turned to look at her. 'For a smart, sexy lady you sure seem to have chosen some tossers to go out with.'

'Present company excepted, I suppose?'

At last the trademark grin slid back across his face. She was surprised at how much she'd missed it. How much it was growing on her. Just like he was.

'But of course,' he was saying. 'I may be many things, but I'm not a tosser.'

'What are you then, Scott?'

'Good question.' Sitting back against his seat, he eyed her steadily. 'Based on feedback, I can say for certain that I'm a decent lawyer.' Light eyes burned into hers. 'And a first-rate lover.'

Incredulous laughter bubbled out of her. 'Jesus, Scott.' She shook her head. 'Just when I'm starting to think you're okay, you come out with a cheesy, arrogant line like that and reinforce what I originally thought about you.'

He shrugged and opened the car door. 'Hey, I can't help it if that's what I've been told. Maybe one day you'll be brave enough to find out for yourself if it's true.'

'Brave enough or foolish enough,' she mumbled in reply but he wasn't listening. He was walking around the bonnet to open her door. As he calmly took her hand and helped her out of the car, she found herself bristling slightly. Manners, like too much charm, made her uneasy. If a fellow officer held the door open for her at the station, her first thought wasn't, *how kind*, but, *what does he want now*?

'Calm down,' he whispered as he kept hold of her struggling hand. 'Taking my hand won't automatically turn you into a simpering female, ready to succumb to my every wish.'

'You bet it won't.'

As she walked rigidly by his side into the restaurant, he turned to study her. 'You know I used to think it was just me you had an issue with, but I'm starting to wonder if it isn't all men.'

Megan took a moment to look down at the strong hand that held hers and then up at the handsome profile of the man it belonged to. What the bloody hell was wrong with her? Why was she continuing to fight this man when every cell in her body was crying out for his touch? Fighting was making her feel like a shrew and she didn't want him to think of her like that. She wanted him to see her as he had when she'd opened the door to him this evening. With lust in his eyes. Because, truthfully, it was enormously flattering that such a gorgeous man was attracted to *her*. So what if he only wanted to take her to bed? Why couldn't that be enough? She had no room in her life for a relationship, anyway. But the occasional dinner date could be fun. So could sex. At least from what she could remember of it.

'I don't have an issue with you or with men in general,' she told him as they were shown to their table. 'I'm sorry if I gave you that impression.' She paused for the waiter to finish fussing around them. 'I've been hurt in the past and I'm afraid it's made me cynical. It doesn't help that I work in an environment full of men, so I know exactly what they think of women.'

'Oh no you don't.' He shook his head. 'What men say in the company of other men,' he smiled, 'or honorary men, isn't necessarily what they mean. It's just what they think other men want to hear.'

'And men think women are complicated?' Giving a despairing laugh, she picked up the menu and began to study it, all the while her mind drifting back to her earlier thoughts. Those of sex. Hot writhing bodies. Scott proclaiming his skills as a lover. The more she thought, the harder it was to work out what on earth she wanted to eat. Steamed sea bass or steamy sex? She made the mistake of looking over at Scott. Thank God he was studying the menu, holding it lightly with his tanned, long fingers. How would they feel holding her? Running smoothly over her naked skin? With a groan of frustration she thrust the menu down on the table.

'Perhaps you're right,' she said into the silence, avoiding

his eyes. 'I shouldn't let past experiences put me off what can, at times, be a mutually satisfying, healthy connection between two consenting individuals.' She hesitated for a fraction, then plunged straight in. 'I'm seriously considering giving it another go. Sex I mean.' Finally she dared to look up and directly into his startled eyes. 'With you.'

Scott had never felt so utterly thrown off balance in his life. He knew shock must be etched all over his face but was too damned flabbergasted to wipe it off. Finally, the result he'd been angling for. One he was certain he'd blown all chance of achieving during the car journey here. But there was something in the way she'd worded it that left him feeling far from thrilled. In fact it had him confused and not a little put out. *I'm seriously considering giving it another go* wasn't exactly the same as *Scott I want you. I have to have you.* No, it was more an admission that she needed to get back into dating again and was thinking of using him to test the waters. Hell, she was making him feel like a flipping gigolo. Irked, he rubbed at his freshly shaven chin. A stark reminder that getting her into bed with him had been exactly what he'd wanted as he'd dressed tonight. He'd be a fool to jeopardise the chance by being too sensitive.

Clearing his throat he reached for his glass and took a long gulp of water. 'Well, if I can help in any way, with your serious considering, let me know.'

'I will.' Looking down at the menu, she smiled, her dimples almost winking at him in the candlelight. 'Of course I'll be remembering your claim from earlier.' She peeked at him from under her lashes. 'You know, the part about you being a first-rate lover.'

Scott allowed a slow smile to creep across his face. Totally at ease now, he stared back at her, his grey eyes smouldering. 'I won't disappoint.'

Megan wriggled uncomfortably in her seat. Suddenly she felt too hot. Her blouse too tight. Her bra too rough against her nipples. What was that saying about not playing with fire if you didn't want to get burned?

He gave her another scorching look and she pressed her legs together. How about if she just wanted to get singed a little?

Chapter Eleven

Settling back into the luxurious leather seat of his car for the journey home, Megan could honestly say she'd enjoyed the meal. The food, the company and the conversation. Scott was definitely smooth, but he was also very knowledgeable, easy to talk to and surprisingly funny. So much so that her sides were actually aching from laughing at his tales from court. She'd expected him to be erudite. She hadn't expected him to have such a dry, wicked sense of humour.

As he climbed in beside her, she smiled at him. 'What is it about you and transport, Scott? I can almost understand the extravagance of the car, or the bike, but *both*?'

About to start the engine, Scott stopped and turned to look at her. 'Can I help it if I love to play with beautiful things?'

Of course he was talking about machines, but it didn't stop her breath hitching at the dark, intense look he gave her. It made her believe, for one moment, that he thought she was beautiful, too. Clearly she wasn't. Built more like a boy than a girl, she had what was at best described as an interesting face. Some men had called it unique; while that wasn't exactly flattering, it had at least been better than *pixie features*, a phrase used by her first boyfriend who'd lasted a week. But when she looked in the mirror at her pointy chin and nose that turned up slightly at the end, she had to concede he'd had a point. The way she wore her hair – short and cropped – sadly didn't help the situation. It did, however, make it easier to get ready for work in the morning.

She brought her mind back to Scott and his huskily worded statement. 'Umm, I think you mean you like to play with fast and beautiful things.'

He smiled and inched his face closer to hers. In the dark of the car he looked intensely male. 'Yep. Fast definitely works for me, too.'

She shouldn't have been surprised by the kiss. God knows the heated looks he'd been giving her all evening had been a pretty clear warning sign. But apparently not clear enough. As his mouth settled over hers, hot, searing, melting, the breath seemed to rush from her body in a sharp gust. Then his lips were nibbling at hers, and his incredibly clever tongue was finding its unerring way into the depths of her mouth. He was, without doubt, a fabulous kisser. Of course he'd had a heck of a lot of practice, but, oh wow, it was almost indecent what he was doing now. What he was making her feel with just a kiss. She sucked in a breath as she felt the heat of his hands sliding under blouse and then under her bra. He wasn't stopping at a kiss.

A moan tore out of her instinctively, the same way her back arched as his deft fingers rubbed lightly over a taut, sensitive nipple.

'Do you like to have your nipples touched?' he asked softly, undoing her blouse with his other hand.

'Umm ...' How the hell was she supposed to talk? To have any coherent thoughts when he was making her brain feel like mush? Briefly his hands disappeared to expertly undo the catch on her bra. Then his mouth left hers and the tongue that had stirred up so much desire when in her mouth now turned its attention to her nipples.

Megan knew she was in a car, in a restaurant car park. It didn't seem to matter. All that mattered was that he carried on doing whatever he was doing with his tongue. She placed her hands on his soft, silky hair and pushed him closer to her, wanting more of his mouth, his tongue, wanting him to suckle her forever. Her breasts, which had always been too small, too unfeminine, were now giving her more pleasure than she'd ever experienced.

'Oh, God, Scott.' Another groan, this time as his hands

loosened the waistband of her jeans and crept inside her knickers. She had no time to wonder which ones she'd put on as his fingers delved into her heat. With a moan of sheer bliss she gave in to the pleasure he seemed intent on giving her. The dual sensation of his clever fingers moving with the same rhythm as the tongue on her nipples soon had her crying out as an intense orgasm ripped through her body. Shattered, she collapsed against the seat.

Scott moved his lips to her face, teasing her with gentle kisses. 'I want you,' he told her huskily. 'More than I've ever wanted anyone.' She must have looked panicked because he smiled. 'No, not here. That was just to give you something to think about. To weigh in with all those considerations of yours.'

'Yes,' she breathed, still battling to regain her breath.

'I guess it's time we were heading back.' The thickness of unsatisfied desire hung in his voice. Was still notable inside his jeans.

Megan nodded weakly. She'd just allowed Scott to make love to her in a car park. Christ. How had it happened that the cool, indifferent woman who'd been steadfastly pushing him away only a week ago was now a spent puddle on his passenger seat?

As he drove them home – the confident, sure hands that had brought her such pleasure a moment ago, now resting on the steering wheel – she suddenly remembered Sally. Where was her mind? She'd let this man dominate it so much she hadn't given a thought to her sick daughter, until now. Wracked with guilt she hastily pulled out her phone.

'Mum, it's me. We're on our way back. How's Sally?'

'Darling I don't want you to panic, but she's still very feverish so we've called the doctor out. He's with her now.'

'Oh my God.' Slumping down into the seat, Megan held a hand to her head, mortified. While she'd been groaning in ecstasy, her daughter had been burning a fever.

'What's up?' Scott cast a quick glance at her, his concern evident.

'The doctor is with Sally. She's still hot.'

He nodded and she felt the subtle surge of power as he put his foot down on the accelerator. 'We'll be there in a minute.'

Nothing dampened ardour more than the thought of a sick child, Scott thought as he sped through the streets. Minutes ago his mind had been full of Megan. He'd been imagining her body, hot and naked, beneath his. Moving with the same uninhibited grace as it had just now. Only this time with him inside her. Now all he could picture was Sally's pale face.

As he brought the car to a stop on the drive, Megan leapt out and ran towards the front door. She seemed surprised when she found him right behind her.

'Thanks, Scott. It was a good evening. Sorry to end it like this …'

He followed her into the house. 'I'm not going anywhere yet.'

'Look, Sally's ill, we're going to have to call it a night.' She started running up the stairs. Resolutely he followed her.

When she reached the top of the stairs and gave him a hard look, he suddenly realised what she was thinking. 'Don't tell me you think I'm hanging round just to pick up where we left off?' he asked bluntly, shaking his head in utter astonishment at the look on her face. A look that told him that was *exactly* what was going on in her head. Feeling as if she'd kicked him in the stomach, he was about to vehemently deny her silent accusation when he realised where they were standing. He had no right to hound her outside her daughter's bedroom, no matter how offended he was. 'I'll wait downstairs,' he told her tightly. 'I want to hear how she is.'

He was pacing the floor of the hallway when Megan appeared at the top of the stairs. 'The doctor advises that we take her to hospital, just as a precaution.'

'I'll drive you.'

'Thank you,' she whispered, and despite his annoyance, his heart went out to her. Even more so when she reappeared, holding Sally in her arms. Worry was etched across her face. A face that was now almost as pale as the daughter she was clutching.

He bounded up the stairs, two at a time. 'Here, let me carry her.'

Though she hesitated fractionally, she obviously thought better of it and shifted Sally into his arms.

The journey in the car was quiet. Sally slept on Megan's lap in the back seat and Scott concentrated on getting them to the hospital quickly and in one piece.

Once there he again took hold of Sally as Megan went on ahead, rushing to the A&E desk. Thankfully the on-call doctor had already phoned ahead and they were shown straight through to a nearby ward.

'I'll wait out here,' Scott told her when he'd settled Sally on to the bed.

She shook her head. 'Thanks so much, Scott, but you don't need to wait now. It could be hours before we know anything more. I'll be okay.'

'As I said,' he replied firmly, 'I'll wait out here.' Did she really think he could leave them both now? Two people he'd become surprisingly attached to in such a short space of time.

Two hours later, Megan was feeling a lot happier. The doctors had seen Sally, pronounced that it was a virus, nothing serious, and set her up with an intravenous drip and some stronger medicine to bring the temperature down. That had been a while ago. Now she was feeling cooler and sleeping peacefully.

Figuring she wasn't going to wake in a while, Megan wandered out of the ward to stretch her legs. She stopped in her tracks at the sight of a tall, broad-shouldered man, sat on one of the hard plastic chairs in the family area outside. His head had dropped forward on to his chest, and despite the uncomfortable position, he looked fast asleep. God, she'd forgotten all about Scott – had naturally assumed he'd gone home. Slowly she walked towards him, cringing inwardly as she recalled how she'd initially thought he'd wanted to hang around just to finish what they'd started in the car. It was becoming increasingly clear that Scott Armstrong wasn't at all the man she'd first believed him to be. He was a much nicer, kinder man. A better man. One she could easily start to like, God help her. Really, really like.

As she neared him he stirred and opened his eyes. 'Hey, how is she?'

Megan smiled as she watched him struggle to sit up, his once crisp white shirt now looking as if it had been slept in. Which it had. 'She's good, thank you. The doctor said it's a virus. Her temperature is already coming down and she's fast asleep.'

'Phew.' He stretched out his long, denim-clad legs. 'Scary stuff, eh?'

'Yeah, scary all right.' Hesitating just a moment, she went to sit next to him, acutely aware of his body as it touched against hers. 'Thanks for hanging around, Scott. I didn't expect to see you here still.'

'Why not? You're still here.'

She smiled at his baffled look. 'Yes, but she's my daughter.'

'And you're my date.'

Jesus. His expression was so serious, as if he couldn't understand why she'd believed he wouldn't stay. She felt a gentle tug at her heart. 'I'm sorry you had to spend the last part of the evening dozing off on a plastic chair in a hospital,' she found herself whispering. 'I'm guessing it isn't the way you were hoping it would end.'

Once more he regarded her steadily, as if his glorious grey eyes could see into her very soul. 'No, not exactly, but you don't have to apologise. I stayed because I wanted to. As I keep telling you, I'm not like the other men you've known. Don't always expect the worst of me.'

'Tonight's not ended the way I'd hoped, either,' she admitted, trying to stifle a yawn but failing. Before she knew it he was gently draping an arm around her shoulders, pulling her towards him and settling her against his solid chest.

'Why don't you close your eyes for a bit? Have a sleep. It'll do you good.'

Megan shifted a little to make herself more comfortable and then started to close her eyes.

'And anyway, how can you say this isn't the way I wanted our evening to end?' he whispered into her ear. 'You're sleeping with me, aren't you?'

She laughed softly, and promptly fell asleep.

Though his body felt stiff from the angle he'd been dozing, Scott didn't dare move. He didn't want to disturb Megan, who was now breathing quietly, snuggled against his shoulder. As he looked down at her, his heart filled with a tenderness he hadn't expected. What had started out as a desire to simply get this feisty, attractive female into his bed had taken a totally new direction. One he'd never envisioned it taking. Women simply didn't have a serious place in his life, so it was hard to understand this aching feeling he had in his chest while he watched Megan sleep. He hadn't even made love to her, for crying out loud. Not properly. Not where he could take time to enjoy her. To satisfy them both. But that would happen now. He knew it. What he was interested to find out was where it would go afterwards, when the initial lust had been quenched.

He let out a short exhale, gobsmacked that he was even thinking that far ahead. He never had before. Then again, Megan was unlike any woman he'd ever met before. A woman in a man's world, she was stronger, tougher and more stubborn than any he'd previously dated. But contrasting with that was her soft, tender, fun side. The one he'd seen when she was with Sally. And then there was the sexy, passionate side he'd glimpsed in the car. That was a side he knew he could bring out even more, if only she'd let him.

All in all, she was a whole lot of woman, he mused to himself. Then, closing his eyes, he drifted back to sleep.

Chapter Twelve

'You never did tell me how your date with the attractive lawyer went,' Megan's mother remarked as she and her parents sat in the lounge the following evening.

The glow from the fire – not really necessary with the warm spring weather, but appreciated all the same – and the knowledge that Sally was a million times better tonight, thanks to sleeping most of the day, had relaxed Megan so much that the question took her off guard. 'Really well,' she replied unthinkingly before catching the dart of satisfaction in her mother's eye. Damn. Now, if she wasn't careful, Mum would be buying the hat and planning the wedding.

'He seems pretty solid.' That was praise indeed from her far more protective father.

Though in Megan's eyes the jury was still out on the term solid, she had to admit that last night had gone a long way towards changing her opinion of Scott Armstrong. It had been almost four in the morning before the hospital had found Sally a private room and she'd been able to sleep on the put-up bed next to her. Only then had Scott, crumpled and stiff from dozing upright on the hard hospital seats, made his way home.

'He certainly came up trumps last night,' she agreed, though the cynical side of her, the side hardened by previous experience, still worried that Scott was simply skilfully manipulating her into his bed. Which didn't mean to say she couldn't enjoy that. As long as she did so with her eyes wide open. 'I think I'm going to see him again.'

Her mother was trying hard not to look smug. 'I'm glad,' was all she said.

For some reason, Megan felt the need to justify her previous doubts. 'Of course everything I said before is still true. Sally's at a vulnerable age. One where she'll be inclined to see a prospective father in any man she comes across. I don't want her forming an attachment to a man who has no intention of being a permanent part of our lives. Frankly, it's the last thing I need, too.'

'But you still need to live,' her mother added firmly. 'If you don't stick your neck out now and again and take a risk, it makes for a very dull life. One filled with *might have beens*.'

'I agree it's time for me to unbend a little,' she conceded, picking at a piece of stray fluff on her jumper. 'Plus, Sally's already infatuated with Scott, so it seems stupid to keep fighting the inevitable. As long as I'm careful and have no higher expectations than having a good time, it should be possible to enjoy his company without me getting hurt.'

The sound of the phone ringing interrupted any further conversation, much to Megan's relief. Talking about matters of the heart was always hard for her, whoever it was with. Even her darling mum. Putting her mug down on the coffee table, she went to answer it.

'Ah, the delicious Detective.'

'Scott.' The sensible part of her knew he was merely being an outrageous flirt. Another side of her seemed to turn into a giant marshmallow at his words.

'I was phoning to check on Sally. How is she doing?'

His question took her by surprise, though it shouldn't have; he'd spent the better part of last night in the hospital, waiting for news on her. 'She's much better thanks. Slept most of today, but she was almost back to her old self this evening.'

'Good.' There was a pause. 'And how are you? Recovered from spending most of the night in my arms?'

That was more what she'd expected to hear from him. He could turn the charm on like a switch: a slightly lower voice, husky overtone, suggestive words. It all combined to cause an answering flash of heat deep within her. Worried that her parents might be able to read her reaction, she turned to face the wall. 'I'm a bit tired, but grateful she's okay,' she replied, endeavouring to keep her reply neutral. 'How about you? Did you manage to get some sleep?'

A deep chuckle drifted back down the phone to her. 'No, I can't say I did. I kept picturing you as you were in the car park, only this time with me properly inside you. An unbelievably hot image, but it didn't do much to help me sleep.'

Oh God. Her breath caught in her throat. How was she supposed to reply to *that*? Especially with her parents in the same room. 'I—well—umm.' She gave up.

He laughed into the silence. 'Hey, at last I've rendered you speechless. I didn't realise all it took was some dirty talk. I'll have to try that again. So, while the platform's mine, so to speak, I'll take the opportunity to ask if you're doing anything tomorrow.'

'Evening?'

'Well, no, I had the daytime in mind, but we can include the evening too, if you're free.'

'I ...' Irritatingly, she was floundering again. Was she now on the verge of spending all of Saturday with him? Day and evening? Lawyers. They tied a person up in knots, getting them to agree to things before they had a chance to work out what it was.

'Excellent. I figured a trip to the seaside might work. Forecast says it's going to be a lovely day. A bit of sea air should finish Sally's rehabilitation off nicely.'

'You're asking *both* of us?'

'Sure. I thought Sally might enjoy a trip to the pier. I presume, knowing her mother, that she's not afraid of the rides.'

The man really did leave her tongue-tied. He was calmly planning a whole day with them by the sea, as if taking a child on fairground rides was a perfectly normal way for him to spend his weekend. 'Are you certain this is what you want to do?' she asked bluntly.

'Why wouldn't it be?' Now his smooth voice carried an edge of irritation.

'Look, Scott, it's a really kind offer, but really, you don't have to plan a day for Sally. You and I can see each other in the evening, if you like.'

There was a long pause, during which she heard his deep sigh. 'Megan, I enjoy Sally's company. And yours. What's wrong with wanting to spend some time with both of you, together?'

'Well, nothing, but ...'

'You still think I'm a heartless bastard who's only interested in your daughter so that I can get to you.' Over the last minute his voice had gone from irritated to downright annoyed. 'In your view of the world I'm going to toy with you both and then ditch you as soon as I've had what I want.'

Ouch, when he put it like that, it sounded cruel. Whatever else he might be, he wasn't that. 'No, I don't think you're after me through Sally.' She really didn't. Not now. Any man with half a brain could see he didn't need to befriend her daughter to get her into bed. She was there already. It was no longer a matter of if, but when.

'Good. I'll pick you up around eleven.'

Slowly Scott put down the phone and reached for his bottle of beer, gulping the rest down in one go. When he'd finished he wiped a hand across his mouth and swore eloquently. The woman was driving him nuts. Oh, to be attracted to an easy-to-read woman who was soft and pliable, not opinionated and stubborn. One who actually thought he was a decent bloke, not some slimy lowlife who got kicks from manipulating women. Sure, she'd denied she thought he was using Sally to get to her. At least he might have convinced her on that one. She hadn't refuted the rest though. The words *of course I don't think you're a heartless bastard* definitely hadn't been uttered. Running a hand through his hair in frustration, he was forced to concede it didn't seem to matter. Whatever she thought of him, there was no getting away from the fact that he couldn't get her out of his head.

Irritated with her and with himself, he yanked another beer out of the fridge and flipped off the top. Maybe, if he drank a few more of these, her opinion wouldn't hurt so much.

The phone rang as he was tackling his third bottle. Snatching it up, he barked into the receiver. 'Armstrong.'

There was silence. Just the faintest sound of someone breathing.

'Hello?'

Then he heard it. The soft, heartbreaking sound of crying. 'Mum? Is that you?'

The sobs continued and he fought his instincts to throw the phone against the wall. God, he was already feeling good and sorry for himself as it was. He didn't need a call from his mother to ice that particular cake. Then again, he reminded himself as he clutched the receiver tightly in his hands, at least now he knew she was alive. It was a step up from yesterday. What he needed to do now was tread cautiously. Coax her into talking to him, not yell and scare her off.

'Mum, please, are you okay?' he asked with what he thought was pretty admirable control. 'Where are you?' His questions were met with silence. 'Can I come and get you?'

'No, I'm fine,' she finally replied, her voice croaky and slightly slurred.

'Let me know where you are, please.' He'd beg, if that's what it took.

He heard sniffing, then a deep breath. 'I can't. I don't want you to find me. I don't want you to see me like this.'

Slumping down on the sofa, he shut his eyes, rubbing his free hand across his face. Christ. 'Have you been drinking again?'

'Yes.' It was the faintest of replies, but enough to make his heart sink.

'Mum, I thought this time you were going to really try.' The last time he'd seen her, he'd checked her into a rehabilitation clinic. That had been two months ago.

'I'm not strong like you,' she mumbled. 'I can't do it.'

'You are strong, Mum.' God knows, she had been – until alcohol had sucked all that strength from her. 'You've had a lot to put up with. Stuff that would have sunk most women.' He took in a deep breath, tried another tactic. 'I've met someone, Mum. Another strong lady. I think you'd like her.' Not that the two would ever meet. He loved his mother from the bottom of his heart, but she represented a part of his life he wanted to keep hidden. At least until he could convince Megan he wasn't the man she thought him to be. Turning up with an alcoholic mother wasn't going to help his case.

'That's good.' A few more sniffles and then the sounds of fresh weeping. 'You're a good son, Scott. I'll make sure I keep out of your way.'

'No,' he replied sharply. 'That's not what I want. I want you here, with me, so I can look after you. Please, come home.'

'I can't, Scott.'

The line went dead. Letting out a long, deep sigh of frustration Scott carefully put down the phone, his eyes resting on the half-drunk bottle of beer sitting on the coffee table in front of him. Suddenly the thought of it made him sick. Grabbing it, he marched to the kitchen and drained the rest down the sink.

When she'd put down the phone, Cathy Armstrong put her head in her arms and wept. She cried for the life she'd once had but could never get back. For the husband who was no longer with her. For the son she loved more than anything, but was too ashamed to go and see. Raising her head she scrutinised her face in the mirror. Haggard, pale, far older than her years. She was a wreck, and she knew it. She'd tried, God knows she'd tried, but she couldn't seem to get beyond the thought of another drink. Nothing else in her life seemed to matter enough. Not even her son, which was an awful thing to have to admit to. Certainly not her self-respect. That was something she'd lost many years ago. Once she'd been a proud woman, married to a proud man. Now she was just pathetically grateful to have found a lover who not only didn't knock her around, but who seemed to understand her need to drink. Better even than that, Reg had introduced her to tablets. The drink helped her to function, but the tablets actually deadened the pain. Sometimes they even made her want to smile.

As she continued to study her gaunt image in the mirror, Cathy acknowledged that if Scott could see her now, he would be distraught. Distraught and utterly ashamed. And who could blame him? He was an important man. A barrister. There was no way he'd want his alcoholic mother to lurch back into his life, as she had been doing off and on over the last few years. Certainly he wouldn't want anything to do with the woman who looked back at her now. She would be an embarrassment. The very last thing Cathy wanted was to shame her son any further.

'Cathy, you up there?'

It was Reg. Reg with his expanding waistline, thinning hair and sometimes rather cold, hard eyes. Eyes she managed to ignore when he was pouring her another drink.

'Why don't you come down here,' he shouted up at her. 'I've got you something that'll perk you up, my darlin'.'

Cathy picked up a brush and straightened out her limp, dyed-blonde hair. Then she powdered her nose, rubbed some blusher into her too-pale cheeks and followed his voice downstairs, her mind already anticipating the buzz she might get from whatever it was he was going to give her. In her heart she knew she was degrading herself even further by turning to drugs. They might only be soft drugs at the moment, but she had a feeling it was only a matter of time before she'd be begging for something harder. It didn't seem to matter what her heart was saying though, her head needed the pick-me-up that only chemicals could provide. Cathy Armstrong was in a long, dark, deadly tunnel. One she'd lost the will to find her way out of.

Chapter Thirteen

Megan couldn't believe she was walking along Brighton promenade next to a man wearing a bright pink shirt. For some reason she'd always laughed at the thought of men wearing pink. Maybe it was because all the men she'd ever known were determinedly macho. She remembered once buying Luke a pink T-shirt, more as a joke than anything else. He'd thrown it back at her and told her to keep it: only girls wore pink.

Under her eyelashes she shot another surreptitious glance in Scott's direction. Clearly it wasn't only girls who could wear pink. Tall, dark-haired, ridiculously attractive men could wear it, too. The colour might say *girl*, but there was nothing remotely feminine about the man who was wearing it. Of course it helped that he wore faded, low-slung jeans that hugged the hard contours of his muscular thighs. And his bum. She'd certainly noticed that.

'Mum, look at the waves.' Sally tugged at her hand, bursting into her lustful thoughts. Thank God. She might have decided that she wanted to make love to this man. Perhaps tonight. But first she had a whole day to get through. Time to take her mind off Scott's undeniably hot backside and on to her clearly excited daughter.

'Do you want a paddle?' she asked, looking down at Sally's animated face. Though it wasn't warm enough for swimming, Megan figured her daughter could probably get away with dipping her toes in.

'Can I?' Sally glanced up at her, her expressive eyes like those of a puppy, desperate for a walk.

Before she had a chance to reply, Scott was picking Sally up and throwing her over his shoulder. 'I'm not sure about a paddle,' he shouted, jogging across the pebbles towards the sea. 'Why don't we just drop you straight in and be done with it?'

Sally shrieked. Megan was pretty certain it was with delight, but she ran up alongside her anyway, just in case Scott decided to go through with his boast. There was an unpredictable edge to him, one that added to his attraction, but definitely made her nervous when it involved her daughter and the cold sea.

She needn't have worried. Having swung Sally over the water a couple of times he relented and dropped her gently on to the beach next to him. 'Last one in is a smelly armpit.'

Giggling happily, Sally immediately plonked herself down on the pebbles and began to tug off her trainers.

Unzipping his boots, Scott stared up at Megan. 'What are you doing standing there? It includes you as well.'

Megan shook her head. 'I'm quite happy being a smelly armpit. At least my feet will be warm.'

She stood by and watched as they finished taking off their shoes and began to roll up their trousers. Megan was about to crouch down and help Sally, but realised that Scott was already there, methodically hitching her white jeans over her knees before going to work on his own. She didn't even pretend not to watch as his well-defined calves appeared, dusted with dark, wiry hair. Perhaps, if she ever did get to see him naked, she'd find a part of him that wasn't damn near perfect. She hadn't seen one so far.

As he plunged his feet into the water, Scott sucked in a deep breath. 'Sh—sugar,' he yelled, altering the exclamation just in time. There were lots of things he had to get used to when in the company of a child. Making certain he didn't swear was one of them. There was also the fact that, although he'd been wanting to do so for hours, ever since she'd opened the door to him that morning, he couldn't yank Megan against him. Couldn't cover her mouth with his and kiss her until her head swam. His had been swimming all day – paddling his feet in the cold sea was a flipping good idea.

As Sally came to join him he lifted her by the arms and

pulled her up high over the waves. She seemed to enjoy it. At least the smiles wreathed across her face indicated as much. It was odd. He'd never thought kids could be so much fun. To him they'd always been a nuisance. Little people who got under his feet when he was trying to dash somewhere in a hurry. Screaming terrors on an aeroplane that ruined an otherwise pleasant flight. A flight they and their parents had no doubt boarded ahead of other, full-fare paying, adult passengers. Boy did that cheese him off. Then he looked over at Sally. Clearly there was another side to children. Or maybe it was just that Sally was special.

'Are you ready for the pier?' he asked a little while later as he attempted to dry off their feet with the tissue Megan had provided from her handbag. 'I see your mother was too scared to venture into the water. Maybe she'll manage one of the rides instead?'

'Mum's not scared of anything,' Sally pronounced as she stood up. 'Are you, Mum?'

Megan shook her head. 'Life's too short to spend time being scared.' He arched her a look and she blushed, clearly recalling, like him, her earlier admission that he made her nervous.

'So you won't leap into my arms when we go in the haunted house?'

'Unlikely.'

'Not even if I make a really loud noise just when the ghost pops out?' he probed, enjoying teasing her.

Again she shook her head. 'Nope, not even then.'

'What about if I kiss you?'

He heard Sally chuckling as Megan swallowed, hard, then darted him a loaded look. 'Is that your technique for scaring off unsuitable suitors? Threatening to kiss them?'

He laughed, the wind blowing his hair across his brow. 'No, that's how I attract the women I want to make out with,' he countered effortlessly.

'Smug bastard,' she breathed under her breath, quiet enough so that Sally couldn't hear.

It only made him laugh even harder.

They walked amicably along to the end of the pier, Sally enchanted by the seagulls swooping overhead. At least she was, until her attention was caught by the stalls. 'Mum, look, a shooting range. You've got to win me something.'

Scott eyed his small companion. 'As the only male, isn't that my duty?'

'Nah, Mum should do it. She used to be an AOF.'

'She means AFO. Authorised Firearms Officer,' Megan interrupted.

Sally nodded vigorously. 'She's really good.'

'Well, that puts me firmly in my place,' he countered dryly.

Megan turned and smiled at him. 'Hey, don't feel too bad. It isn't often you come out with the area champion marksman.'

He raised an eyebrow. 'Pretty hotshot, eh?'

'Yep,' she replied cockily. 'But don't just take my word for it.'

Megan reached into her bag for her purse but Scott was already there, thrusting a note under the stall keeper's nose. 'Allow me. At least that way I can say I contributed to the prize.'

She raised the shotgun, eyed her targets and, using the three cork bullets supplied, knocked down each target in turn. No fuss. No fiddling around lining up the shots. Just bang, bang, bang.

As Sally beamed with delight at the giant furry dog thrust into her hands, Megan looked coolly over at Scott. 'Want a go?'

He shook his head. He knew when he was licked. And damned if he wasn't totally in awe of her style. It wasn't just the fact that she could shoot like a champion; it was the manner in which she'd done it. Clinically. He realised she would be the same in a real-life situation, if faced with a real gun. Cool, calm, unflappable. He hadn't considered that side of her before. The side that sometimes came across danger. That dealt with hardened criminals. Men who wouldn't hesitate to intimidate. To shoot first, ask questions later. She'd never seemed more strong and tough to him than she did at that moment. Or more downright sexy.

In a bid to reassert his masculinity, Scott had a go at the basketball stall. The cuddly dinosaur he won might have been smaller and altogether less impressive than the stuffed dog Sally was proudly carrying, but he tucked it smugly under his arm nonetheless. When Megan smirked and gave him a knowing stare, he merely shrugged. 'I was in the university basketball team.'

Her eyes laughed at him. 'I played county netball at school.'

He stared at her, trying to work out if she was bluffing, then decided it wasn't worth the risk. If he insisted on her having a go and she beat him at that, too, the day would be over for him. So, potentially, would the evening. He wasn't totally sure whether she'd decided to sleep with him yet, but he had a horrible feeling he might struggle to perform if she took away much more of his manhood. 'Lunch, I think,' he pronounced.

After lunch they tackled the rides, both of them taking it in turns to sit with Sally. No attraction was left out, irrespective of how big or small, timid or downright terrifying. Sally happily carried the furry dog around all afternoon, with Scott left feeling like a total plonker clutching the purple dinosaur. When he once again caught Megan slyly grinning at him, he shoved it further under his arm.

'At least it doesn't clash with your shirt,' she said.

'Ha ha.' He winced at his lack of a decent comeback, but right now his mind wasn't focused on quick repartee. It was too full of thoughts of what a really perfect day it had been. One in which he'd felt like part of a family. Shit ... he felt his heart literally still in his chest and wondered where on earth *that* had come from? His days of playing happy families were well and truly over, had been since he'd turned seven. He had no plans to resurrect them again with a family of his own. He simply wasn't the settling down type. And yet, whilst he could dismiss the notion of family life, he couldn't dismiss the warm feeling around his heart as he thought of the day he'd spent with this woman and her child. He wanted more days like today, even though the thought of how much he wanted that scared him half to death. Far more so than any of the rides he'd just been on.

Walking slowly back towards the car, Scott noticed Sally dragging her feet a little. Not surprising, poor girl. Only two days ago she'd been in hospital. Maybe spending so long out today hadn't been a great idea, after all. 'Fancy a ride on my shoulders?' he asked, gently mussing her hair.

She didn't need to reply. The relief and pleasure shining from her eyes was enough.

Thrusting the purple creation at Megan, quickly followed by the ridiculously large dog, he swung Sally up and on to his shoulders. 'How's the view from up there?'

She giggled. 'Cool. I can almost touch the sky.'

Left holding two embarrassing toys now, Megan supposed she should have felt miffed. Instead, she was touched by Scott's sensitivity. That he'd noticed Sally was tiring was one thing. That he'd solved it so quickly and simply was another. 'You're a nice man, Scott Armstrong,' she murmured.

His eyes darted quickly to hers. 'Nice?' He appeared to mull the word over in his mind. 'It's not bad, but can't you think of a description that's a little more ...' He scratched at his jaw. 'Rugged? Manly? Definite even?'

'You should be pleased with nice, buster,' she replied archly, though her lips were twitching, a sure sign that if she wasn't careful she'd soon be giggling like her daughter. 'It's a big improvement on how I might have described you a couple of weeks ago.'

He screwed up his face, as if in pain. 'Yeah, okay, I'm not sure we want to go there again.'

'What description were you hoping for?' she asked after a moment. 'Gorgeous? Incredible? Hunky?'

He might have a sensitive side, but it didn't mean he wasn't insufferable sometimes. 'Do you want me to lie?'

With an exaggerated sigh he gave in. 'Okay, let's stick with nice for the time being. I'll try and like it.' Then he shot her a sideways glance, winked and lowered his voice to a husky murmur. 'You never know, by the end of the day you might be thinking of some better descriptions.'

Distracted, Megan almost tripped and had to grab on to his arm to stop herself from falling.

By the time they arrived back at her house, Sally was fast asleep in the back of the car, clutching at both the furry prizes. It was a sight to soften the hardest of hearts.

Scott turned off the engine and looked over at Megan, his expression unreadable.

'Are you coming in or going straight home?' she asked.

'That depends.'

'On what?'

'On whether you're going to come back with me,' he replied softly.

Suddenly there was no doubting the expression on his face, or the sentiment behind the words. She might have known Scott wasn't the type to beat around the bush. He knew what he wanted and he went straight after it. Now it was up to her to decide whether she was prepared to be as bold. She, too, knew what she wanted.

'Yes,' she replied quietly, her heart racing. 'I'll come back with you.'

His mouth curved into a huge grin. 'In that case, I'll come in while you settle Sally and then I'll go home. With you.'

Chapter Fourteen

Scott would never know how he got through the hour of polite conversation with Megan's parents while she was off getting Sally ready for bed. All he kept thinking about was the order in which he was going to strip off Megan's clothes. And whether he would, actually, be able to wait until he stripped her naked before he made love to her. Right now, the bedroom seemed an awfully long way away. He might have to take her in the hallway, first. Yeah, that could work. Get all this pent up sexual frustration out of their systems in one quick hit, so he could then concentrate on really making love to her. Slowly, sensuously.

Steadfastly getting in the way of his delicious thoughts were Megan's parents, who insisted on wanting to know about the day. Where they'd gone. What they'd eaten. To say it was her *parents* who were interested was stretching it a bit: it was her mother who kept firing off the questions. Stanley remained silent, though Scott knew he was listening to every word. Adding the pieces of information to those he'd already gleaned. Putting together a picture of the man he knew damn well was probably going to have his wicked way with his daughter tonight. No wonder he was looking so stern.

At last Megan came back down the stairs. She looked from her parents to Scott and smiled slightly. Knowingly.

'Right, I'm off to have dinner at Scott's. I, um … might be back late.'

'Don't worry, darling, you both have a good evening. We won't wait up for you.'

It was a none too subtle signal of her mother's approval. Perhaps even encouragement.

Stanley stood up to give his daughter a kiss and Scott a hard glare. One that said *you look after my daughter, or else.* He might have accepted the situation, but it was grudgingly.

When they were finally in the car, Scott let out the breath he'd been holding. 'Jesus, I bet your father was a great cop. With a look like that, he'd terrify the hardiest of criminals into submission.'

'Sorry, that was a tad awkward, wasn't it?' She shifted in her seat. 'This hasn't happened for a long time. Dad's not sure how to handle it.'

He glanced at her as he drove. 'What hasn't happened for a long time?'

'Me going back to a man's house, with the obvious intention of doing more than have dinner.'

There was a slight pause, during which Megan died a thousand deaths. Then he nodded. 'Good.'

'Is that all you have to say? Good?' Now she'd taken the leap and admitted her sexual desert, she was a bit miffed at his nonplussed reaction.

'It might be one word, but it covers a lot of bases.' He was concentrating on the road, eyes fixed ahead, so all she could see was his striking profile. 'I mean it's good that there aren't a lot of other men sniffing around. I want you to myself. And it's good that you haven't made love for a while, so you won't be able to make too many uncomplimentary comparisons.' Briefly his eyes drifted over to hers. 'Most of all, it's good that we're on the same wavelength. That you realise exactly what I have in mind as soon as we open the front door.'

Jeez, speaking of good, he was damned good at this. At turning her on with his words. She clasped her hands together on her lap, all too aware of the squirming sensation taking place beneath them. 'Will I get dinner?'

He grinned. 'Eventually, when we find ourselves needing more sustenance.'

The house he pulled up outside of was totally different to what she'd expected. Far from a bachelor flat, it was an elegant, substantial family house. Before she'd had a chance to take it in though, he'd opened her car door, grabbed her arm and rushed her towards the front door.

In no time at all he was turning the key in the lock, bundling her inside, slamming the door shut behind them and bringing his mouth fiercely down on hers. 'You can get a tour later,' he murmured, in between trailing hot kisses over her face and down her neck. 'For now the only thing you need to be concentrating on is me.'

That was incredibly easy to do when he was kissing her like he was, she thought. His mouth felt so soft, yet he felt so hard, so very male. She had to get rid of his clothes. Get her hands on that firm, hot flesh. She was starting to tackle his buttons, and getting frustrated by her inability to slide them open easily, when his phone sprang into life, crashing into the intimacy.

'I'll let it ring,' Scott muttered, his own hands making much better progress at undoing her blouse. 'Nothing's more important than this.'

The answer machine clicked in, Scott's deep voice asking the caller to leave a message.

'Scott ...' There was a quiet sob.

Immediately she felt Scott stiffen. He pulled away, gave her a quick look of apology and dashed to pick up the phone. 'Mum? Are you there?'

Megan heard the sound of a click as the person on the other end of the phone ended the call.

'Christ.' He slumped on to the sofa, looking down at the phone, and swore.

'Was that your mother?' she asked quietly, noticing how pale he'd become and how grim his expression.

Rubbing his hands over his face, he sighed. 'Yeah. I think so.' Clattering the phone back on its stand he swore again.

She could see he was distressed. It was more than plain worry she could read in his eyes. 'Do you want to go and see her?'

He laughed, but unlike the richness of his usual laughter, this had a hollow sound. 'Chance would be a fine thing.' Then he surprised her by hanging his head. 'I don't know where she is, Megan,' he muttered when he finally looked up again. 'So there isn't a damn thing I can do.'

His eyes looked full of pain and her heart went out to him. He was hurting and helpless, two things she would never normally have associated with him. 'I think I'd better go.' With a mixture of intense disappointment and aching sympathy, she bent to pick up her bag.

'No.' He stood up quickly, walking over to her, laying a hand on her arm. 'Please stay.'

'I can see you're worried, Scott. I don't mind making my own way home. We can do this another time.'

At last a little of the grimness faded from his face. 'I finally get you into my house and you think I'll let you go?' He shook his head. 'Not a chance. Another day you might come to your senses and realise I am the arrogant git you thought I was all along. I'm not taking that risk.'

She sighed and, with the instincts of a nurturer, put her arms around him and pulled him to her. 'I promise I won't.'

They stood there for a while, holding each other tight, their bodies firmly pressed against each other. It wasn't long before it became very obvious that Scott was no longer thinking about his mother. Gently he pulled away but not before placing his hands on either side of her face, turning her head up to look at his. 'It hasn't been the ideal start to the evening, but I think you could say I'm back on track with my original intentions. Would you come upstairs with me? Please?'

She'd been planning on going up as soon as she'd felt him harden against her. The fact that he'd asked rather than demanded, and had even added the word *please*, hadn't made a damned bit of difference to the outcome. But it had done funny things to her heart.

His bedroom was a man's room. Dark wood, navy curtains,

sleek sound system, enormous bed. She wasn't going to think about all the women who'd slept in it before her. Slept? Who was she kidding? She doubted any of them had done much of that.

'Second thoughts?' He drew her against him, circling her waist with his arms, pressing her against the throbbing length of him.

'No.'

'What then?'

His eyes were searching hers, concerned. It left her slightly unnerved. She didn't want his kindness. Not when she was feeling so vulnerable. 'I'm just wondering if I'll remember what to do.' She tried to laugh. 'Three years is a long time.'

She felt his surprise. 'Three? What not since …'

'Sally's father. No.'

Suddenly Scott was aware of the enormity of the step Megan was taking. Whereas before he'd felt rather slighted at the thought of being used to get her back into the dating game, now he felt unbelievably honoured. She wouldn't have been without offers during those intervening years. He knew that. Yet his had been the only one she'd accepted.

Gently he lowered his lips to hers and nuzzled. 'It's like riding a bike.'

'I can see that. I mean the part about having something hard between my legs.'

It surprised a laugh out of him. 'And here's me trying to create an intimate atmosphere.'

'Scott.' She rested her head against his chest. 'I'm worried that after all this chasing, I'm going to be a crashing disappointment.'

He quirked an eyebrow in astonishment. Outwardly she was all ballsy and strong. Inside she was much softer. Much more vulnerable. What a woman. One it wouldn't take much of a nudge for him to fall head over heels for.

Tenderly he smoothed down her hair. 'Megan, if what

happens between us is disappointing, it'll be my fault.' Then he forced her to look at him and met her worried eyes with his trademark grin. 'But don't you remember me telling you about the two things I'm really good at?'

Finally the anxious look in her eyes began to recede. 'Umm, law and making love. Based on feedback, if I remember. Not just the crowing of an arrogant man.'

'I know I sit on the wrong side, but would you say they're right about the law part?'

She cocked her head to one side, taking her time to consider the answer. Although he'd intended the question as a joke, he found himself holding his breath as he waited for her reply. 'Yes,' she conceded finally.

Ridiculously pleased, he took her hands and raised them to his lips, kissing each of her knuckles in turn. 'Well then, we should be in for a night to remember, shouldn't we?'

Her shoulders went down a notch, her mouth softened into a smile and Scott knew she was finally his for the taking.

While his lips found hers, and his tongue began an intimate exploration of the inside of her mouth, he made short work of undressing them both. There would be time for the tantalising, slow reveal another night. He'd make certain of it. Right now he wanted her naked, in his bed, before she changed her mind. Or he received another phone call.

Having unwrapped the exquisite package in front of him, Scott picked Megan up and lay her down on the bed. She was so unlike the brash, voluptuous women he'd taken to bed in the past. And far, far sexier. Right now she was watching him shyly, her small pert breasts sitting up, beckoning him to take them in his mouth. He ran a hand over her arms, noticing the toned, smooth feel of them. He was used to soft. Now he wanted firm, strong. Moving to sit astride her, he bent to suckle at a rosebud pink nipple, rejoicing when it tightened and she started to moan.

He wanted more. He snaked his tongue down over her

taut, flat stomach. He knew she was as obsessive as he was at working out. It paid off. At least as far as he was concerned. He delved lower, delighted as she began to writhe beneath him.

'Scott, God, please ...'

Smiling he brought his head back up. Her eyes were clouded with passion. He doubted even she knew what she was asking for. 'Please what?'

She made a thrusting motion with her hips under his, telling him quite clearly what she wanted.

Scott found he was in no mood to tease. He'd wanted to get inside her the moment he'd seen her. He wasn't about to deny himself any longer. He quickly covered himself with a condom and set about settling between her legs, relishing the feel of her hardened nipples against his chest as he lowered himself on to her. His body needed no help in guiding its way deep into the very heart of her. One slow, hard thrust and he was in. Oh, God. He sucked in a deep breath when he realised how tight she was. How hot and moist. He had to stop moving. After all his boasts, the last thing he needed now was to explode the minute he'd entered her. But boy, was he in danger of doing just that.

'You feel incredible,' he told her after a moment, pushing back the hair from her face, staring deeply into his eyes.

It made her smile. 'You feel pretty good, too.'

'It's almost too good,' he murmured, softly kissing the lips that stared up at him so invitingly. 'Do you mind if we just ...' He closed his eyes, trying to think of something other than how much he wanted to thrust hard inside her and just come in one massive explosion. 'Talk algebra to me,' he demanded thickly.

Surprise, puzzlement, amusement. He watched them all flit through her beautiful eyes. 'Really? Algebra turns you on? Two x plus three y equals ten z?'

Scott laughed, shaking his head, pretty sure he was now

back in control. 'Nope. You turn me on, Megan. Just you.' To prove his point he started moving inside her, in and out, setting up an easy rhythm.

Megan lay beneath his magnificent body as it rocked into hers and knew finally why risks were taken and hearts broken over sex. It wasn't for the lukewarm feeling she'd thought sex to be, but for this. There simply weren't words to describe how he was making her feel. Sure it had been a long time, and her memory might not be what it was, but if sex had ever felt like this before, she'd have damn well remembered. And she wouldn't have waited so long to do it again. She gazed up at the man leaning over her, his eyes burning into hers, his strong, handsome face reflecting his focus and concentration. And the desire he never tried to hide. Was this actually about sex, or was it about him? The way he made her feel.

She'd never felt so utterly desirable. Or wanted so much. The thrust of his powerful body was like the most delicious torture, each deep lunge intensifying what she was feeling so that soon she was just one giant mass of highly sensitised nerve endings.

Finally, clutching at his taut buttocks, she pulled him towards her and came in an explosion of feeling, arching her hips and crying out his name. As she slowly came down to earth she felt him buck inside her as he, too, achieved his shuddering climax.

'Beautiful,' he whispered into her ear on a ragged breath. 'Fantastically, amazingly, beautiful.'

The warm glow of satisfaction that had settled throughout her body doubled at his words. She hadn't let him down.

'Yes, it was, wasn't it,' she agreed on a sigh.

Resting on his elbows, their bodies still joined, Scott tenderly kissed her forehead. 'It was, but actually I was talking about you.'

She shook her head, moved by his sentiment, but knowing it wasn't strictly true. 'Me? No way ...'

He silenced her, very effectively, with another deep, drugging kiss. 'Are you calling me a liar?'

She rolled her eyes. 'No, I'm not, but ...'

'Then you need to believe me when I tell you that you're beautiful.' His voice was low and seductive, his breath warm against her skin. 'Maybe not in the conventional sense, but who wants conventional when you can have enticingly, excitingly, gloriously different?'

Megan shook her head. He was too much. It wasn't enough that he'd captivated her body, now he was dazzling her mind. She'd have to be so careful he didn't make inroads into her heart, too. 'I can't believe I'm here, with you, in your bed,' she told him, trying to keep things simple.

'I can.'

She looked up at the face so close to hers. God, he was a handsome brute.

It was no wonder he oozed self-assurance. 'You really did believe we'd end up like this, didn't you? I must be so pathetically weak.'

With his hands he smoothed back her hair. 'Not weak. Intelligent. I knew you'd soon realise what you were missing out on.'

She expelled a noisy breath, half amusement, half exasperation. 'You know, sometimes I can't believe the words that come out of your mouth.'

He looked slightly miffed, but there was enough of a twinkle in his eye for her to realise he was playing with her. 'Hey, can you deny you're smart?'

'Oh, for the love of God, put a sock in it, Scott. I'm not going spend all night arguing with you.'

The amusement in his eyes turned to something darker, hotter. More intense. 'Good, because I have something much more interesting planned.'

He lowered his mouth back to hers and began to kiss her again, playing with her lips, his tongue darting teasingly into her mouth. She felt him moving against her, hardening, and raised an eyebrow. 'I guess I'm not getting dinner just yet.'

Running his hands down the length of her body, he whispered into her ear. 'You guess right.'

Chapter Fifteen

Monday morning and Megan was back at work and finding herself on the wrong end of a grilling from a fellow officer about how she'd spent her weekend.

'Well, things have certainly moved on from the last time we spoke,' Ann gently mocked over a cup of coffee in the station canteen. 'What happened to *we're just friends?*'

Megan squirmed in her seat. 'What can I say?' she answered with a shrug of her shoulders. 'It seems I'm as gullible as all the other women who've gone before me.'

'Good looks and charm won the day, eh?'

Wincing, Megan took a gulp of the brown stuff in her cup. To call it coffee was stretching the imagination too far. 'It's galling to admit, but yes, I guess they did. In the end I succumbed, just as he predicted I would.' Was it her imagination, or did the coffee taste even more bitter than usual?

Ann looked at her with concern. 'Do you really think that's all this was? A competition?'

She didn't know the answer to that. She really didn't. When he'd taken her to bed Saturday night, it had felt so perfectly right. He'd been the lover of her dreams: attentive, passionate, tender. When he hadn't been making her body tingle with his touch, he'd been making her mind spin with his lavish compliments. But now, in the cold light of a Monday morning, none of it felt real. 'Who knows?' she answered truthfully. 'I don't even know how I feel, never mind how he feels.'

'Do you want to see him again?'

'Yes.' She hadn't needed time to think about that. 'Oh God, Ann, when I'm with him I know there's so much more to him than the charming but shallow man I had him down as. But when I'm away from him, I wonder if that's just me desperately wanting to see something in him that isn't there, to justify my attraction to him.'

'Considering how badly hurt you were by the charming but ultimately insincere Luke, that's hardly surprising. It seems to me there's only one way for you to find out though. See him again.'

Easy for Ann to say, but Scott hadn't phoned since she'd left his bed in the very early hours of Sunday morning. Nor was she certain what she'd say if he did. Her body wanted to see him again, that was for sure, but the rest of her was more hesitant. Scott was dangerous. She prided herself on her common sense and self-discipline, yet both had gone out of the window since he'd started his charm offensive on her. It alarmed her to think how easily he'd started to push through her defensive barriers. Downright terrified her to think how he might, if she continued to see him, rip those barriers clean away.

Later that morning Megan received a call that forced all thoughts of Scott Armstrong firmly into the background. A body had been discovered, dumped in a ditch. The body of a six-year-old girl. Immediately her heart had leapt into her mouth and she'd had to quickly remind herself that Sally was at school. She'd dropped her off herself. She was fine.

Now, as she trod warily through the damp, eerily quiet woods towards the body in the ditch, her thoughts were focused not on her own daughter, but on someone else's. Through the clearing she saw a small group standing round a prostate body and readied herself for what she was about to see. Slipping silently alongside the pathologist, she joined the huddle and stared down at the victim. Her lifeless body was hideously pale, the skin covered with blackish bruises and dried blood stains. Megan shivered and was forced to shut her eyes for a moment to steady herself. Nothing could ever prepare her for the sight of a dead child. The reality was always far more horrific than anything her imagination could conjure.

Steeling herself, she glanced back down at the victim. There was no doubt in her mind that this poor girl had been murdered. The bruises, she suspected, were old. Evidence of previous abuse. The stab wounds on her chest, however, were fresh. Her stomach churned violently, threatening to spew up the contents of her breakfast.

'Megan?' The pathologist was looking at her, concern in his eyes. 'Are you okay?'

She blinked, swallowed, and pulled herself together. She couldn't help the poor girl now. It was too late. The best she could do was find the monster who'd done that to her. 'Sorry, yes, I'm fine. It's just ...'

'The kids are always the worst, aren't they?' He shook his head sadly at the battered, twisted body and then patted her arm. 'We'll finish up here. You start working on catching the bastard. I'd estimate time of death to be around 9 p.m. last night. When I've got more details, I'll let you know.'

Together with her small team, Megan worked on the murder case for the rest of the day. Through school registers and questioning they discovered who the girl was. That she'd grown up in a dysfunctional family. Her mother a drug addict, father unknown. On a hunch Megan brought in the mother for questioning and found out who her latest boyfriend was. They tracked him down, only to end up frustrated when he wasn't at the garage he'd been working at recently. The mechanics told her they'd expected him in that morning, but he hadn't shown up. Interesting.

The hairs on the back of her neck started to prickle as she put the pieces together. It fitted a sickening but sadly all too familiar pattern. Addict mother, in need of her next fix, overlooks the safety of her daughter. Infatuated with the boyfriend, or more particularly the highs he provides her, she fails to notice her daughter is becoming withdrawn, her body showing signs of abuse. Megan would put this month's salary on her hunch that the boyfriend murdered the little girl. Perhaps because she finally fought back, perhaps because she threatened to tell her mother.

'We'll find him, Sarge.'

She looked up from her desk to find one of the junior detectives standing outside her office. Briefly she nodded in agreement before turning back to her computer. Too bloody right they would. If she had to work all day and all night for the next few weeks, she'd track the scum down. Right now, however, she couldn't do any more. Her head was pounding, and her mind far too full of images of the tragic young girl. All she wanted to do was go home and hug her daughter. Her beautiful, perfect, very much alive, daughter. Circling her shoulders to release some of the tension, Megan finally turned off her computer and tidied away the files from her desk. With a heavy heart she walked into the corridor. And came face-to-face with Scott.

'Hey.' He reached out an arm to steady her as she literally bumped into him. His eyes narrowed as he took in her exhausted appearance. 'Rough day?'

'You could say that.' She didn't want to deal with Scott right now. She was too raw and emotional.

'Well, I've got the perfect solution. You, me, two steaks and a good bottle of wine. What do you reckon?'

It was all about the timing. This morning, before the phone call telling her of the body, she'd have been very tempted by the invitation. Not to mention flattered and relieved that he wasn't quite ready to cross her off his list now he'd bedded her. Now, however, the thought of doing anything other than spending the night with Sally in her arms left her cold. 'I'm going home to be with my daughter,' she told him bluntly. Her tone was too harsh, but right now she couldn't manage soft, or apologetic. She wanted to go home, and Scott, with his large frame and annoying questions, was standing in her way.

She attempted to shoulder past him, but he caught her by both arms and pulled her back. 'Not so fast, Detective.' When he was satisfied that she wasn't about to run away, he released one arm to hold her by the chin, forcing her to look up at him. 'What did I do?'

'Christ, Scott.' She expelled a harsh breath, part frustration, part anger. Not with him, but with the world. 'Not everything is about you.'

Scott winced as the words cut through him. Despite the time they'd spent together, she still had him down as self-centred and arrogant. 'What's wrong?'

She tried to jerk her arm out of his hold. 'Leave me alone, Scott.' Then, as if as an afterthought, 'Please.'

He hadn't intended to let go. At least not until she told him why she was looking so distressed. Why her face was so drained of colour and her eyes so flat. But the please, together with the pleading light in her eyes, had him dropping his hand. 'Okay. You know where to find me.'

She wasn't listening. She was rushing down the corridor as if her life depended on it. Scott let out a frustrated sigh. Women. How the hell was he meant to understand them? Was she cross because she'd expected him to call earlier? He let out a snort of disgust at his own vanity. She'd looked far too cut up for it to be about him. There was clearly something far deeper tearing at her. What really upset him was that she hadn't been prepared to share it with him. He'd been good enough to share her body with the other night, but wasn't, it seemed, good enough to share what was on her mind. In previous relationships he would have looked at that as a blessing. Now, with Megan, the thought was anything but. It hurt.

Wearily he made his way back to his car. It looked like it was going to be steak for one, in front of the football. His mobile rang as he was throwing his briefcase into the boot.

'Armstrong.'

'Hey, it's Nancy. How are you?'

Pissed off, frustrated. He checked himself. 'Fine. Just on my way home.'

'Ah. I was hoping to catch you about the Kevin Rogers case. I've got some more information I want to go through with you.'

Scott thought of the dull evening ahead. He might as well work it. 'Well, if you don't mind coming round to mine, we can discuss it there.'

'Great, thanks. I'll see you in a bit.'

So now, instead of a romantic meal with his lover, he was going to spend the evening working with an ex. Bloody perfect.

Nancy and he spent the following few hours going through her meeting with the prostitute who'd previously gone on record as stating that Kevin Rogers assaulted her, and then mysteriously withdrawn her statement.

'Eventually she admitted she'd been told by her pimp to make the original statement. He'd promised to see her right if she did this favour for him. But the closer it came to the trial, the more she'd worried about telling the lie, until she finally withdrew the allegation a few hours before it came to trial.'

Scott nodded and tried to ignore the growl of his stomach. Tried not to think of the fat, juicy steaks sitting in the fridge. 'Did she have any idea why this man wanted her to lie in the first place?'

Nancy shook her head. He noticed that she'd let her hair down and it was falling over her shoulders, wisps of it trailing into her cleavage. A cleavage she was amply displaying. He had a worrying feeling the hair had come down in his honour. As had the button on her blouse.

'No, not really. She thought the lie was for someone else. There were rumours of a vice cop he was friendly with. One who turned a blind eye to what they were doing. Maybe it was for him.'

'If he exists,' Scott replied dryly. Finally he could ignore his hunger no longer. 'Look, Nancy, I'm starving.' He thought how easy it would be to ask her to stay and share the steaks with him. But what he really wanted to be doing was eating with Megan. Eating, drinking, talking. Making love. He sighed. No, it wasn't fair to ask Nancy to stay. She would get the wrong idea. 'Why don't you quickly take me through the rest of your notes. We can discuss it further on the phone tomorrow, once I've had a chance to digest them.'

The look of disappointment on her face made him extra glad he hadn't asked her to stay. He was finding his new relationship enough of a challenge. There was no way he wanted to get entangled in an old one.

Chapter Sixteen

While Scott had been going through his case with Nancy, Megan had been spending the evening with her daughter, cuddling her until she fell asleep in her arms. Now she was standing in the kitchen, going through the process of making a cup of tea she didn't actually want to drink.

'What's on your mind, Meg?' Her mother drew up alongside her. 'And don't tell me it's the case, because I think there's more to your frown than work.'

Megan gave her a half-smile. 'Scott offered to cook for me tonight. I snapped his head off.' At her mother's questioning look, Megan sighed. 'Bad timing.'

'Well, the night is still young. Time enough to make amends, if that's what you want to do.'

Silence hung in the kitchen. Megan could hear the swish of the trees against the window as the wind picked up. 'I think I do,' she replied at length, afraid of quite how strongly she did want that. 'God knows, I wish I didn't. I really don't think we're going anywhere, but ...' she trailed off, chewing on her bottom lip.

'You want to find out, just the same?' She nodded. 'Yes. I do.'

Her mother turned to study her. 'What was he offering to make?'

Megan glanced back at her, starting to smile. 'Steak.'

Chuckling, her mother put an arm around her waist and hugged her. 'Well, decision made. There's only macaroni cheese on offer here tonight.'

Half an hour later, Megan hovered outside Scott's house, second thoughts crashing through her mind. The hand that clutched a bottle of wine was beginning to sweat. Shifting the bottle to her other hand, she swore to herself. Then, for good measure, she swore at Scott. This was his fault. The moment he'd thrown the words *you know where to find me* at her, he'd very cleverly kicked the ball firmly into her court. Up till then he'd done all the chasing. Now, if she wanted to see him again, it was up to her. It frightened her that she did want that. She wanted it so much she was now standing on his doorstep and ringing his damn bell. Totally uncertain of the greeting she'd receive. Or even if he'd be in.

He opened the door.

'Detective.' For a brief moment his eyes lit up with pleasure. Then he carefully set his expression to neutral. 'What brings you here?'

Slowly she withdrew the bottle from behind her back. 'I was wondering if the offer of steak was still on?'

It was as Scott opened the door wider to let her in that Megan noticed Nancy. The woman was sitting at the kitchen table, an empty wine glass in front of her, a look of surprise on her face. No doubt it equalled the one on Megan's. In the seconds it took for her to absorb the cosy scene, Megan's heart stuttered. How could she have been so stupid? A man like Scott didn't just sit around and wait for a woman to come to her senses. He went out and found someone else willing to spend the evening with him instead. Angrily she shoved the wine bottle at him, turned on her heel and started back down the steps.

'What the—' Scott swore. 'Where are you going now?'

'I can see you already have company,' she replied stiffly. 'Please, accept the bottle as a gift. Consider it thanks for services rendered the other evening.'

She'd reached as far as the bottom step when he lunged at her. 'What the hell are you talking about?' he demanded fiercely, for once not the smooth, controlled operator. Anger shot out of his usually cool eyes like darts.

'I would have thought that was obvious,' she retorted,

glancing back at Nancy who was still sitting at the table, watching them argue with great interest.

Again he swore. 'Nancy is here because we're working on a case together. As I found myself with a free evening, I invited her to work here rather than in the chambers.' Thrusting a hand through his hair, he let out a bitter laugh. 'Is this how it's going to be between us, Megan? You expecting me to let you down at every turn?'

'I ...' She didn't know what to say. Her eyes blurred with tears and, though she bit her lip, she found she couldn't help it. She burst out crying. Great wracking sobs she had no hope of controlling.

Instantly, she was wrapped into a pair of strong arms. 'Hey, shh,' he soothed, gently propelling her up the steps and back into the house.

The next thing Megan knew, she was sitting on his battered leather sofa and a glass of wine was being thrust into her hands.

'Here, have a drink. You brought it and you look like you need it.'

She looked around. 'Where's Nancy?'

He let out a wry smile. 'Funnily enough, she took one look at you and fled.'

Megan clutched at the wine glass and swallowed a big mouthful. 'I'm sorry if I ruined your evening.'

He exhaled in frustration. 'For God's sake, Megan. There was no evening. You put an end to that, if I remember correctly. So I decided to work instead. End of.'

She'd cocked up, well and truly, Megan thought numbly to herself. Firstly, she'd bluntly turned down his offer of dinner. Then, having come round to apologise, she'd accused him of being about to take another woman to bed. She couldn't blame him for being angry at her. She was pretty angry at herself, too. 'Are the steaks still on?'

He perched on the arm of the chair, studying her. 'Yelling at me makes you hungry, huh?'

The hint of a smile began to play around his lips and the grey eyes turned from angry to amused. It was at that moment that Megan realised how wrong she'd been to turn down his original offer. This man, strong, virile, dangerously attractive, was exactly what she needed after a day like today. He reminded her she was alive. That, while there was an awful lot wrong with the world, there was also an awful lot to be thankful for. 'I guess it does.'

Taking her hand he pulled her to her feet. 'Right then. I'll go and put the steaks under the grill while you talk me through what the hell happened to you today.'

They ate and talked. Although she couldn't discuss the full details of the case, she found it surprisingly easy to share what she could with him. Maybe it was because she'd been through it once already, with her parents. Or maybe it was because he was a good listener. One who worked in the same circles as she did but looked at things from a different perspective. Tonight they weren't on opposite sides. He simply contributed his own thoughts, helping her piece together the parts of the puzzle. It was useful. As helpful, in its own way, as talking to her parents had been.

As she pushed her empty plate aside and took a final sip of wine, Megan sat back and smiled. 'You make a fine steak.'

'One of my many talents.'

A few weeks ago such a boast would have irritated her. Now she laughed. 'I didn't expect to be ending the day like this.'

Quietly he cleared away the plates and then, taking her hand, drew her up against him. 'I'm glad you came round.'

'So am I.' She sighed and flung her arms around his waist, hugging him. 'I'm sorry about earlier today. I was so wrapped up in the case—'

He interrupted her. 'I understand. But you have to know that you can talk to me. We don't always have to be on opposite sides.'

For a few minutes they simply stood with their arms around each other, holding. 'And I'm sorry about assuming you and Nancy, you know.'

He drew away and looked at her. 'Megan, I know you don't think much of my morals, but I never have, and never will, sleep with more than one woman at a time. When I'm with a woman, I'm committed.'

And she should be, Megan thought to herself as she burrowed back into him. She should be committed to some sort of institution for the mentally insane, allowing herself to develop these sorts of feelings towards him. But God, when he held her like this, warm, comforting, strong, she wanted to believe they really had a chance. That the man who was holding her was for real and not another Luke. A feckless playboy who would play with her heart and then drop it.

'Isn't this the part where you promise me you won't go out with other men while you're going out with me?'

His teasing question cut into her dark thoughts. 'What, none of them?' she asked innocently.

With his mouth he gave her a gentle nip. 'I mean it, Megan.'

As if he really had to worry about the legions of men anxious to take her to bed. 'I promise, if I get a better offer, I'll talk to you first before I sneak into their bed.'

'That wasn't exactly the way I'd hoped you'd express it, but I guess I'll have to settle.' Then suddenly he was scooping her up and into his arms.

'Hey, what are you doing?'

'Isn't it obvious?' he growled, climbing up the stairs. 'I need to make sure you know there won't be any better offers than mine.'

The last time, he had made love to her. This time, Megan was determined to have her say. So when he unceremoniously dumped her on his bed and started to undo her clothes, she used her self-defence training and quickly turned the tables, ending up astride him.

He looked surprised, but not displeased.

'I want to undress you, this time,' she told him as she started to peel away at his shirt. God, the man had an amazing body. Of course she knew that. She'd seen glimpses of it two nights ago. But tonight was the first time she'd been able to study it properly. Once she'd stripped away his shirt and had a satisfying ogle of his chest, she ran her tongue over the well-defined muscles, lingering over his dark brown nipples.

'Christ, Megan,' he groaned, arching his hips automatically towards her.

It was immensely satisfying to watch how much her touch affected him. It made her realise that perhaps he was enjoying this as much as she was. So after completing her assessment of his upper chest, she moved from the taut pectoral muscles down to his impressive six pack.

'You're starting to drive me crazy,' he rasped, taking hold of her head and trying to bring it towards him.

'Good,' she replied, moving away from his hands, not ready to relinquish control just yet. She licked at his belly button and smiled as his taut muscles quivered and his groan became even louder. Then she started to undo the buttons on his jeans, a task made all the more difficult by the rigid bulge straining underneath.

When at last he was free, she pushed the jeans and boxers off with her feet while she feasted her eyes on the naked body she'd revealed. The ripped chest, dusted with sexy dark hair. The taut abdominal muscles, firm thighs, impressively large arousal. Gently she rubbed her body all the way down his, delighting in the way his chest hairs tickled at her sensitive nipples.

'Megan, you're killing me.'

She smiled at the thickness of his voice, at the pleading in his eyes and was about to lower herself on to him when he suddenly reared up. Taking her into his arms, he swiftly reversed their positions. 'This has to end, now,' he muttered as he thrust into her.

The speed with which he took back control, and the furious pace of his thrusting hips, was her undoing. It wasn't long before she was exploding around him, a huge orgasm ripping through her body. He was right behind her.

'Jesus, Megan.' He collapsed on top of her before rolling over on to his back, taking her with him so she ended up snuggled up against his chest.

'Pretty good, eh?'

Scott didn't think he had the energy left to even look down at her. He knew if he did, he'd see a smug look on that gorgeous face of hers. 'That's an understatement,' he answered dryly, remembering how she'd made him lose control. When was the last time a woman had done that to him? Hell, he'd torn into her like some sort of savage. The idea of it made him wince. 'I didn't hurt you, did I?'

Leaning on his chest she put her face close to his and looked into his eyes. 'No, you didn't.' Smiling, she kissed him. 'That was exactly what I needed after today.'

He'd dealt with enough murders to understand what she meant. It sickened him to think of what she'd seen today. Made him realise once again how tough she was. 'Any time you want to use sex to release some of that inner anger, you know where I am.'

She grinned and planted soft, sexy kisses all over his chest. It was enough to cause his body to twitch once more. Unbelievable.

'Scott, I've been thinking.'

Whoa. Immediately he tensed. In his experience, nothing good ever came out of a woman's mouth after the words *I've been thinking*. 'What?'

'I'm pretty certain who killed that girl. All we have to do is find him. It shouldn't take long. But when we do, and it comes to court—'

He covered his mouth with hers, silencing her. He knew exactly what was on her mind and, thanks to the Cab-rank rule, he was powerless to prevent it. If he were given the case, he'd have to take it, unless he had a damn good reason why not. And he didn't. Besides, why wouldn't he want it? *Every* man was entitled to a defence, was innocent until proven guilty, even those suspected of murdering a child. He nibbled at her bottom lip, distracted by the soft fullness of it. Tonight wasn't the night for another discussion over justice. It was a topic they were always going to clash over. 'Let's just wait and see what happens, shall we,' he murmured in between kisses, trying to pull her mind back to pleasanter thoughts. 'Can you stay the night?'

She shook her head, just as she had last Saturday night. Although he knew the reasons, it left him feeling frustrated. 'What time does Sally wake up?' he asked.

'Anywhere between six and half seven. I know what you're thinking. Some days I go to the gym at that time, so I'm not always around when she wakes, anyway.' She sighed. 'And you're right. But I went to the gym today, so I won't be going tomorrow.'

'How about if I set the alarm for 5 a.m.?'

'Well, yes, that would work, but it'll mean waking you up. It's easier if I just get in my car now.'

She was starting to move out of the bed, but he hauled her back. 'Not so fast. I've not finished with you yet.'

'Scott ...'

'Megan, I want to spend the night with you. To sleep with your sexy little body snuggled up against mine. To wake up next to you. Is it too much to ask?'

'Well, wow.' She smiled and settled herself back against him. 'If you put it like that ...'

When the alarm finally sounded at five, he was already in the middle of waking them both up. Neither of them heard it.

Chapter Seventeen

For the rest of the week, Megan knew little but work. Though she had several cases ongoing, her priority was the child's murder. It took all her focus and energy. They'd found and questioned the boyfriend the following day. He didn't have an alibi for the time of the murder. Not only that, but forensics were able to find his DNA all over the victim's body. Though it was pretty clear he was the murderer, Megan was terrified the evidence they had wouldn't be enough to convict him. The defence could argue that the man was her stepfather. Of course they would find his DNA on the child. It didn't mean he'd killed her. So Megan wasn't taking any chances. She was talking to the people who knew him, and knew the family, building up the case, proving the type of man he was and the relationship he'd had with the child. Only when she'd done that would she charge him. That was why she was in her car, on her way to the girl's school, when Scott phoned.

'Fancy lunch, Detective?'

'Lunch?' She glanced at the clock on the dashboard. Could it really be that time already? 'I'm in the car, working on the murder case. By the time I'm done it'll be nearer tea than lunch.'

'Are you putting me off?'

'No, I'm busy catching the bad guys.'

'Okay. When you've caught them, give me a call. If it's too late for lunch we'll do afternoon tea. I'll even buy you a scone.'

As her face broke out into a goofy grin, she could only thank God there was nobody else in the car to witness her lapse into infatuated female. Scott wasn't just chasing her, he was romancing her. She'd bargained on them having quick sexual encounters at his house, or in a hotel room. Never in her wildest dreams had she pictured them meeting for afternoon tea.

'Okay, throw in cream and jam as well and you're on.'

He whistled over the phone. 'Jeez woman, you drive a hard bargain. I'll wait for your call.'

Thoughtfully Scott put down the phone and returned his attention to the computer. For a man used to women jumping when he said jump, he was finding Megan, who seemed to always do the opposite of what he wanted, more than a little exasperating. Already she'd turned him down twice this week, claiming she was too busy. Perhaps she was, but Scott was starting to realise that getting Megan into his bed had been the easy part. Keeping her there was far more difficult. So was handling the thought that he actually wanted to do that. To keep her in his bed. In his life.

Soberly he looked down at his fingers on the keyboard, noticed their slight tremor. Hell, the thought of making a permanent commitment to one woman was enough to make his whole body quake with terror, never mind his fingers. Over the last couple of years he'd sometimes caught himself wondering if he was even capable of having real feelings for a woman. Feelings that went beyond the sexual and into the emotional. At least now he knew he was. The fact that the woman he was falling for was guarded, bloody-minded and always thought the worst of him should have him running a mile. So should the fact that she had a child and still lived with her parents. Instead, it seemed to make him more determined to show them all he wasn't the playboy heartbreaker they had him down as. Which just went to prove he was well and truly, alarmingly, smitten.

It was after three when Megan finally called him. He drove by the station, picked her up and took them to a nearby hotel. It had her eyebrows rising when he parked the car.

'You can take your mind out of the gutter, Detective Sergeant,' he told her as they walked into the lobby. 'This is the only place I know that does a full afternoon tea.

Sandwiches, cakes, scones, the lot.' He glanced over at her. 'I don't know about you, but I'm bloody starving.'

Megan was used to skipping lunch. Not because she watched her figure. In fact, as far as that went, eating more was actually what she should be doing. She was too thin. If she put on weight, she might gain breasts and look more like a woman. 'I could eat,' she replied, happy to give it a go. Especially in these rather glamorous surroundings. It sure beat the station canteen.

The afternoon tea, delivered on the traditional three-tier cake stand, lived up to its name. To Megan's eyes it looked like a mountain of food, but as she watched, Scott proceeded to wolf down two sandwiches in a single bite. Perhaps it wouldn't take them long to get through it, after all.

'You didn't have to wait for me,' she remarked as he munched his way through another two. There was something really incongruous about the dainty sandwiches in Scott's large, manly hands. 'I wouldn't have minded if you'd told me you'd already eaten.'

'What, and hand you another excuse not to see me?' He poured out the tea and took a large swig. 'No way.'

Midway through picking up a salmon and cucumber sandwich, she paused. 'I haven't been making up reasons not to see you.'

'Haven't you?'

She thought back to his last two phone calls. 'Scott, I really have had a lot on. If I'd gone out, I would have been lousy company.'

'Next time, let me be the judge of that.'

Megan was momentarily stunned at his defensive tone. Wasn't this the man who blithely assumed all women fell at his feet? Did he really think she'd been shunning him? And was he really that bothered if she had been? 'For the record, as you would say, I don't need to make up an excuse to turn you down. If I don't want to see you, I'll just tell you straight.'

He nodded. 'Okay.' Then his eyes fixed greedily back on to the cake stand. 'So I take it the girl's murder has been taking up most of your time this week.'

'You're right. We've just charged the boyfriend with murder.'

'I know.'

She looked up quickly and put down the scone she'd been about to put into her mouth. Her heart was beating wildly in her chest. 'How?'

'Penny, our clerk, is an ace at ferreting out *hot-off-the-press* information. I understand Nancy is his solicitor.' He finished his mouthful and stared directly into her eyes.

Megan felt her blood run cold. She knew the implications of that. Scott was a highly experienced criminal defence barrister. If Nancy wanted him for her client ... swallowing hard, she looked down at her plate. 'I see.'

'It won't necessarily be me who gets the case,' he told her quietly. 'There are others in chambers with just as much experience.'

'But it could be you.' She knew he'd defended murderers before, but somehow this was worse. There was a child involved, the same age as her daughter.

'If I was given the case, I wouldn't be defending what he did, Megan,' he continued in the same calm, patient voice. 'I would simply be making the prosecution prove their case. Making sure there was sufficient evidence to convict him.'

'I know.' She really did understand the importance of a defence. Not just to the person being tried, but to the whole justice system. But how could she possibly date a man whose job it could be to defend this monster?

Silence hung between them. Megan couldn't eat any more. She pushed away her plate.

'What did you think of the scone?' Scott was looking at the half-eaten fruit bun on her plate. 'Worth the wait?'

Megan stood up. 'It's late. Sorry, but I need to get back to the station.'

With an exclamation of pure exasperation, he tugged at her arm. 'Come on, don't be like this. Stay a little longer. At least finish your scone.'

She looked over at him, her blue eyes sombre. 'I'm not hungry any more.'

'So that's it, is it?' Scott demanded, rifling through his wallet to find enough cash to leave on the table. 'We don't discuss this like civilised adults. You just get angry and storm off.'

Megan knew she was being unfair, but right now it didn't help. Despite knowing better, she'd become personally involved in the case. She couldn't bear to think of that poor dead girl not receiving justice because of some clever legal argument. 'I'm not angry. I'm upset.' Her voice was scratchy and she had to swallow hard to clear her throat.

'Is it me who's upset you, or what I do?' He was alongside her now, looking down at her from his imposing height.

As they walked through the hotel lobby Megan took a deep breath and tried to calm herself. Think rationally. But images of that poor tortured girl kept flooding back. 'It's what you might do.'

'What am I supposed to say to that?' He moved to stand in front of her, blocking her path. 'If I'm given the case, you know I have to take it.'

Numbly, she nodded. 'Do you want it?'

'Honestly?' He hesitated, then looked her square in the eyes. 'Yes. Murder trials are challenging. Interesting. It doesn't matter to me who the victim is. I don't think of it like that. I'm simply there to make sure the people who go to jail deserve to have their freedom taken away from them.'

Shoving his hands into his pockets, he moved aside so they could continue their progress to the car. Hell, he didn't know what else to say. It hurt that Megan couldn't understand his point of view. That no matter how many times he'd tried to explain himself, she still saw him as the bad guy. He had an ominous feeling that if he took the case their relationship would be over. With that crushing thought in mind, he yanked open the passenger door for Megan and then skirted round the bonnet and jammed himself into the driver's seat. So much for finding a woman he could finally start imagining a future with.

The journey to the hotel had been full of banter. The journey back to the station was undertaken in an uncomfortable silence. Megan's rigid body language was a pretty good indicator that she was still upset with him. So was the sight of her white knuckles as she gripped her hands together in her lap.

As he pulled up outside the station, he turned to her. 'We're both on the same side, Megan. Both fighting to make sure justice is done.'

She shook her head. 'I'm sorry, but right now I can't see it like that. All I can see is that I've worked myself to the bone gathering evidence to prove that man bullied, abused and then murdered a six-year-old girl. But when it goes to court, you're going to do your damndest to methodically rip it all apart.' She raised her eyes to look at him. The accusation in them tore at his heart. 'How can you call that being on the same side?'

'Because I'm thinking with the cool detachment of a lawyer, not the emotional sensitivity of a mother,' he snapped, then immediately regretted it. Not exactly the tone of the cool and detached lawyer he'd just claimed to be. Certainly not the way to get her to understand his point of view.

'Maybe you're right,' she replied quietly as she climbed out of the seat. 'But at least I care enough to want to make sure he pays for what he did to her.'

She slammed the door shut, taking satisfaction in knowing that would make him wince. At that moment she hated him and what he stood for. Marching back into the station she made a promise to herself. No matter what it took, she was going to make sure this case was so bloody watertight nobody would be able to pick it apart. Even a barrister as clever as Scott Armstrong.

Megan was surprised to find she was still fuming when she arrived home. She didn't usually take her work home with her, but then again, this wasn't just about work. This was about feeling betrayed.

'What's got you all in a tail spin?' her father asked as they sat together in the living room that evening, Sally safely tucked up in bed.

'Is it that obvious?'

'It is to me.'

Megan looked at his craggy but still handsome face. One so dear to her that at times just the sight of him made her eyes well. She wished with all her heart she'd been able to give Sally a father like she had. Maybe there was still time. Involuntarily her mind skipped back a week or so to the day she'd spent with Scott by the sea. How he'd lifted Sally on to his shoulders with the naturalness of a father. Then she laughed at the way her thoughts had progressed. Ridiculous. Scott was never going to be a permanent fixture in their lives. After the way their afternoon tea had gone, she wasn't even sure they'd see each other again. 'It's the murder case. The little girl,' she told her father as she leant back against the sofa. 'We've just charged the boyfriend. His solicitor is a friend of Scott's. He might be asked to defend him.'

'Ahh.'

'Exactly.'

'I don't need to ask you how you feel about that.' He stood up and went to sit down next to her, taking her hand. 'What has he said?'

She shrugged her shoulders. 'Oh, he reminded me that if he's given the case, he has to take it. I know that. But he's not even apologetic about it.' She looked up into her Dad's understanding eyes. 'He *wants* the case. Said it would be a challenge.'

'Have you not considered that he views it as simply doing his job, Megan? Just like you're doing yours?'

Shocked, Megan stared at her father. 'Dad, I thought you of all people would understand my side of things.'

He squeezed her hand. 'There was a time when I was young and fiercely driven, just like you. Full of passion and determination to round up all the criminals and make the world a safer place.'

'And what's wrong with that?'

The wrinkles deepened on either side of his eyes as he smiled back at her. 'Nothing. But as you grow older you realise not everything is black and white. There are thousands of shades of grey. Not every man you charge is guilty, despite what the evidence seems to be telling you. Sometimes, not often, but crucially *sometimes* evidence can point you in the wrong direction.'

'You're starting to sound like Scott.'

'All I'm saying is there are two sides to every argument. A phrase that holds true in real life and in court. You need to hear both sides before you can really understand who's right and who's wrong.' He kissed her on the cheek and rose from the sofa. 'In court, it's up to a judge and jury to determine that. In real life you have to work it out by yourself.' He walked towards the door and then turned. 'Sometimes you can both be right. You simply view things from different perspectives. Goodnight, Meg.'

She watched her father leave. The last thing she'd expected was for him to see things from Scott's point of view. It made her think. If she wanted to continue a relationship with Scott, she had to get past his choice of career. She had to understand his side of things. The question was, would she be able to do that? Megan wasn't sure. But the thought of not seeing him again was too painful to even contemplate. In the few short weeks since they'd started to date, he'd become a hugely important part of her life. She loved his phone calls. His ability to make her laugh and take away the stress of the day. Then there was the way he looked at her like she was the most desirable woman he'd ever seen.

Unfurling her legs, she stood up. Perhaps she should talk to Scott again. To understand why he did what he did. What drove him? Everyone had a story, and hers was simple: she was following in her father's footsteps. She wondered what's Scott's story was. It was about time she found out.

Chapter Eighteen

Scott hadn't heard from Megan since their ill-fated afternoon tea two days ago. Not that he'd expected to. Hoped would be a better term. Call him a foolish optimist, but he'd taken to yanking out his mobile phone with incredible speed whenever it rang. None of the calls had been from Megan.

He consoled himself with the thought that she'd probably been knocking on his door at home, and dropping into his chambers instead. Neither of which he'd know about because he'd not been around. Asked to defend a case in a court several hours' drive away, he'd taken the option of staying the night. The way Megan had slammed the car door in his face the last time he'd seen her had pretty much told him there wasn't much point in dashing home.

Now he was on his way back. The trial had been mentally draining. The guy he'd been defending kept changing his story at the last minute, making putting together a case pretty damned difficult. He'd lost, but Scott felt no personal slight. He'd done his best under very trying circumstances. Still, the whole two days had been exhausting, and he was grateful to be putting a lid on it all.

As he pulled off the motorway, his mobile rang again. And yes, his heart was suddenly leaping into life once more: clearly it wasn't undeterred by the last forty-eight hours of non-Megan phone calls. Despairing of himself he pressed answer on the hands free set.

'Armstrong.'

'Scott, it's Megan.'

Well knock him down with a feather. With a small smile of relief, mixed with a large dose of pure satisfaction, he relaxed the hands that had unconsciously tightened on the steering wheel at the sound of the phone. 'DS Taylor. Good to hear from you,' he replied with what he hoped she could hear as warmth and feeling. It really was great to hear her voice.

'I'm not sure it will be.'

He frowned. Since when had Megan ever sounded hesitant? Not in his experience. 'What's wrong?' he asked instantly.

'Nothing. Not really. It's just ...'

Again there was a pause. He shifted from uneasy to downright worried. 'Spit it out, Megan.'

'I've been informed by one of the uniforms that they've —' She cleared her throat. 'We're holding your mother.'

'My *mother*?' Shit, now he was alarmed, getting near to panicked.

'Yes. Apparently she was causing a disturbance, so they brought her in.' Again there was a pause. 'She's sleeping right now, but before she crashed she asked them to call you.'

His hands clenched once more on the wheel, only this time they were in danger of snapping it in two. Jesus Christ. His mother. Drunk and disorderly. Megan hadn't said the words out loud, but he could read between the lines. And now she was in a police cell. Bloody fantastic. 'I'm in the car. Tell them I'll be there in around an hour.'

'Yes, okay. I'll wait.'

'No.' That was the last thing he needed, Megan to witness his humiliation. That she'd heard about it was bad enough. 'You go home.'

He ended the call before she had a chance to argue. Jabbing at the radio, he found a station that played heavy rock and turned up the volume to try and drown out his thoughts. It didn't work.

Back at the station, Megan sighed and glanced up at the clock on the wall. Only five minutes since she'd last looked, but fifty minutes since Scott had put the phone down on her, telling her to go home. As if she could. She rose out of her chair, turned off the computer and walked back down to the police cells. The officer on duty gave her a sympathetic smile as she went to look into the cell where Scott's mother was being held. Catherine Armstrong was still fast asleep, sprawled out across the bench. On Megan's insistence, they'd given her a blanket and pillow. It was, she thought to herself, the least she could do for the poor lady. And for Scott.

From the instant they'd phoned her to tell her that a drunk they'd brought in was insisting she was Scott Armstrong's mother, Megan had died a million deaths for him. She'd hated having to phone him, but had hated the thought of another officer phoning him even more. She knew he'd be mortified. That his mother was clearly an alcoholic must be hard enough for him to bear. She'd seen with her own eyes how cut up he'd been after simply hearing her voice on the answer phone. Now it wasn't just his secret to endure in private. Now she knew. The whole station knew.

'Where is she?'

She snapped her head round and saw Scott bearing down on her, his handsome face lined with fatigue, concern and no small amount of embarrassment.

Megan motioned towards the officer who nodded and went to fetch the key. She watched in silence as Scott pushed his way into the small room and darted towards his mother, cradling her in his arms. 'Mum, it's me,' he told her, smoothing down her dyed-blonde hair. 'Come on, wake up.'

'She was three sheets to the wind when they brought her in,' the officer told him. 'Probably more than just alcohol pumping through her system.'

As Megan cringed for him, Scott remained with his back to them, gently holding the woman in front of him. 'Mum, come on, I need you to wake up. I want to take you home.'

When there was no response, he finally turned to face Megan. It was as if he'd drawn a shutter over his eyes in a determined effort to keep at least something private from them, even if it was only his feelings. Usually clear and bright,

right now his grey eyes were flat and expressionless. Just like the voice he used when he spoke. 'Are you charging her?'

Megan looked sharply at the officer, who shook his head. 'No. She was causing a bit of a fracas, but really we brought her in for her own safety. You're free to take her home when she wakes up.'

He shook his head. 'I'm taking her home now. I'll carry her to the car.'

'Fine. If you can just sign the paperwork?'

As Scott followed the officer out, Megan looked down at his sleeping mother.

There wasn't much of a resemblance, though she guessed if the cheeks hadn't been puffy from alcohol abuse, the sharp bone structure was probably there. Perhaps, if the eyes had been open, they too would have been a startling light grey.

She turned as Scott came back into the room. For a fleeting moment she saw the anguish in his face before he once again controlled his expression. 'I'll come with you,' she told him quietly.

About to bend down, Scott stopped and faced her. 'Thank you, but there's no need. I'll take care of her.'

Megan wanted to shout. To cry. To throw her arms around him and comfort him. If they hadn't argued the last time they'd met, if she'd phoned him earlier in the week to apologise, as she'd told herself to, she might have been able to do all of those things. Instead she was left watching as he gently lifted his mother into his arms and carried her out of the police station. She went ahead, opening the doors for him, determined to do whatever she could to help. As he eased his mother's sleeping form into the back seat of the car, her heart went out to him. She would have understood if he'd been cross. If he'd shown signs of annoyance or anger towards his mother. Hell, if her mother had ended up in a prison cell, out of her head on alcohol and drugs, she would have been both. But if Scott was angry, he didn't show it. He treated his mother considerately, tenderly. Lovingly. It was enough to melt any woman's heart, never mind Megan's already fragile one.

'Are you sure you don't want me to come home with you?' she asked as he finally closed the passenger door and moved to the driver's side.

'What, and spend the evening babysitting a middle-aged woman with a raging hangover?' He smiled tightly. 'I think not.' He was about to get in when he hesitated. 'But thanks for the offer. And for making sure they didn't charge her.'

Then he lowered himself into the driver's seat and disappeared out of view.

Scott was livid. With his mother, with himself, with life in general. How had it come to this? How had he come to be picking her up from a police cell, with heaven only knew still circulating round her blood stream? How had she got herself into this state? More to the point, how had he let her? He was her son, for God's sake. He should be there to protect her. Help her. He thumped his fist on the coffee table, noting even that didn't disturb her from her slumber on his couch. He'd failed in his duty as a son. He could only hope he hadn't found her too late. That there was some way back for both of them.

It was several hours later before she finally stirred. Scott, who'd been reading a brief while watching over her, heard the moment she woke up. He immediately put down the file and sat down on the coffee table, gently putting an arm on her shoulders to stop her as she tried to sit up.

'Mum, you're at home. Don't make any sudden movements. Try to get up carefully while I fetch you a glass of water.'

Slowly she came round. 'How are you feeling?' he asked as he tucked a pillow behind her back.

'Like death,' came the whispered reply.

She looked like death too, Scott noted. Her skin was

sallow, her grey eyes dull, her hair lifeless. 'Where have you been?' he asked, knowing it was the last thing he should say, but he couldn't help himself. He needed to know what she'd been doing to get herself into such a mess.

As he'd expected, she turned away from him, unwilling or unable to meet his eyes. She wasn't about to tell him where she lived, or what she did with her life in between the occasional visits home.

He sighed. 'When did you last eat? Are you hungry?' When was it that he'd turned into the parent in their relationship? He couldn't remember. It felt like it had always been that way.

She shook her head. 'Not yet. Maybe in a while.'

'Okay. Why don't you head on upstairs and I'll run you a bath. Perhaps after that you'll feel more like eating.' And talking, he hoped. Because soon his patience was going to grow very thin. He couldn't take seeing her like this. Gradually she'd been getting worse. Her visits home more infrequent. When they did happen she looked older, more fragile. It was why he'd sent her back to the rehabilitation centre. Fat lot of good it had done her.

Having bathed, changed and eaten some toast, she was at last looking a bit better. Well enough, Scott considered, for a serious conversation. 'You know we can't go on like this, don't you?'

She eyed him warily.

'You're in a mess, Mum. I don't know where you disappear to, who you're hanging out with, but wherever it is, I don't want you going there again. It's killing you,' he told her bluntly.

'I know,' she replied, her voice heavy with regret. 'I seem to have lost my will power.'

'I've got enough for both of us.'

She shook her head despairingly. 'It doesn't work like that. I have to do this on my own.'

'You're not on your own, Mum.' He almost shouted the

words, but at the last second held himself in check. Yelling at her was not the way forward. Softly, gently, that's what she responded to best.

'I know, darling. I know.' She smiled weakly at him. 'You're a good man, Scott. I always knew you would be. Just like your father. He was a good man, too.'

'Yeah.' She'd always believed in his father, even when others hadn't. 'But he isn't around to help. He hasn't been for a long time. I want you to let me help you, instead. If it was him telling you to go into a clinic, dry yourself out, wean off the drugs, get your life back, you'd do it.'

That had been the one solid throughout his whole, sorry childhood. Scott had always known how much his mother had loved his father. If anything, it had been too much. When he'd left, it had broken her. Since that day, she'd never been the same. Scott had tried. God how he'd tried to make it up to her. To make her smile. To make her see that life was worth carrying on. That there was still someone there who needed her. Who loved her. Sadly, it hadn't been enough. From the day his father had disappeared from their lives, it was as if his mother had, too. At least in spirit. Only her sad body had remained, going through the motions of living, nothing more. His love for her hadn't been enough to make up for the loss of her husband. It hadn't been when he was a small boy and he knew it wasn't now. And there wasn't a damn thing he could do about it.

He looked up and saw that she'd fallen asleep again. Cursing, he got to his feet. What a marvellous few days this had turned out to be. Damned by Megan for his choice of career, losing his case, and then picking up his drunk, spaced out mother from a police cell. In full view of the girlfriend he'd been hoping to spend the evening making up with. Sometimes life could be a real bitch.

Chapter Nineteen

She was knee deep in witness statements, but Megan knew she had to make this phone call. At least if she wanted any chance of seeing Scott again, other than on the inside of a court. And she did. There was no point in lying to herself. She was hooked. She tried his chambers first, but was told by the clerk that Scott was working from home today. Megan had a pretty good idea why, and tried his mobile instead.

'Armstrong.'

She wondered if she'd ever get used to hearing his voice. If it would ever fail to make her pulse race. 'It's Megan. I was phoning to find out how your mum is.'

For a few seconds there was silence. Megan was beginning to wonder if he was going to put the phone down on her when he finally replied. 'She's fine, thank you.'

Well, at least he was talking to her, sort of, though his short reply didn't bode well for a lengthy conversation. 'Good.' Neither did her even shorter response. Come on Megan, this isn't that difficult, she berated herself. A few days ago they'd been able to talk to each other for hours. They were still the same people. 'Have you found anything further about where she's been living?'

'No.'

His replies were getting shorter and cooler. Not really the answers of a man who was dying to make up with her. 'Scott, I know you've got your mum staying with you at the moment, but how about I come over and cook you both a meal? I'm not bad, you know. I could probably manage to make an entire dinner without any of us getting food poisoning.'

There was a heavy sigh. 'Now's not a good time, Megan. In fact, I was thinking ...' Silence. A faint scratching sound that she guessed was him raking a hand across his chin. Unshaven, if the noise was anything to go by. 'Perhaps we should cool it for a while. Go our separate ways. Give us both time to think about things.'

'What things?' she blurted, stunned by his statement.

'About the fact that you hate what I do, for starters.'

A sudden chill swept through her. She should have phoned him earlier, before all this mess with his mother made everything so much more complicated. 'Sometimes I don't understand it, that's all.'

'That wasn't the impression I got the other day.' Another sigh. This time even deeper. 'Look, we've both got a lot going on in our lives right now. Neither of us needs any further complications.'

'Is this your way of saying you've had enough?' she interrupted, her tone unnaturally clipped. 'Thanks, but I've had what I wanted, and now I'm looking to get out?'

'No,' he replied sharply. 'Don't twist my words—'

'I'm not the one who's clever with words, Mr Barrister. You are. But I am good at reading the signs. Right now they seem to be saying go away.'

A third sigh. 'Look, Megan—'

'Do you want me to go away, or not?'

'Yes.' The single word bounced through her brain, causing pain wherever it touched. 'But not a permanent yes,' he added quickly. 'Just until things settle down.'

'I see.' But she didn't. Either he wanted her in his life or he didn't. He seemed to be saying he didn't. 'Well, I guess I'll see you around then.'

After putting down the phone she picked up her handbag and walked slowly towards the ladies. It was only when she shut the door on the cubicle that she sunk on to the toilet seat and allowed herself to cry.

For several minutes she wallowed in self-pity, weeping tears for the woman who'd finally let another man in, only to find he was already bored of her.

Emerging from the cubicle, she blew her nose, splashed water over her face and went back to face the world. She wasn't going to let another man hurt her like Luke had. Sure, she might be upset for a few days, but she'd get on with her life.

On her way back to her desk, she bumped into Ann, who took one look at her face and tugged her into the nearest vacant office. 'What happened?' she asked, pushing her down on a chair.

Clearly her attempts at patching up her face hadn't been successful. 'Nothing. I just had a bit of grit in my eye.'

'Bollocks.'

The earthy phrase, coming from the lips of a woman who often reminded her of a school teacher, managed to make her smile. 'True. Okay, I'll give you one guess.'

'You and Scott had a falling out?'

Miserably, she nodded.

'Is this the same Scott who apparently has a diary clash that makes him unable to take up the child murder case?'

Dazed, she gaped at Ann. 'I—he—what did you just say?'

'I said, Scott isn't going to be defending that case. It'll be Peasbody, who, whilst he's good—'

'Isn't anywhere near as good as Scott.' Her mind began to spin. He hadn't taken the case. Earlier he'd told her he wanted it. Now apparently he didn't have the time to commit to it. A diary clash. She knew enough about the workings of a chambers to know that barristers sometimes claimed other commitments to avoid a case. It wasn't strictly within the rules, but it was hard to prove it wasn't true. At least with any barrister as busy as Scott. Was she reading too much into it, or, if it weren't for her, would his diary have been free enough for him to take on such a high-profile case?

'Does this change anything?' Ann's kind eyes were watching her.

'I don't know. We'd had a falling out over it, but then matters took another nose dive.' She loved Ann like a sister, but she wasn't going to be the one to betray Scott's privacy. 'In the last conversation we had a few minutes ago, he told me he wanted to end things.'

'Did he say why?'

Actually, now she thought about it, Megan realised he hadn't put it like that. 'He said we should cool things for a while,' she recalled slowly. 'I think his phrase was *give us both time to think*.'

Ann looked as puzzled as she was. 'About what?'

'I'm not sure.' Megan frowned, trying to recall what had happened between Scott wanting to see so much of her and the phone call today. Two things stood out. The first was their argument over the child murder case. Well, he'd managed to neatly sidestep having to take that on, so surely that couldn't be the driving factor? The only other thing that had happened had been the appearance of his mother.

'Do you want me to go and box his ears? Arrest him? Threaten him? All of the above?'

Megan didn't need to look at Ann's face to know she was serious. The lady was fiercely loyal when it came to looking after those she cared about. 'Thanks for the offer, but I'm good. I'm wondering if the problem isn't between him and me after all. If it's actually about something else.'

'Well, I'll stand down for now, but the offer's there if you need it.' Ann rose from her chair and gave her a quick hug. 'Don't let this one hurt you, Megan. Watch your back, and if you can't, I will.'

Megan didn't like to tell her friend it was too late. She was already in too deep, getting hurt was almost inevitable. Especially as she was about to offer help to a man who most certainly wouldn't want it, and probably wouldn't accept it. But there was no way she was going to let him go through this alone.

The moment he set foot back in the eerily quiet house, his arms laden with groceries, Scott knew his mother had disappeared again. Dropping the bags he ran up the stairs but, as he'd feared, her bed was empty. Disgusted with himself, he punched at the door frame, barely feeling the pain as his knuckles crunched against the hard wood. How the hell had he been so stupid, leaving her alone? It had only been half an hour. Thirty minutes in which he'd driven at breakneck speed to the nearest supermarket to stock up on the essentials. Milk, bread, cheese. Some foods he knew his mother liked in a bid to get something nutritious down her. But it had been thirty minutes too long.

His eyes fell on a sheet of paper left on the coffee table. She'd scribbled a quick note. *Don't worry about me, Scott darling. I feel better now. I'm staying with a male friend. I'll call you. Love, Mum.*

Shouting a stream of expletives, he ran back down the stairs and straight to the cabinet where he kept the whiskey. Without thinking he drained what was probably the equivalent of a quadruple shot into a tumbler. Grasping the glass, he jerked it up to his mouth and was inches away from downing it in one, when he suddenly realised what he was doing. Way to take away the pain of having an alcoholic mother: become an alcoholic himself. Slamming the untouched contents back on to the coffee table, he sunk on to the sofa, buried his head in his hands and wept.

An insistent ringing on the doorbell finally penetrated his consciousness and he warily raised his head. God, how long had he been blubbering like a baby, for Christ's sake? Dragging himself off the sofa he sloped to the downstairs bathroom and looked in the mirror. Bloody hell. What a wreck. Cupping his hands under the tap, he splashed water over his face, trying to remember when he'd last sought refuge in tears. As a boy, in the sanctuary of his bedroom, when nobody else was around to witness his humiliation, he'd sometimes wept. But since he'd reached adulthood? Other than a few tears when he'd buried his father, which was surely understandable, he'd never felt the urge to cry. He had his life and his emotions under control now. At least he thought he had, until today.

The doorbell continued to ring. Scott took one last glance in the mirror, decided that at a push he could put his appearance down to a monster hangover, and went to answer it.

'Megan.' He stumbled backwards in shock. She was the very last person he'd expected to see. Looking and feeling like he did, he wasn't sure he wanted to see her, either.

Remaining where she was, she studied him. No doubt took in the red-rimmed eyes, the drawn face, the heavy stubble. 'You look awful.'

He ignored the comment. There was no way he was going to be drawn into a conversation about his appearance, or how he'd come to look like he'd spent the last half an hour weeping away like a baby. 'What do you want?' he asked belligerently.

'Is that any way to greet a friend?' She pushed past him and into the house. 'Where's your Mum? Sleeping it off still?'

'I don't know.'

She turned quickly back to look at him. '*You don't know*?'

And now the two days of crap was taking an even further plunge downwards. 'No,' he replied tetchily. 'I went out to get some food. When I came back, she was gone.'

It was then that Megan realised why Scott looked as terrible as he did. He'd been crying. There was no other explanation for the red eyes. But while he looked like he needed a friend, and she was desperate to put her arms around him and provide whatever comfort she could, his guarded expression stopped her, reminding her they weren't in that place right now. 'Do you know where she is?'

'No.'

He stood with his arms crossed, his feet slightly apart and his back ramrod straight. Defiant, as if mustering the last dregs of his pride. It almost broke her heart.

'Didn't you look through her handbag, find any clues?'

She received a pointed glare. 'Of course not. I don't make a habit of going through women's handbags.'

'You'd never make a detective.' He didn't even attempt to smile. Just stood, stony-faced. She tried a different tactic. 'How long has she been gone?'

He looked down at his watch and shrugged his shoulders. 'I left about an hour ago to go to the supermarket. I was gone half an hour, max.'

It didn't take any detective skills to work out what he'd been doing since. She eyed the whiskey glass and he must have seen the direction of her gaze.

'Like mother, like son, eh?' he asked bitterly, turning his back on her and slumping down on his sofa.

'How did she get out?' she asked, ignoring his barbed comment. 'I mean, did you lock the door after you?'

He looked incredulous. 'Lock up my own mother inside the house? Are you crazy?'

Megan stared at him. 'No, it's what I'd have done. Handcuffed her to the bed, padlocked the door. Anything to make sure she didn't escape again. At least until I'd found out where she was living.'

'Jesus, Megan, she's my *mother*. I can't treat her like a criminal.'

His voice started to break and she immediately kicked herself. This wasn't another case. This was deeply personal. 'Sorry, you're right. I wasn't thinking like a daughter. I was thinking like a cop.' Her words sounded very similar to words he'd uttered a few days ago, when he'd defended his right to accept the child murder case. He'd been thinking like a lawyer on that occasion, and her like a mother. Now the tables were turned. 'She's not been gone long. We can go for a drive around, see if we can find her.'

He shook his head and slumped even further down the sofa. 'No. She clearly doesn't want me around, or she wouldn't have fled in the first place.'

Megan found it hard to believe what she was hearing. He sounded so down, defeated. Where was the man who was always so maddeningly sure of himself? As he ran a hand through his already dishevelled hair, Megan realised with a start that this was a totally different side to Scott Armstrong. With his cocky manner and smooth good looks it was easy to assume he was shallow. She had. But the man sitting before her now, vulnerable, uncertain, hurting because his mother didn't appear to want him in her life, was far deeper, far more complex, than she'd ever given him credit for. And she was falling for him.

Chapter Twenty

Scott beckoned Megan to sit down. He didn't have the energy to stand, and he wasn't prepared to keep looking up at her. What on earth was she doing here? After she'd seen the state of his mother in the police station, he wouldn't have blamed her if she'd never contacted him again. Many women would have seen it as the time to get out. God knows, he'd certainly given her the opportunity to do exactly that. Yet, despite what he'd said, she'd still turned up on his doorstep, proving what a warm, caring woman she really was. Right now though, he couldn't handle that kindness. Nor could he bear the sympathy in her eyes. 'Look, Megan, I appreciate the house call, but there really isn't anything you can do. It's my mess and I'll deal with it.'

'Do you think that's the only reason I came round? To see if I could help with your mother?'

'What other reason is there?'

She took the seat opposite, staring at him with her huge blue eyes. 'Tell me, why did you turn down the murder case?'

Ah, so she'd heard about that had she? 'It was a big case. I had too much on. I couldn't devote enough time to it to do the client justice.'

'That's the only reason?'

Those eyes of hers weren't looking away. They were fixed on him. Heck, she was just like her father. The same interrogation technique. Coolly stare the other person down with those magnificent eyes until they'll admit anything. 'It's enough of a reason.'

'No, it isn't. You turned the case down because I didn't want you to do it, didn't you?'

He could lie and say no, but what was the point? She knew what the answer was anyway. 'I had a diary clash, Megan,' he replied sternly, 'and if you call it anything different I'll be had up before the Bar Standards Board.'

Immediately she smiled. Such a gorgeous smile. It lit up her eyes and caused his heart to flip in his chest. 'Of course.' Still smiling, she moved to snuggle down next to him, wrapping her arms around him, pulling him close against her. 'This is what I came over to do.'

God help him, his bloody eyes started to fill with tears again. As he sank into her embrace, he bit on the inside of his cheek in an attempt not to break down. He'd embarrassed himself enough in front of this woman. But the hug felt so good. So exactly what he needed. Lifting his arms, he placed them around her and squeezed her back.

When he was sure he had a handle on his emotions again, he pulled away. 'Thanks. That was ...' Might as well admit it. 'Just what I needed.'

'So why do I get the impression you still want me to go?'

Go? Was she mad? Of course he didn't *want* her to go. What he wanted was something entirely different. It involved him taking off her clothes and burying himself inside her until he couldn't think or remember anything but her and how wonderful she was. 'I don't want you to go,' he admitted.

'But?'

He exhaled slowly. 'Megan, I appreciate you coming round. I really do. But my life is one hell of a mess at the moment and I don't want you getting mixed up in it.' He moved further away from her. Far enough that she wouldn't be able to read the shame in his eyes. 'I meant it when I said we need to cool it. To think about what we really want. And frankly, the last thing I want is for you to stay here out of some misguided sense of charity.'

'Charity?' The disgusted expression on her face was almost laughable. 'That's why you think I'm here? Poor Scott is going through a bad time, and though I really don't like him any more, not now I know he's got an alcoholic mother, I'll come round and give him one last roll in the sheets. It's the least I can do for those hours he's spent servicing me.'

He raised his eyes to the ceiling. 'That wasn't exactly how my thought processes were going.'

'Weren't they? I'm not sure who to feel insulted for. You or me.' She leapt up from the sofa and began to pace the room like a trapped bobcat. 'I don't need time to think about what I really want, Scott. I know perfectly well what I want. I want you.' He swallowed down the lump in his throat. 'And yes, some of what I'm feeling for you right now is sympathy. Jesus, who wouldn't? But that's not the only reason why I'm here. I care for you, Scott. A lot. Enough to want to help, in any way I can. If it isn't by tracking down your mother, which I could do, very easily, if you'd let me, then it's by being here for you. A shoulder for you to lean on. Someone who'll make you a hot meal, if you want. Take you to bed, if you want that, too. At least I hope you want the last part. I was pretty much banking on that bit.'

He didn't know what to say. His reputation for fast thinking was in tatters. Her words left him speechless.

'So, what's it to be?' she prompted.

Racking his brain, he desperately tried to remember what she'd said. The bits in between *I care for you* and *I want to take you to bed*, that was. He had no trouble remembering those. 'Can we start with the last part?' he finally croaked out. 'Then maybe work up to the other two later.' He moved to stand in front of her. Clasping her by the shoulders, he bent his head and started to explore that enticing mouth of hers. 'Probably a lot later.'

Still with his mouth fastened on to hers, he lifted her into his arms and carried her up the stairs. 'And just so we're clear,' he told her as he laid her on the bed. 'I care a lot about you, too.' He suspected his feelings went far deeper than caring. That they were actually merging into love. But he wasn't ready to admit that to himself yet, never mind her.

* * *

'When did your mother start drinking?' Megan asked a couple of hours later as they cleared away the plates from the meal they'd just shared.

They'd done the making love part. Twice – once in the shower. Then she'd made a quick pasta dish with the food he'd bought for his mother. Now, he guessed, she was doing the shoulder to lean on bit. Except much as he enjoyed leaning on her, preferably with his whole body, naked, he wasn't ready to talk. Not about this. It was too painful, too shaming. Too likely to rock the relationship boat that they had only just managed to stabilise.

'When my father left us. When I was seven.'

'I'm sorry.' She took his hand and led him towards the sitting room. 'Is that why you took up drawing?'

Scott was a man. He loved to talk about himself. But not about *this*. 'I guess, yes. It gave me something to do in the evenings.' When his mother was drowning her sorrows in the bottom of a vodka bottle. Even now, Scott couldn't touch the stuff.

'When I first came in and saw the whiskey glass, I thought …'

'I was going down the same slippery slope?' He sighed and looked down at their joined hands, her fingers entwined in his. 'I might do, one day. I don't know. I try to restrict my drinking to just a couple of times a week. I don't drink to excess. This afternoon was the first time in a long while I've reached for the whiskey bottle in anger. Usually to let off steam I go for a beer or two. I remember putting the glass to my lips and then seeing her face.' He looked over at Megan. 'That was how she started. So upset and angry with life that she reached for the bottle.'

'But she didn't have the strength to stop herself.' Megan reminded him. 'You do.'

'Perhaps. Or perhaps my troubles are very minor compared to hers.'

'Why did your father leave?'

That was the million dollar question. One he simply couldn't, wouldn't answer. Instinctively he released his hand from hers. 'He left,' he replied bluntly. 'That's all that matters. It broke her heart.'

'So you would draw while she drank.'

'Pretty much, yes.' He rubbed a hand over his face. He still hadn't shaved. Something Megan had reminded him of as he'd kissed the soft, sensitive skin of her breasts. 'I don't want your pity, Megan,' he ground out as he saw sympathy swim once more in her eyes. 'She was a good mother. She held down a job to provide for me. I always had clean clothes on my back and food in my stomach.'

'And what about love?' she asked softly. 'How much of that did you have?'

How could Megan read him so easily? 'Enough,' he replied shortly. Enough that he knew his mother cared for him. Just not as much as she'd loved his father.

Megan saw his face close up and knew she wasn't going to get any further with that line of questioning. Years on the force had taught her when to continue probing, and when to change tactics. 'Scott, about what I mentioned earlier. Tracking her down. I can do that, you know.'

'I know.' She heard him take in a deep breath, knew he was wrestling with what to do. 'I'm worried she's started to fall in with a bad crowd. That she's taken up with a drug dealer,' he admitted. 'Before it had only ever been alcohol. Now ...' he trailed off, looked at her with haunted grey eyes. 'She's on a downward spiral. I'm terrified this can only go one way.'

'Then let me help you,' she pleaded, taking hold of his hands and gripping them tightly. 'Come on, Scott. At least let me find out where she's staying.'

'I can't have the police hunting down my mother,' he replied in a tortured voice. 'Christ.'

She reached for his face and smoothed out the furrowed

lines on his brow. 'It won't be like that. I'll do it discreetly. Nobody else involved but me.'

'You've got enough on your plate.'

'What, too much to help you? Too much to help stop a woman from eventually killing herself? No, I don't think so.' She knew what she was offering was difficult for him to accept. His lover tracking down his alcoholic mother. It wasn't hard to understand how humiliating that was for him.

'I'm frightened of what you'll find,' he finally admitted to her, avoiding her eyes.

Frankly, so was she. 'I know. But sitting here and hoping shit won't happen doesn't stop it happening. Isn't it far better to know what's going on, rather than second guess? At least, if we can find her, it'll be a start. You'll know what you're up against. Be able to begin fighting back.'

'Yeah, you're right.' He finally met her eyes and smiled. It wasn't his usual, confident grin, but at least it was something. 'God, you're a tough one, Megan. How can something so tough come in such a small, cute package?'

'I'll overlook the cute part, if you take me to bed one more time before I go.'

'I can do that, but I'd rather you stayed. Sleep with me tonight. Come with me to the gym tomorrow. You'll still be home to have breakfast with Sally.'

Megan wasn't going to argue this time. These last few days all she'd dreamt of was spending the night in Scott's arms. At one point she hadn't believed she'd ever be doing that again. So while Scott went to the bathroom, she quickly phoned her parents and warned them she wouldn't be back until breakfast. Perhaps it was a slippery slope, staying the night, but Megan was too relieved to worry about that. The future would take care of itself – for now she had Scott back in her life. A different Scott to the one she thought she knew. Deeper. More vulnerable. Altogether more loveable.

Chapter Twenty-One

Once again Scott found himself biking over to Megan's house for a family meal. This time it was Sunday roast. Not something he was going to turn down in a hurry. It felt good to be part of a family, no matter how small a part it actually was. Probably because his own family life had turned out so catastrophically bad.

According to Megan's sources, Scott's mother had chosen to live with a notorious drug dealer instead of her son. Reg someone or other. When Megan had told him, it had taken all of her considerable powers of persuasion to stop him from jumping on to his bike and having it out with the man.

'Macho posturing isn't going to help,' she'd told him in no uncertain terms. 'It'll just make things worse. He'll see you as the enemy, which, trust me, is the last thing you want. And there's no way your mother will respond to you telling her what to do. She has to work that out for herself. You know where she is now. You know that at least she has a roof over her head. If she's with Reg, she's physically safe. He won't let anyone harm what's his. What you need to do now is work out how to get her to see where her life is heading.'

Easy to say. A bloody sight more difficult to actually fathom out how to do, he didn't even know where to start. Again, Megan had come to the rescue. She knew some good counsellors who'd be able to help. Before he knew what was happening, she was making him an appointment to meet with one the next day.

Right now, however, as he roared on to their driveway, he made up his mind that he was going to put the whole sorry mess behind him. Live for the moment.

'Scott!'

There was a sight that would go a long way towards helping

him do exactly that. Sally had already opened the door and was jumping up and down, yelling his name. He wasn't sure when they'd gone from greeting each other with a smile to full-blown hugs. Whenever it was, he was glad. He wrapped his arms around her tiny body and lifted her up. 'Hello, Titch.'

'I'm not small,' she protested as he brought her safely back down again. 'I'm one of the tallest girls in my class.'

'Maybe so,' he smiled, ruffling her hair. 'But you're a titch compared to me.'

'That's because you're too tall.' She looked up at him, craning her neck. 'It must be lonely up there.'

He laughed and squeezed her dainty hand. It was lonely at times, but it had nothing to do with his height. The truth was he hadn't even realised he was lonely until he'd met Megan. Now the days he spent apart from her felt like a giant void. To say it was unnerving was putting it politely. Even worse was the knowledge that sometimes he actually caught himself counting down to the time he'd see her again, and the void would be filled.

As Sally ran up the stairs to gather together her latest artwork, he poked his nose in the kitchen and found Dot, up to her elbows in pastry, the radio blaring out classical music. She gave him her warm, twinkly smile. The one that made him realise with a sharp tug how much he wished his own mother would greet him that way. 'Do I get to eat that later?' he asked, once he'd kissed her on her flour-dusted cheek.

'If you're good,' she replied with a dimpled grin.

'And what constitutes good in your book?'

'Eating everything I put in front of you will do, for a start.'

He laughed. 'Well, in that case, I can promise you I'll be as good as gold.'

She waved him away and he went in search of Megan, who he found arguing with her father over some police matter in the living room.

'Scott.' It did his heart good to see the welcome on her face.

To have her walk over to him and kiss him, even though her father was in the room. 'I didn't hear the doorbell.'

'That's because your daughter beat me to it.'

She smiled. 'She's been looking out for you.'

'So I guessed. She's also been drawing more pictures.'

'It's worrying to see the effect the Armstrong charm has on the Taylor women.'

Scott found himself grinning like an idiot, though he was also conscious of her father in the background, his rather stern face telling him the Taylor male remained to be convinced.

After a few minutes of small talk, Megan drifted off to help her mother and Scott was left standing with her father. The silence stretched out between them, becoming more and more awkward. Why, suddenly, couldn't he think of anything to say?

Thankfully Stanley started to talk. 'I think this is where I'm supposed to ask you if your intentions towards my daughter are honourable.'

Scott froze. Well then. Swallowing down the quick burst of terror, he told himself that would teach him to leave the conversation up to her father. Slowly he crossed his legs at his ankles, making a determined effort not to look panicked. 'I have to admit, most of my intentions fall in the dishonourable category,' he finally replied, trying a little humour. A glance in her father's direction confirmed his fears. There was no reassuring smile. Not even a glint of amusement: humour was the wrong tactic. He changed gears and slipped into lawyer mode. That way he could answer anything that was thrown at him. 'Mr Taylor,' he began again, deliberately choosing the formal title in an effort to convey his sincerity. 'I can't say I know where my relationship with Megan is going to end, but I can say for certain that I'm not playing any games. I have no intention of hurting her. She means too much to me.'

Stanley nodded, seemingly satisfied, but Scott was still aware of the tension between them. But, whilst they were already wading knee deep in dangerous topics, he might as well get everything out in the open. 'I know you don't think much of me.'

'I didn't say that,' the older man replied steadily.

'No, but detectives aren't the only ones good at reading between the lines. Lawyers do it, too.'

Stanley considered him carefully, with the same steady gaze Scott had received before. The one that made him feel like a specimen under a microscope. 'I don't have anything against you, Scott.'

'Perhaps not, but I also know I'm not the man you imagined your daughter going out with.' He paused, but saw no hint that Stanley was going to contradict him. 'I can only say I plan to reverse your opinion of me. To grow on you.'

Was that a small smile on his face? Or was he seeing what he wanted to see?

'I'm sure you will, Scott. I'm sure you will. But I meant what I said earlier. I don't have anything against you. Megan finds it hard to accept what you do for a living, but I don't. My only concern is for her. She's been badly let down in the past. I won't have her, or Sally, going through that again. Not if I can help it.'

Scott was saved a reply by the entrance of the little girl herself. Still, he looked Stanley in the eye and nodded. Message received, loud and clear.

No doubt feeling his mission had been accomplished, Stanley then rose from his chair and left the room, leaving Scott with Sally. A far easier companion.

'Here's a picture I made for you,' she announced proudly, pushing one of a handful of her latest masterpieces over in his direction.

He looked down at the colourful artwork, just about making out the sea and three figures.

'It's you, me and Mum by the beach. Next to the pier we went on.'

The more he studied the picture, the more it touched him, and terrified him, in equal measures. She'd drawn them all holding hands, Sally in the middle, and they looked like a real family. As his heart lurched, he wondered frantically if that's how Sally saw them. A family. 'Have you shown this to your mum?' he asked softly, feeling a crazy surge of raw emotion. One he wasn't sure he could explain.

Sally shook her head and Scott thanked God. He was pretty certain it wasn't a picture that Megan would want to see. It would no doubt terrify her as much as it did him, though for entirely different reasons. The terror on his side came from the fact that he could easily imagine them as a family, spending lots of similar days together. But family days out with him weren't likely to be on Megan's to-do list. She'd given him several none-too-subtle hints that, while she was enjoying her time with him, it had an expiry date. His moral compass didn't fit with hers and there were parts of him she didn't understand and didn't even like. Sure, he was making some progress in changing her mind, but he had a horrible feeling it wasn't going to be enough.

While Scott had been receiving his grilling from Stanley, Megan, too, had been on the wrong side of a grilling. In her case, from her mother.

'How is that poor boy doing?' she asked as she put the finishing touches on an apple pie.

Megan had never met anyone who was less like a *poor boy*. 'By poor boy I assume you mean Scott?'

'Of course. Such a terrible business. Has he seen his mother again since, you know, that night?'

'The night she was brought into the station, you mean,' Megan replied dryly. What had happened was now common knowledge, which made her mother's attempt at being discreet all the more laughable. 'No, he hasn't. I told him to back off and talk to an expert in dependency first, before charging in like a raging bull.'

'It can't have been easy for him, growing up as he did.

No father and an alcoholic mother who, from the sound of things, didn't really take much notice of him.'

Megan studied her mother. 'You've fallen under the man's spell, haven't you?' she accused. 'I can't believe you're now repeating his sob story to me. What are you trying to do? Make me feel so sorry for him that I jump into bed with him? I hate to say this, Mum, but that ship has already sailed.'

'I worked that out for myself,' she replied tartly. 'I was only making conversation. Telling you that I approved of him, if my opinion matters at all to you.'

Knowing she'd gone too far, Megan bent to hug her. 'Sorry. Of course your opinion matters to me. It matters a lot. It's just …' She sighed, and rested her head against her mother's. 'I'm in real trouble, Mum. I like him so much.' She wasn't going to admit to the other L-word, not yet. 'I know it's going to hurt badly when it all comes to an end.'

Gently her mother shifted away so she could look at her. 'Oh Megan, why do you assume it will end?'

'Because he's not the type who thinks long-term.' Tears filled her eyes and she had to blink rapidly to stop them from escaping. 'I knew that when I went into this relationship. It's why I fought it for so damned long. But then I thought, why not? I can have a little fun. I just have to be careful.' She tried to laugh. 'I've forgotten how to be careful.'

Her mum reached down and squeezed her hand. 'Darling Megan, you can't spend all your life being careful. Sometimes you just have to live it and see where it takes you.'

Megan sighed and closed her eyes for a moment. Of course her mother was right. Mothers often were. But she had the horrid feeling that this particular road was taking her right back to searing heartbreak. A place she'd promised to never revisit.

It had been a lovely evening, Megan reflected as she stood in the hallway waiting for Scott, who'd bounded upstairs to say goodbye to Sally. All her favourite people had been gathered around one table. It had almost been too lovely, carrying with it the danger that she would start to believe such evenings could become a permanent fixture.

Stop thinking so much, she scolded herself. Live for now. As Scott came back into view, his long limbs bounding back down the stairs, she automatically reached for his black leather jacket and handed it to him.

'Hey, thanks. I could get used to such service.' Giving her a quick, maddening grin, he shrugged it on.

'I only provide it to make sure our visitors actually leave,' she retorted distractedly, her mind more focused on how the jacket hugged his broad frame.

As he was zipping up she noticed a sheet of paper falling out of his pocket and reached to take it. 'What's that?'

'Ahh.' Without looking at it, he took it from her and pushed it back in. 'Just a picture Sally drew for me.'

'Really? Let me see.'

The glance he gave her was fleeting, but long enough for her to see the hesitation in it and start to wonder. What exactly had Sally drawn that was making him look so uncomfortable?

'Hand it over,' she demanded in her commanding police sergeant voice. It worked. Within moments she was staring down at a touching family picture. And immediately regretted asking to see it. 'Shit, shit, shit.' The words flew out of her mouth at the same rate her heart sunk in her chest. As she continued to stare at the three figures, noting the care Sally had put into the picture, she felt ripples of raw panic. She didn't want Sally to get hurt. Something she seemed to have lost sight of while allowing herself to be dazzled by Scott.

'I didn't think the drawing was that bad,' Scott remarked, his flippant words totally at odds with the rigid expression on his face.

'This is what I was afraid would happen,' she shot back, trying to keep her voice down so the rest of the house couldn't hear. 'Sally getting the wrong idea. Starting to think of you as a father figure.'

'And that's such a terrible prospect because …?'

She glowered at him. 'You don't need me to answer that question.'

For a brief moment she thought he actually looked hurt, which made her wonder if she'd got it all wrong. But how could she when he'd openly admitted that his idea of a long relationship was measured in weeks? She guessed he was feeling slighted because she'd implied he wasn't a good prospect for a father, when the truth was he'd never be around long enough for either of them to find out.

His eyes flickered and his jaw tightened. Before she realised what was happening he was pulling her towards him, his mouth crushing hers. It wasn't a gentle goodnight kiss. It was rough, bruising and bordering on animalistic. It was as if he was staking his claim on her. Given no opportunity to respond, all she could do was absorb the potent heat as it seared every part of her body. Finally, his breathing ragged, he pulled away.

'What was that for?' she hissed, annoyed to find her breathing as shallow as his.

'To make sure you think about me tonight.'

Then he was gone. Jamming on his helmet, throwing a leg over his bike, he vanished into the dark, leaving her standing alone on the driveway, angry and hurting. Angry mainly with herself, because instead of pushing him away, she'd clung to him like a limpet while he'd savaged her mouth. Totally undone by the fierce heat of a kiss she hadn't needed as a reminder to think about him. She'd have done that anyway.

Which brought her to the part that hurt. Scott Armstrong was a man no woman could tie down, though many had tried. It hurt like crazy to know that she, too, had ended up falling into that trap. Wanting more from him. And if she hadn't already guessed that wasn't in his plans, his furtive attempt to hide Sally's picture had made the fact glaringly obvious. And left them both where, exactly?

Chapter Twenty-Two

Scott waited until the middle of the week before he called Megan. It took him that long to work through his muddled emotions. Every time he thought of her, and that was too damn much, he saw the look of horror on her face when she'd looked at the picture Sally had drawn. He must have been good enough to go out with now and again, to practise tangling in the sheets with, but nowhere near the mark when it came to anything serious, like being a potential father for her daughter. He was amazed how crushed that made him feel. Two months ago, if someone had told him that one day he'd want to be thought of as a potential father, he'd have sneered. A wife, children. A family. Give him a break. After his own experience of family life, he'd be nuts to want to go down that route.

But then he'd started dating Megan. Spent time with her daughter.

Now he'd fallen for them both, totally, utterly. So much so that he couldn't imagine life without them. It was incredibly sobering to realise that finally, at the age of thirty-two, he'd fallen in love. And apparently being in love made a person do stupid things. Like picking up the phone to talk to a woman who didn't have a place for him in her long-term plans. But what was the alternative? She wasn't going to phone him. That was patently obvious. So if he wanted to see her, he had to call her. And he more than wanted to see her. He needed to see her. His mother wasn't the only one with an addiction. Hers was alcohol. His was a short, sexy detective.

With that sobering thought in mind, he dialled Megan's mobile.

'Are you free for lunch?' he asked, pushing aside the pleasantries. The last time they'd seen each other, he'd kissed her in anger. He doubted any affable greeting on his part was going to cut it with her.

There was a long silence on the other end. Was she smiling or frowning? 'I might be.'

He took solace from the fact that, even though her voice was cool, she hadn't said *no*. He'd been prepared for a *no*, so a *might be* was a pleasant surprise. 'What would make the difference between you being free or not?'

It was a long, agonising moment before she replied. 'An apology could work.'

'I'm not going to apologise for kissing you,' he replied quietly. 'But I will apologise for doing it in anger. And for not phoning you sooner.'

'Too busy?'

'No, damn it …' He paused, reminded himself that getting angry again wasn't going to help. 'Forget it. I'm phoning you now. You have a choice. Enjoy a leisurely lunch with a sexy lawyer, or go to the station canteen and eat with a bunch of boring coppers.'

'Who's the sexy lawyer?'

He let out a laugh, relieved she was making a joke. At least he hoped it was. 'I thought that was obvious.'

There was a slight pause and he heard a rustle of paperwork. No doubt she was deciding whether she had time in her busy day to squeeze him in. 'Okay, I'll meet you but it has to be quick. An hour max.'

Before picking up the phone, he'd have taken any crumb she deigned to offer, so an hour for lunch was a pretty good result. But why did she have to make it sound like she was doing him a favour by seeing him? Why couldn't she want to see him, too? 'Fine,' he replied shortly. 'I'll make sure I don't take up any more than sixty minutes of your precious time.'

Putting down the phone, Megan sat back in her chair and looked up at the ceiling. What was she to make of the man?

One minute he was striding away from her, the next he was calmly inviting her to lunch. He was tying her up in knots.

Ann tucked her head inside the office. 'What are you rolling your eyes over?'

'Men,' she replied succinctly, then rubbed at her neck and frowned. 'No, that's not fair. One man in particular.'

'Is Scott still giving you the run around?'

Megan took one look at Ann's face and almost laughed. 'You've got the look of a Rottweiler, prepared to go into battle. I'm almost tempted to say "down boy".' Ann opened her mouth to speak, but Megan held up her hand. 'It's not Scott's fault. It's mine. I knew what we had wasn't going to be a long-term thing. I didn't even want it to be. I might have fancied him, but I wasn't sure I actually liked him all that much.'

'And now?' she asked, quietly closing the door.

'Now I've fallen in love with him.' There, the words were out in the open. The bald, naked, terrifying truth. 'Which is totally ridiculous. I mean, we haven't even got anything in common. He's a defence lawyer. I'm a cop. If that isn't enough reason to put the brakes on now, there's also the small matter of how we see our relationship unfurling. I want something long and stable. He's probably already planning his escape exit.'

'Oh, Meg.' Ann moved to squeeze her arm. 'How can you be so certain?'

Glumly Megan put her head in her hands and recounted the tale of Sally's drawing and Scott's reaction to it.

'You know his instinct to hide the picture doesn't automatically mean he was horrified by it. He might just have needed some time to think before showing you. It probably took him by surprise as much as it did you.'

'Is that your polite way of saying I should know better than to try and second-guess a person's motives?'

'Yes. The less than polite version is *talk to the bloody man.*'

Ann gave her a look filled with sympathy. 'You really love him?'

'Looks like.'

'Then he's a very lucky guy. And if he doesn't realise that, I'll make him realise.'

Torn between laughing and crying, Megan went to hug her friend. If only it were that simple.

He'd chosen a small bistro for lunch, just five minutes' drive from the station. When he picked her up he was stiffly polite towards her; perhaps not the most positive of starts, but maybe he felt as uncertain of their next step as she did. Not that Scott and uncertain were a combination she'd ever imagined. As they sat down on the elegant leather chairs and scanned their menus, Megan's eyes kept drifting to the man sitting opposite her. It was so hard not to simply reach over and cover his gorgeous face with kisses. She tried to harden her heart. Tried to convince herself that actually he wasn't the most stunningly attractive man she'd ever met. That his silver grey eyes weren't the most beautiful eyes she'd ever gazed into. That one look from them didn't have the capacity to melt her bones.

'Did you see the counsellor about your mother?' she asked when they'd ordered, directing the conversation to a reasonably safe topic.

He nodded. 'Yes. You were right. It was a very useful experience. He told me she's probably suffering from depression as well as alcoholism, which is why it's proving so hard for her to beat it.' Finally those light eyes glanced over at her, their look so sincere her heart flipped. 'It was the first time I'd heard that, so thank you.'

Megan found it hard to find her voice. 'Have you heard from her?'

'No.' His long, tapered fingers started to fiddle with the placemat and Megan could see this was hard for him. 'The counsellor told me I shouldn't go and see her. The fact that she hasn't let me know where she's staying is a big hint that she's ashamed of it. The last thing she needs is for her son to see her living in a hovel.' He swallowed, his Adam's apple moving slowly up and down. 'I have to be patient. He said he was sure, as she's always come home, that she will do again. If she does, he's suggested a few questions I can ask. Things I can say to help get her to think about her situation. To understand that there is a way out.'

'Okay, good.' Unable to remain detached, she found herself aching for him. This must be so painful. Especially the waiting.

'If it hadn't been for you, I'd have rushed straight over there and probably scared her off for life.' His eyes searched out hers. 'Thank you.'

No, she couldn't hold that gaze. It was too heartfelt. Too painful. Too likely to suck her in even further. 'Yes, well, I'm not sure I did much but, if it helped at all, I'm glad.'

Their conversation halted as they were served their food. A burger and chips for him. A pasta for her. 'So, how's work?' she asked finally, knowing that he would prefer not to talk about his mother any more.

'Good. Busy.' He squirted sauce on to his burger and took a bite. 'In fact you might be able to help me. I'm defending the Kevin Rogers rape case.'

'Yes, I know him. He's been brought in for questioning a few times, but we've never been able to make anything stick, until now. A thug, if ever I met one.'

'I agree that he isn't a particularly nice man. No doubt, as you say, a bit of a thug. It doesn't make him a rapist, though.'

His words were calm and measured and Megan made a determined effort to bite her tongue. She didn't want to fight with him. Certainly not over someone as pathetic as Rogers. 'How did you think I could help?'

'Rogers insists he's been set up. He claims it's common

knowledge that there's a cop in the vice squad who's, how shall I word this? I believe the phrase is bent.'

And just like that, her appetite vanished. Wherever this conversation was heading, she knew it was going to end badly. 'I see. And you believe everything a man like Rogers tells you, do you?'

'No, of course not.' He stopped eating for a moment. 'Just like you, I listen to what my client tells me, what the witnesses tell me and finally what the hard evidence tells me. Rogers believes the cop has it in for him, and that he's behind his arrest. Witnesses tell me the girls he likes to frequent are fed up with him because he's crude, at times aggressive and owes them a lot of money. They've told their pimp to sort Rogers out. Now I'm wondering if there's a connection between that, and Rogers' arrest.'

'Right. You always get the truth from the mouths of prostitutes and scumbags. What about the hard evidence? What does that say?' Oh God, why did they always end up fighting?

He sighed. 'Look, I'm not here to go through the whole damn case with you. We've got far better things to talk about. I just mentioned it in case you'd heard any rumours yourself.'

There was a crashing sound as Megan clattered her knife and fork down on to her plate. Boy, he was smooth. 'Do you really expect me to tell tales on a colleague in order to help you stop a rapist going to jail?' Feeling suddenly sick, she pushed her plate out of the way.

'For God's sake, Megan. Why do you always turn these things on their head?' The muscle of his jaw flexed. 'I haven't asked you to tell tales. I just wanted to know if you knew of any rumours. It's not the same thing. I'll arrange for someone to go to the station and ask around anyway. I just thought, as we were talking about it, I'd mention it now.'

Megan was no longer sure of anything. His phone call after days of silence, the way he'd eased his question into the conversation – it all seemed too convenient. 'Is that really how it happened?' she asked tightly. 'Or did you realise this morning that you needed to find out the name of the cop, and what easier way to do that than to take me out to lunch?'

'Wow.' Scott looked at her thunderstruck. 'You really think that was my only interest in seeing you?'

God, she hoped not, but after the angry way they'd parted, and the knowledge that it was only a matter of time before he called a halt on their relationship, she really didn't know. 'Wasn't it?'

'You were the one who raised the subject of my work, Megan.' He took two deep, steadying breaths. 'I phoned you because I wanted to see you.'

'Why?'

'Isn't that obvious? I missed you. I enjoy seeing you, talking to you.' His voice lowered. 'Making love to you.'

'The last one, I can understand. The others? I can't see why you'd enjoy that any more. All we do is argue.' Tears were starting to fill her eyes and Megan wiped at them viciously with a napkin, determined not to let him see her cry. 'You know what, I can't do this any more.'

'Do what?' he asked quietly.

'You and me. You were right.'

For once in his life, Scott really didn't want to be right. 'About what?'

'About us going our separate ways.'

'Hey, now, I didn't mean that—' he started to protest. He'd said that because he'd been ashamed about his mother, for God's sake.

'You told me we needed to think about things,' she interrupted. 'In particular about whether I could cope with what you do for a living.'

So that's where this was all going. Again. Scott cursed his big mouth. Why the hell had he brought up the Rogers case today? Why hadn't he just said *fine*, in response to her idle question about how his work was going? 'What are you telling me, Megan? That you're not prepared to see past my job when you look at me? That the person I am beneath that doesn't matter to you?'

'Stop using your clever words again,' she shot back. 'This isn't about how I view you. It's about us. How we both look at things from totally opposite sides. I didn't think it would matter so much, but it seems to. We spend too much of our time together arguing. It isn't any fun, for either of us. I can't see how we can move on from here. How we can ever work as a couple.'

'I thought that's what couples did,' he interjected softly. 'Argue. That's why they invented making up.'

Megan's heart was breaking. She couldn't bear to sit opposite him any longer. To hear him try and charm his way into continuing a relationship he knew, just as well as she did, had no future.

'I need to get back to work.' Standing up, she slid out from her seat and pushed it back under the table. 'You stay and finish up. I'll get a cab back to the station.'

He lunged to his feet, his chair making a loud scraping noise as he shoved it back in order to get out. 'I'll take you,' he ground out, flinging some notes on to the table.

Once more they drove back in silence. When he parked up she quickly got out of the car. 'So, this is goodbye?' he asked flatly, his face totally impassive.

'Yes.' The word came out in a whisper. 'And if you're honest with yourself, when the dent to your ego has healed, you'll thank me for it.'

Fighting against her instincts, she gently pushed the door shut. She wasn't going to get upset. That meant no slamming doors or bursting into tears. She was Detective Sergeant Megan Taylor. If she could cope with rapists and murderers, she could cope with a little blip in her love life. Turning sharply, she strode back into the station.

Being a police detective was part of who she was, she told herself as she settled back at her desk. Something she was proud to have achieved. It was worth a few sacrifices in life, even when it came to matters of the heart. The first man she'd loved, Luke, had found it really unnerving being with a cop. It probably helped explain why he'd taken up with other women. That and the fact that he'd been immature and totally self-centred. Now, with Scott, the job had interfered again, but in a different way. It had stopped her from being able to understand him. Prevented her from being able to fully accept what he did for a living.

Even if they'd been able to work through that, though, a man who measured his relationships in terms of weeks was never going to be hers for long. So, all in all, better to end it now before she'd been torn apart any further by their arguments. Or by his excuses for ending it. It should be easier this way, she told herself as she rubbed at her chest. A pitiful attempt to ease the crushing pain in her heart.

Chapter Twenty-Three

Megan made it through two meetings, a witness interrogation and tea with her daughter without breaking down. But by the time she put Sally to bed she felt as if she was walking on a tightrope. One false move and she'd come crashing down.

It was her father who finally pushed her over the edge. He'd taken one look at her as she walked back downstairs and, calmly putting an arm around her shoulders, had hugged her. That was all it took for the wrenching sobs to finally erupt. He sat with her on the sofa as she cried them all out. Cried for the love that might have been. It didn't help that she'd known all along it wasn't going to last. The man had bulldozed his way under her skin and then slid, quietly, into her heart.

'Want to talk about it?'

She raised her head and looked out through puffy, bleary eyes. 'Sorry, I didn't mean to detonate on you like that.'

'That's what I'm here for.' He pulled her against him and she felt his reassuring strength. 'So, are you going to tell me what all that was about?'

'I think you can guess.' She looked at him with a wry smile on her lips. 'There are only two times in my adult life I've sobbed my eyes out. Both times there was a man involved.'

'Ahh.' His body tensed slightly, as if he was all geared up to go out and punch the living daylights out of the man who'd caused her to be so upset. Her father, her hero. 'What did he do?'

'He didn't do anything. This time it was me,' she quickly reassured him. He might be seventy, but she knew it wouldn't take much for him to get into his car and turn up on Scott's doorstep, demanding retribution for upsetting his daughter. 'I finished things, so there's no need for you to challenge him to a duel.'

He drew a finger under her chin and looked tenderly down at her with his sharp blue eyes. 'If it was your decision, why are you so upset?'

Exactly. 'Because I don't want it to be this way,' she admitted on an unladylike sniff. 'Because I fell in love with him, despite the fact that I knew better than that.'

'I know I'm a mere man, but I don't understand why you ended a relationship with someone you love.'

'Oh, Dad.' She reached over to the coffee table and dragged out a box of tissues. 'Sometimes love isn't enough, is it? Scott isn't the sort of man who has an eye on the long-term. He's a charmer, flitting from one woman to the next in the bat of an eye. I knew that, but I slept with him anyway.'

'Are you saying there was someone else involved?'

'No.' It wasn't surprising her Dad didn't understand this. When she spoke it out loud, even she was having trouble grasping her reasoning. But she was talking about feelings here. Not hard facts. 'There isn't anyone else. Not at the moment at least, though it wouldn't have been long before someone else caught his eye. That's the way with men like him.' She shut her eyes against the sudden flashback to that moment she'd opened the door on Luke and another woman. 'God, I should know.'

Her father ran his hand up and down her back, soothing her as he had done when she'd been a child. 'Honey, just because Luke let you down, it doesn't mean Scott is destined to,' he said after a while.

'Logically, I know that's true. But ...' She bit at her lip in an effort to stem the tears that threatened to erupt again. 'God, Luke hurt me, Dad. I don't ever want to live through pain like that again,' she finished on a whisper.

'I know, Meg, I know.' He paused for a moment. 'And sadly there are no guarantees in life. But I got the impression that Scott cared a lot for you. Why else would he have come round here and suffered a couple of meals with your stuffy old parents? Or made such a fuss of Sally, for that matter?'

'You're not stuffy.' She gave him a weak smile before letting out a deep sigh. 'I don't know, Dad, perhaps you're right, perhaps he cares, but is that enough?' She blew her nose and leant back against him.

'Well, they say, with age, comes wisdom.' He patted her hand. 'There doesn't seem to be any reason why you two can't get back together, if that's what you want. Just let the dust settle for a couple of days and then give him a call.'

It sounded easy. Far too easy to take things back to where they were. But if she did, nothing would have changed. 'No, Dad. It's more than simply who Scott is. It's what he does, as well. We argued all the time about it. Hardly surprising, really, when you think about it. I mean, I spend my days gathering evidence to convict someone. He spends his days finding ways of rubbishing that evidence. I know it wasn't personal, but still, I couldn't get past it.'

There was quiet for a while, just the sound of the steady tick from the grandfather clock in the corner of the room. 'Did you ever ask him why he went into law?' her father finally asked. 'Defence, in particular?'

Megan thought back through their conversations. It was the question she'd kept meaning to ask, but hadn't. 'No. I didn't.'

He patted her knee and went to stand up. 'Perhaps you should.'

She glanced up sharply at him. She was a cop, and the daughter of a cop. She could tell when someone was holding something back. 'What is it? What do you know that I don't?'

'I'm not sure. It's not my business, so I've not said anything, but I think I remember a case with a Donald Armstrong.' He looked over at her. 'He wasn't from round here, but you should be able to find it on the database. If I'm right, and he was Scott's father, it might help you to understand.'

Megan avoided the gym the following morning, choosing to run from home instead. She wasn't feeling strong enough to face Scott just yet. It was enough that he was constantly on her mind, as were the words her father had spoken last night. So it wasn't a huge surprise to find herself ignoring her usual coffee stop, and heading straight for her computer terminal instead. Straight for the central criminal database.

There were a lot of Armstrongs, but when she narrowed it down to Donald only a few came up. She immediately discounted three as they were too recent. Which left two. One was a case of fraud. She skimmed through the notes quickly, but there wasn't anything in there that seemed to point to what her father had hinted at.

The second was a case of murder. As she read through the file, two things screamed out at her. The first was that this Donald Armstrong had been sentenced to life for the murder of his brother. The second was that his sentence had been revoked seven years ago on appeal.

Weakly, Megan sat back in her chair, staring at the computer. She could feel the thump, thump of her heart against her ribs. Good God, was this Donald Armstrong his father, or were the names just a coincidence? She pulled up a picture of Donald Armstrong's face and her heart nearly cartwheeled out of her chest. There was no way this was a coincidence. The man in the picture looked almost the spitting image of Scott. It had been taken at the time of his conviction, when he wasn't much older than Scott was now.

Suddenly, with aching clarity, pieces of the Scott Armstrong jigsaw puzzle started to fall into place. He'd told her his father had left when he was seven. By left, she'd naturally assumed he'd separated from his mother and gone to start a new life. She hadn't bargained on him having been sent to prison. But the dates matched up. There was no doubt about it. What she was reading here weren't just the dry facts of an old case. It was something Scott had lived through. No wonder his mother had turned to drink: the loss of her husband added to the shame of having him locked away for murder.

Part of her didn't want to read on. It was too harrowing. If felt like an invasion of Scott's privacy, and no doubt it was. After all, if he'd wanted her to know about this, he would have told her. He'd had the opportunity, but he'd settled for half-truths. The detective in her, however, wanted to know more about the case. Why his father had been sentenced. Why the sentence had been overturned. The file told her only so much, but it did at least shed light on why Scott had turned to law. It was obvious, from the dates of the appeal, that the case had come to court not long after he'd qualified. If she'd have to guess, she'd say Scott had gone into law with the express purpose of helping to overturn his father's conviction.

So what, if anything, did all this mean to *her*, she pondered as she finally made her trip to the coffee machine. Did knowing it make any difference to their compatibility? The short answer was no. It was true that at last she could understand why Scott did what he did. Why he was always so adamant that his job was to stop the innocent from going to prison. To stop what had happened to his father. If that had been the only problem between them, then maybe the knowledge of what he'd lived through might really have made a difference. It wasn't. Scott was still Scott. Utterly gorgeous, charming. A total heartbreaker. There was more depth, more substance to him than she'd ever guessed, but he was still a man who didn't put down roots. Who definitely didn't settle with one woman. So he was still a man she was better off without, no matter how much that might hurt right now.

Scott was in his chambers, ploughing through the brief on the Rogers case. He'd been working on the damn thing all day. All long, dreary, day. Foolishly, in hindsight, he'd started the morning with a degree of optimism. Yes, he'd had a restless night, filled with vivid dreams and too little sleep, but he'd really believed that work would be his salvation. That it would stop him from thinking about Megan.

He'd been wrong.

Every time he attempted to cram his brain full of details of the case, cram it so full there wasn't room for anything else, his mind would rebel, flinging up images of Megan for him to alternately lust and cry over. Not that he was actually crying. God forbid he was going to do that again. It was bad enough crying over his mother. To cry over a lover? No way. He wasn't going to do that. Occasionally his eyes felt tired. That was all.

Thankfully the ringing of his phone put a halt to his pitiful thoughts, and not a moment too soon.

'Scott, it's Nancy. I was just wondering how you were getting on with the Kevin Rogers brief?'

'Still working on it.' He omitted telling her that he'd be getting on a lot faster if he wasn't spending so much of his time brooding like a lovesick fool.

'Good. I've found the name of the pimp Kevin says runs the girls. He's called Reg Blake. Apparently he's also the local drug dealer, which I guess—'

Scott was aware of Nancy's voice still echoing through the speaker, but he'd almost stopped listening at the mention of *Reg* and had definitely stopped when she'd followed that up with *drug dealer*. As she wittered on, his mind whirred into overdrive. What were the chances of there being two drug dealers in the area with the same name? Infinitely small. Christ. He rubbed a hand over his face, not surprised to find it wasn't the least bit steady. The man his mother was shacking up with wasn't just a dealer. He was a ruddy pimp. Suddenly his face felt clammy and a bitter taste of bile was surging towards the back of his throat. He tried to swallow it down, but he couldn't fight off the feeling of acute nausea.

Any minute now, he was going to puke up all over his bloody case notes.

'Nancy, I've got to go. I'll call you later.'

He slammed down the phone and made an anguished dash down the corridor and into the gents. Moments later he was emptying the contents of his stomach into the ceramic white toilet. Long after he'd finished retching, he continued to lean over the bowl, placing one hand against the cubicle wall to support his weak and trembling body. His mother, living with a pimp. God. Wiping a hand across his mouth he made an effort to stand up straight. It had been hard enough to take in when he'd heard this man of hers was a drug addict. Now it felt a million times worse. What if she was on the game? If Reg was making her sell her body? The thought had him quickly bracing his hands on his knees as he once more wretched into the toilet bowl.

He'd started the day telling himself that things couldn't get any worse. He'd been wrong. And God help him, the day wasn't over yet.

Chapter Twenty-Four

When he'd finished furnishing the toilet with his lunch, Scott rinsed out his mouth and walked bleakly back to his desk. His instinct was to get into his car, find his mother and drag her back home with him. But as his hand reached for the car key, he recalled the counsellor's words. His mother hadn't told him where she was because she was ashamed. Suffering the ignominy of having her son turn up and drag her away from the git wasn't going to ease her humiliation. It was going to add to it. Still, it was one thing to protect her sensitivities. Another to protect her life. This was far worse than he'd imagined. Sex and drugs could be a lethal combination. His stomach turned once more at the thought of the type of lowlife she must be mixing with. How could she? This woman, who had loved his father with all her heart, was now giving herself to scum like Reg. It was beyond his powers of comprehension.

Frustrated, he balled up the loose paper on his desk and threw it into the bin. Sitting here and stewing about things wasn't going to do either of them any good. Neither was grinding his teeth and clenching his fists. He needed to find a way out of this mess for her. It required him to think, hard. Up to now he'd been waiting for her to come to him. Now he had to manufacture a way for him to go to her. Perhaps he could use the case. He'd go and interview Reg tomorrow. It was a legitimate way in. Nancy may have already done that, but he could no doubt find questions that she hadn't asked. Slightly mollified that at least he had some sort of plan, Scott gathered up his files, deciding to finish working on the Rogers case at home. At least there, if he was feeling sick, the bathroom was close by. And private. As he headed for the car park he realised with grim humour that Nancy's phone call had resulted in one positive outcome. It had taken his mind off his crappy love life.

It was late into the evening before Scott finally put his case files away. Sad, lonely man that he was now, he tossed up whether to watch something inane on the television or just go straight to bed. This is what his life had come to. Going to bed, alone, at ten o'clock. Tomorrow would be different, he promised himself. Tomorrow he'd go and find a bar and get steaming drunk. To hell with his alcoholic mother and to hell with Megan. After today he was done moping after both of them.

A knock on the door caught him as he was about to hike it up the stairs. It was late for a social call. Which meant it was either trouble or ... could it possibly be Megan? She'd had a change of heart? Discovered that, even though it had only been a day, she couldn't live without him? God, was it too much to ask that something good could come out of the day?

With a surge in his spirits, he rushed to open the door. The answer to his question was apparently a resounding, terrifying, bloodcurdling, yes. It was too much to ask for something good. Far too much.

'Christ, Mum.'

He practically pulled her into the house, kicking the door firmly shut behind her. In a daze he turned to look at her, hoping against hope that his initial impression had been wrong. She didn't really have eyes that were glazed and unfocused, a pallor that was deathly pale. Her shaking hands weren't really holding a knife, covered in blood. But shit. It didn't matter how long he stared, how much he concentrated, he couldn't change what he was seeing. His first impression had been right. She had all of those things. There was even blood on her jacket, and a smear of it across her shoes.

'Scott.' Her lips trembled as she struggled to get the words out. Then she dropped the knife with a clatter and buried her face in her hands.

'What is it? What's happened?' Dread clutched at his heart. Dread mixed with a healthy dose of horror. This couldn't be happening. It wasn't real. It was another vivid dream, only this time without a naked Megan. Without any joy.

She looked up from her hands. Some of the blood was now on her face, giving it a gruesome edge. She didn't look like his mother. She was like some horror story caricature. A deathly pale, blood splattered ghost out of *Scooby Doo*. 'Oh Scott ... I think I've killed a woman,' she finally stammered.

He wanted to collapse on the floor and howl, but adrenaline must have kicked in, because that wasn't what he found himself doing. From somewhere deep inside him he dredged up some calm. 'Don't be ridiculous,' he replied with solid conviction. 'Come and sit down. I'll get you a drink. You can tell me what you remember.'

Meekly she went to sit down and Scott automatically went to the liquor cabinet to pull out the whiskey. Anything to rid her of the frozen terror on her face. But as he reached for the bottle, his hand stalled. Jesus, what was he doing? Swiftly he changed direction and walked to the kitchen. Waiting for the water to run cold, his eyes landed on the knife she'd dropped and he swore. He couldn't deny the blood on it, or the blood on her clothes and hands. Whatever she might or might not have done, it was all evidence. Critical evidence. It could work for her or against her. Either way, much as he loved her, he knew he couldn't tamper with it. He had to call in the professionals.

And that brought his mind straight back to Megan again. The only person in the police force he trusted with his life. Or that of his mother's. He was going to have to call her. And wasn't that an ironically shitty twist of fate.

After giving his mother the glass of water, which she took wordlessly, Scott walked back to the kitchen to make the call. The phone rang several times before Megan finally picked it up. For a moment he stood, shutting his eyes and just listening to her voice. When she'd said hello a third time, he managed to find his own. 'Sorry to call you so late. It's Scott.'

'I guessed. Your name's on my screen.'

She sounded hesitant. He couldn't blame her. What woman wants a man she's just dumped phoning her late at night? 'Look, I'm not about to become your personal stalker, it's just ...' God, was he really going to say the words out loud? 'My mother's here. She came to my door carrying a bloodstained knife.' His voice was cracking and he swallowed to try and steady it. 'She says she's killed someone.'

There was an unnerving silence. Just the sound of Megan, breathing. 'Scott ...'

'Shit, no, I haven't been drinking.' He laughed harshly into the phone. 'Not that I couldn't do with a bloody stiff drink right now. What with my blood-splattered mother sitting glassy-eyed on my couch, telling me she's a murderer.'

She must have realised he wasn't kidding. 'God, okay, Scott, don't move. I'm on my way.'

'Don't run off and escape, you mean?' he asked harshly, but she'd already put down the phone.

It was twenty minutes later when he heard the knock on the door. Grimly, Scott went to answer it. Megan was standing on his doorstep tonight, after all. If only it had been her earlier, instead of the poor, broken woman currently slumped on his sofa.

'Scott?' Megan stared up at him. Saw how ashen he looked. How distressed. All her previous hopes that this was just some giant ruse to see her deflated in an instant. This was really happening. 'Where is she?'

He pointed over to the sofa in the living room. 'She's fallen asleep.'

'What did she say, before she went to sleep?'

Taking her arm Scott pulled her into the kitchen, neatly side-stepping the knife in the middle of the floor. 'She was holding that,' he told her, eyeing up the implement as if he couldn't quite believe this was happening. 'Then she dropped it and told me she thought she'd killed someone.' He turned away, slamming a hand on the granite worktop, his whole bearing that of a man teetering on the edge of control. 'I told her to sit down, gave her a drink.' His lips twisted. 'Water, in case you're wondering. Then, after I'd finished on the phone to you, I found her asleep. I thought it best to leave her until you arrived.'

She stared at the knife. 'Scott, you know I have to call this in, don't you?'

He closed his eyes, took in a deep breath, then nodded. 'I know.'

Though it cut her to the quick to say it, she knew she had to. 'If we find a body, we might have to arrest her.'

'She didn't do it,' he countered fiercely, his face looking panicked. 'I'm telling you, whatever this looks like, she didn't do it.'

'Scott.' She ached for him, but she was an officer of the law and had to uphold it. 'I'm just warning you what might happen. Right now, the evidence is saying that she might have.'

'For Christ's sake, she's my mother.' He was lashing out at her. Megan told herself it wasn't necessarily directed at her, personally, but the situation. 'I think I'd know if she was capable of murder or not.'

'I'm not going to get into an argument about this now.' With her heart feeling painfully heavy, Megan turned away and punched the numbers on her mobile. The sooner she called it in, the sooner the others arrived, the better all round.

When she came off the phone she looked round to find Scott hunched down in front of his mother, stroking her hair. The scene was so poignant, she had to look away before she gave into the temptation to wrap her arms around him. She'd relinquished that right. She was no longer here as Scott's girlfriend but as a police officer. It was her job to remain detached and professional. Quietly she walked over to the hallway and waited there until the cavalry arrived.

First thing the following morning, Megan went to talk to her superintendent. Talk was a euphemism. Actually she was trying to walk the tight line between demanding she be allowed to stay on the Armstrong case, and not getting fired.

'You're dating her son, Sergeant. I hardly think you can claim you're impartial.'

'Scott and I are no longer in a relationship, Sir. My judgement won't be compromised.'

'No?'

'No,' she replied firmly. 'The fact of the matter is, I know Scott is a damned good lawyer. If this isn't done absolutely by the book, then if it gets to court he'll murder us,' she winced at her poor phrasing, 'so to speak.'

'And you think you're the only detective I have who can follow correct procedures, do you?'

Inwardly she groaned. The man wasn't a superintendent for nothing. He was notoriously difficult to argue with. 'No, of course I don't, Sir.' She figured a liberal amount of Sirs would win her a few favours. 'But I will make sure mistakes aren't made.' God forbid the police mucked up again and another Armstrong went down without compelling evidence. She was determined that wasn't going to happen. Even if it meant going head-to-head with her superiors.

'Okay. It's yours. But you take one step out of line ...'

He didn't need to finish the sentence. She knew exactly what her punishment would be: loss of the career that meant so much to her. At the moment however, her career wasn't foremost in her thoughts. Scott was. She knew she couldn't let someone else take over this case. If Scott was going to lose another parent to the justice system, she had to make sure it was for the right reasons this time.

Keeping the case was one thing – working on it something else entirely. The woman who might have committed a murder was Scott's mother, for crying out loud. They might no longer be together, but it didn't mean she didn't desperately hope that Cathy had simply suffered a breakdown. That they wouldn't find a body. Because if they did, and she had to end up charging his mother for murder ... she shuddered violently and went off to get herself a strong cup of coffee.

An hour later and her worst fears materialised. A body had been discovered. Lucille, a female prostitute. She'd been found stabbed to death with a kitchen knife in the house she worked from, only yards from where Cathy was living with Reg Blake. As Megan viewed the bloody crime scene, it was easy to come to a quick conclusion. She understood from her preliminary enquiries that Reg ran the group of prostitutes who worked down that street. It didn't take a huge stretch of the imagination to believe that Cathy had seen Reg with the victim. Perhaps ripping more off her than simply money. In a fit of jealousy, fuelled by excessive drink and probably drugs, she'd stabbed the girl to death.

Frankly, much as Megan wanted to keep an open mind, it was very difficult to see any other interpretation. Cathy had turned up at Scott's house around half an hour after the estimated time of death, with the murder weapon. Forensics had confirmed that the victim's blood matched that on the knife and on Cathy's shoes. Cathy herself, when she'd spoken to Scott, had admitted that she thought she'd killed the woman.

'Are you going to charge her?'

She glanced up to see Scott bearing down on her, looking nothing like the distinguished lawyer. After leaving the hospital where his mother had been kept in overnight, he'd obviously gone home, thrown on his oldest jeans and a worn sweatshirt, and come straight out again. His hair was a mess, his face unshaven. Red-rimmed eyes told of a night without sleep.

The combination of his scruffy appearance, the fierce expression on his face and the proud way he carried himself made her want to hug him so much it hurt.

The cool look in his eyes reminded her he didn't want comfort from her any more.

'We're not charging your mother yet,' she told him in her controlled, officer-of-the-law voice. 'But I have to warn you that everything does point to that, yes. We've found a body ...'

If anything, his expression became grimmer. 'She didn't do it,' he told her forcefully. 'For God's sake, Megan, what's her motive?'

She expelled a deep breath. 'Scott, I can't talk to you about the case. Don't put me in a difficult position.'

'I'm not having her sent to prison.'

His eyes turned bleak and Megan looked away, unable to bear the pain she saw in them. God, how must he be feeling? First one parent and now the other. 'I can understand how you feel, but ...'

'Can you?' he interrupted harshly. 'Can you really?' Clearly struggling to keep his emotions in check he turned his face away from her.

'Let's focus on what your mother needs right now.' This was so difficult. Megan ached to touch, to soothe. She could do neither. 'We've talked with the police doctor and he's recommending she stays in hospital to detox. When the drugs and alcohol wear off, she'll be in a bad place. She needs expert care around her.'

'Yes, you're right.' He swore. 'This just gets better and better, doesn't it?' Seeming to gather himself, he stood taller and looked her in the eye. 'Thank you. I appreciate you not detaining her here. The thought of her staying in a cell ...' He trailed off, a muscle jumping in his clenched jaw. 'Right then, I'd better go and check on her.'

He was about to leave when she put a hand on his arm, stopping him. 'How are you doing?' she asked gently.

'Me?' Laughter, harsh and hollow, ripped out of him. 'Oh, I'm just dandy, thank you. The woman I've been seeing thinks the job I do puts me on the same rung of the evolutionary ladder as a leech and my mother, who, by the way, was living with a drug-dealing pimp, is about to be charged with murder. But other than that? Life is great, thanks.'

She recoiled from the anger that lashed at her through his words. 'I guess I asked for that.'

'Find out who really was responsible for this murder, Megan. And keep my mother out of prison,' he replied flatly.

He was hurting. It was understandable, she reminded herself, and took a deep breath. 'I'll do what I can.' About to turn away, she stopped. 'Scott, about what you do ...' Her voice broke slightly, and she was forced to swallow before continuing. 'I don't think it makes you, what did you say, a leech? God, Scott, how could you think that?'

Shaking his head he thrust a hand into the pocket of his jeans. 'Well, it doesn't really matter now, does it? I'm unlikely to be heading up to the top of your *guys-I-want-to-date list* in the foreseeable future, am I?'

She watched his retreating back, wondering about the pain in his voice, in the depths of his beautiful grey eyes. Was he really that upset their relationship had ended, or was this business with his mother simply making all his emotions raw and vulnerable? She'd be a fool to believe it was anything but the latter. But fools could hope, couldn't they?

Chapter Twenty-Five

Scott left the station and walked out to his car cursing himself. If there was one trait he couldn't abide in a person, it was self-pity. So why on earth had he just vented at Megan like that? If he carried on in that vein, he'd have no hope of ever worming his way into her life again. Not that his hopes weren't already gasping their last breath anyway, what with him being not only a bastard defence lawyer, but one with a mother suspected of murder. Thank God Megan didn't know about his father. That would really be the cherry on top of the icing that was already on the blasted cake. Yeah, he was exactly the type of man a second-generation police officer would go for.

The only good thing to come out of this morning was getting his mother transferred to a place where her addictions could be properly assessed and treated. He'd half feared the police would insist on detaining her in one of their cells. She was suspected of murder, after all. Though he'd have fought tooth and nail against it, at least now that was one battle he didn't have to fight. Thanks to Megan. In fact Megan seemed to be coming up trumps all round, and that was more than could be said for him. What a colossal shame he hadn't seen what was going on with his mother years ago. Sure, every now and again he'd sent her to a clinic to dry off, but he hadn't exactly gone out of his way to check that she stuck to it afterwards. He also hadn't insisted she get looked at by a real expert. One who dealt with the mental issues often associated with addiction. If he had ... hell, if he'd paid more attention she wouldn't be in this bloody mess now. A fine son he'd turned out to be.

Riddled with self-loathing, he drove over to the hospital where his mother had spent the night. When he found her on the ward, he had to stop himself from gasping. Never a large lady, she lay back against the crisp white sheets, looking impossibly frail. At least the glassy-eyed look had gone, though he wasn't sure if the sad, defeated look was any better.

'Scott, I'm so sorry to be a burden.'

Not the words he wanted to be greeted with. 'Mum, you're not a burden.' His voice sounded strangled, and he knew he was on the verge of breaking down again. He bought himself some much needed time by moving his chair closer to the bed, so he could hold her hand. 'We'll sort this out, you and I,' he told her quietly after a moment. 'Get to the bottom of who killed the girl and why you were left holding the knife.'

'You don't think I did it?'

He gazed at her, holding her eyes, looking deep into her soul. 'Mum, you're no more capable of murder than Dad was.'

She sniffed and then collapsed, weeping, into his arms.

It was early afternoon when Megan slipped into her car and waited while Ann, who'd thankfully also been assigned to the case, slid in alongside her. Their port of call was a return to the crime scene. She wanted to go back and talk to a few more of the girls who worked in the area. They were bound to give her a feel for whether Reg was cheating on Cathy, which was the only motive Megan had at the moment.

They knocked on the door of a small terraced house. One that had paint peeling from the window frames and weeds growing through the cracks in the path. It looked like it needed a bit of TLC. Then again, so did its neighbours. The vice team believed Reg's prostitutes worked from several of the houses along the street. Possibly all of them, from the look of it. Clearly the girls weren't into gardening or DIY.

The door was eventually opened by a woman with jet-black hair and bright red lipstick. She could have been anything from twenty to forty. Certainly she looked like she was at the older end of the spectrum, but working girls aged quickly. They became hardened to life, and it showed in their faces.

'What do you want?' the woman asked, eyeing them both with suspicion.

She showed her ID card. 'I'm Detective Sergeant Taylor. This is Detective Shaw. We want to ask you some questions regarding the murder of one of your colleagues.'

The woman laughed. 'Well, aren't I the popular one today?' She opened the door wider, giving Megan a glimpse of a tight red shirt and even tighter black skirt. 'You might as well come in and join the party. There's a guy already here wanting to talk about the same thing.' She looked Megan up and down, and did the same to Ann. 'He's real easy on the eye and far more my type.'

Instantly Megan had a horrible feeling she knew who the woman was referring to. It was confirmed when she came face-to-face with Scott in the front room, sitting on a garish red sofa. He didn't even have the grace to look embarrassed. He simply gave her a half-smile of acknowledgement.

The girl looked from Megan to Scott. 'Do you two know each other?'

'You could say that, yes.' Scott stood and pulled out a couple of chairs from the adjoining dining room. 'Sit down, Detective.' He glanced at Ann. 'Or should I say Detectives. Mandy was just about to tell me whether she saw or heard anything unusual last night.'

Giving him a hard stare, Megan sat down stiffly on the chair. 'We'll be asking the questions,' she told them both firmly.

Scott acknowledged her statement with a wry grin. 'The floor is yours.'

'How well did you know the victim?' she began, taking out her notebook.

Half an hour later they walked back outside.

'Ann, would you mind waiting for me in the car?'

Her friend hesitated. 'I think it might be best if I stay,' she replied at length, giving Scott the evil eye.

Trying not to smile, Megan lightly touched her friend's arm. 'I'm okay, honest,' she whispered. 'You can back down.'

After giving Scott one final, pointed glare, Ann walked slowly over to the car.

'I don't think she likes me.' Scott was staring at Ann's back, as if trying to work out what it was that he'd said.

'She's looking out for me. Which is good to know, especially when I have to deal with you, pulling stunts like you did back there. What the hell did you think you were doing?' she demanded, squaring up to him.

'The same as you,' he replied calmly. 'Finding out what really happened last night.'

'This is police business, Scott.'

'No,' he shot back. 'It's my business. You're accusing my mother of murder. It's my business to prove you wrong.'

'Don't you trust me to do my job properly?'

He grimaced and jammed a hand in his trouser pocket. 'It's not a matter of trust. I need to find out what happened. I won't have my mother charged with a murder she didn't commit. Can you imagine what the stress of a court case would do for her?' The emotion in his voice was making it hoarse. 'It will kill her,' he finished quietly.

Megan fought to keep calm and professional. Fought to remind herself that this was a murder investigation, pure and simple. That she had no interest in Scott, or what he was feeling. 'Scott, if you keep getting in my way, annoying key witnesses by talking to them first, it won't help her case.' She put a hand on his arm, noted the rigid way he was holding it. 'This is the part where you need to trust me.'

He hesitated. She could almost see the tug of war happening in his head. She understood why he mistrusted the police, but she wasn't asking him to trust DS Taylor. She was asking him to trust Megan Taylor. To believe in her enough to ferret out the truth. Clearly he didn't. 'I guess your silence speaks for itself.' She turned away, so he wouldn't see how hurt she was.

Scott didn't have to see Megan's face to know she was cross with him, but he couldn't, in all honesty, say he trusted her. No, that wasn't right. He trusted *her*, but he didn't trust in the system. Not after what he'd seen happen with his father. Evidence could be tampered with, statements altered. Whilst he knew for absolute certainty Megan wouldn't do any of that, he couldn't say the same for any of the other detectives who might be working on the case. 'What I need to do, Megan, is vindicate my mother,' he replied softly.

She nodded, but he sensed that somehow he'd disappointed her.

Desperate to put his arms around her, or even just to touch her, he raised his arm. No sooner had his hand touched the material of her jacket than he caught a glimpse of her colleague-cum-bodyguard sitting in the car. Her eyes throwing daggers at him. Sighing, he let go. 'Look, why don't we work together on this?' Megan didn't say anything, but at least he had her attention.

Shoving his hands back into his pockets, Scott chose his next words carefully. 'You're not the sort of detective who only sees things one way. Not the type who's blinkered to other possibilities, who only wants to prove that you were right all along. I know that. You want to uncover the truth. So do I.'

Scott's heart sank as she remained doggedly silent. He realised he wasn't above begging at this point. 'I'm asking you, please, as a ...' he hesitated, 'as a friend. Let me work with you to find out the truth.'

Stripped of the façade of the self-assured lawyer, he was now simply a son, desperate to help his mother. Where once he might have arrogantly demanded, now he was humbly pleading.

It didn't seem to make any difference to Megan.

'You know I can't discuss the case with anyone outside the team, Scott.'

'Yeah, but I'm already involved, aren't I?' he pointed out. 'Surely it couldn't harm to listen to my views, even if you don't tell me anything.'

Megan Taylor wanted desperately to help him, but DS Taylor had to play by the rules. 'This is my investigation, Scott. I'm in charge. Discussing it with you could lose me my job.'

'I know.'

'And what if this comes to court? We'll be on different sides.' He wouldn't be allowed to take the case, but it wouldn't stop him finding a way of orchestrating it behind the scenes.

'I know that, too.'

Never had the gap between them felt more obvious.

His quiet eyes pleaded with her.

'I will listen to you,' she found herself saying. 'I'll consider your perspective. But I won't do anything that will prejudice the case.'

'Agreed.' His face showed no sign of victory. Just a trace of relief, mixed in with exhaustion and worry. 'Who's next on your list?'

Megan sighed. She could just imagine how easy it was going to be to get Scott Armstrong off her back. Aside from the danger he might pose to her career, there was also the danger he'd pose to her mental state. How was she going to cope with seeing him every day? He'd be in her face and in her business, which he saw as his business, too. Damn him, he'd also be in her head and in her heart. She needed to wrap the whole sorry mess up as fast as she could. Find enough evidence to charge Cathy Armstrong or, please God, prove that someone else was responsible for killing the call girl.

'Next on my list is Reg Blake.' She watched him flinch and told herself to harden her heart. 'And no, you won't be coming with me on this one.'

'What, you don't trust me not to punch his eyes out?' Though the words were harsh, his voice carried a hint of self-mockery.

'Frankly, no, I don't.'

He glanced away, into the distance. 'I have to see him, Megan,' he told her quietly. 'The way I look at it, my mother has been framed. So I have to ask myself, who had motive to kill the girl and frame my mother? Reg looks like a pretty hot candidate to me.'

'Why would he want to kill one of the girls who work for him?'

He shrugged. 'I don't know. Which is why we need to talk to Reg.'

'No, *I* need to talk to him. You can wait in your car.' She saw him about to protest and put her foot down. 'You know I can't have you sitting next to me when I interview him, Scott. Talk about totally inappropriate. How can you even ask me?'

'How can I not?' he countered softly.

It was the same voice she'd heard him use many times in court. Calm, professional, dripping with persuasion. She'd cursed it then, as she did now. 'Can't you see how you being too involved could compromise not only the case, but me?'

Finally she'd got through to him, and he slowly inclined his head. 'Okay. I'll be waiting in the car.'

'And make sure you stay there,' she told him firmly. 'If I find you ringing on the bell, inviting yourself in ...'

'You have permission to stamp on my foot.'

'Believe me, it won't be your foot I trample on.'

Scott found his eyes drawn to hers and for a brief moment he forgot all about the hell that was happening around him. Her cheeks were slightly flushed, her blue eyes bright and, despite her irritation with him, a trace of amusement lingered on her very kissable lips. He moved towards her, zeroing in on her mouth, desperate to taste her again.

'Everything all right over there?'

Megan's sidekick, who'd clearly had enough of waiting in the car, was now climbing back out of it. Whatever Megan had told her buddy about him, it wasn't good. She clearly saw her role as protecting Megan from the clutches of the evil lawyer, at all costs.

He took a small step back. What had he been doing anyway, thinking of kissing Megan when his mother was about to be charged with murder? Never mind the fact that Megan had already made it plain she wasn't interested in him any more.

Looking slightly flustered, Megan spun away from him and walked towards her car. 'Everything's fine, thanks. Let's go and find out what Reg Blake has to say.'

Reg Blake was a mean, ruthless, slimy son of a bitch. At least that was Megan's assessment. As she listened to the man answer her questions, she found herself thinking *what does Scott's mother see in this man?* She must be in a very bad place if she couldn't see through the thin veneer of charm to the utter bastard that lay beneath. Megan had met enough criminals in her time to know one when she saw one. Make no mistake, Reg Blake was definitely one. He was also, in her opinion, cold-blooded enough to be capable of murdering someone with a knife, and heartless enough to frame someone else for it.

'How long have you been seeing Cathy Armstrong?' Ann asked.

'Off and on, around six months.' Reg grinned, showing a set of teeth that were too white and too perfect for his face.

'Did she ever work for you?' Megan didn't want to ask it, but you never knew what information would later prove to be important.

He seemed to find the question amusing. 'Nah. She was too old for that line of work. Too old for me, too, but I thought she had a bit of class about her. Just goes to show how poor my judgement is. Nothing classy about a murderer, eh?'

Megan looked over at Ann, who raised her eyebrows. Clearly she, too, had heard all she wanted to from the man. They quickly wrapped up their questioning and shot out of the building.

'Well, he made my flesh crawl,' Ann pronounced as they walked towards the car. Her eyes slid to the flashy vehicle parked behind it. 'Good job he wasn't there with us.'

Megan could only agree. Beneath Scott's polished, easy-going exterior laid a controlled violence she'd seen occasional glimpses of. There was no doubt in her mind that when it came to those he loved, Scott would do whatever he had to do to defend them. Including spilling blood.

'So,' Ann continued, still looking at Scott's car. 'What are we going to do about him?'

Good question. 'Look, Ann, if any shit is going to hit the fan over his involvement in this, it's going to land on me, not you. Make yourself scarce for a few minutes while I talk to him.'

'I don't like this.'

'I know.'

'I'll wait on the condition you let me have a quick word with him.'

Megan knew that glint in Ann's eye. For a moment she wondered about sparing Scott the ear bashing he was about to receive. Then she recalled the clever way he twisted words and smiled. This should be fun. 'Okay.'

She followed a discreet distance behind as her friend tapped on the driver window.

'Detective Shaw? How can I help you?' Megan heard Scott's smooth, unconcerned words and almost felt sorry for him.

'Screw with Megan, and I'll screw with you.'

Well, that was putting it succinctly. Behind her, Megan silently whistled at Ann's words.

'Umm, an interesting proposal.' Scott again, clearly

unruffled. 'As I've already screwed, as you so delicately put it, with Megan, I guess that means that you and I ...'

His voice trailed off as Ann interrupted with a vehemently spoken: 'Don't be such an asshole.'

While Megan tried to hide her laughter, Scott spoke again. 'I'm just playing the part you've got me down as, Detective. That of the philandering lawyer with no heart. Do they teach you that stereotype at police school?'

Ann shook her head and turned to Megan. 'He's all yours. Shout if you need any help.'

She needed help all right, Megan muttered to herself as Ann walked back to her car. The type that could stop her from finding this man so wildly attractive.

'How did it go?' Scott demanded as soon as she opened his car door. He'd felt so damned impotent sitting out here while Megan and her sidekick were asking Reg all the questions he desperately needed to know the answers to.

'You know I can't tell you, Scott.'

'In which case I'll just walk right back over there and ask the very same damned questions you've been asking,' he countered stubbornly. 'I have a right to know what the man is saying about my mother.'

Megan leant against the car and studied the ground. Finally she glanced up and sighed. 'He says he's been dating your mother for about six months.' She hesitated, then added quietly, 'She didn't work for him.'

Relief washed through him, quickly followed by mortification that it was Megan who'd found that out. 'What else did he have to say about her?' he asked grimly.

Megan shook her head. 'I can't say, Scott. You know that.'

'Okay then. Let me guess what he said. All you have to do is reply yes or no.' He screwed up his eyes as he thought through the most likely scenario. 'Right, here it is. Even though he's the most ugly sleaze ball ever to walk this planet, he probably reckons my mother was starting to become jealous of his relationship with the girls and with Lucille in particular. Maybe she saw him enjoying some of the ... what shall we call it? How about perks of the job with our victim. Consumed by a jealous rage, because, hey, what woman wouldn't be when they saw such a magnificent specimen of manhood with another woman, my mother went back to murder Lucille.'

He didn't have to wait for Megan's answer. It was there on her face. In her eyes.

Suddenly the car felt oppressively claustrophobic. Yanking open the door he climbed out and set off down the street, away from Reg's dingy little shop. Away from the whole squalid mess.

But then there was a hand on his arm, tugging him back.

'Scott, wait.' He brought himself to a stop. 'Are you okay?'

She was there by his side, looking up at him, eyes filled with concern. It hadn't been that long ago those same blue eyes had looked at him with desire. Now it was clear she felt nothing but pity. Jerking his gaze away from hers, he nodded. 'I'm fine.'

She narrowed her eyes and gave him a piercing look. One that told him she didn't believe his statement, but she'd let it go. 'Right, well, I need to check back at the station.'

'Yeah, you and your bodyguard.'

She gave him a sharp glance. 'What's that supposed to mean?'

He shrugged. 'Nothing. I just wonder what you've told her about me that makes her want to gouge my eyes out.'

'Just the truth, Scott. That we went out for a while, but found we were incompatible.'

'Whose truth is that? I don't remember any incompatibility when you were writhing under me, calling out my name, begging me not to stop.'

Megan let out a gasp. Incredulity, horror, disgust? He

wasn't sure which. Probably a mixture of all three. Then she turned on her heel and marched back to the car.

Taking a deep breath, Scott followed her. Christ, he could be a total dick at times. 'Sorry,' he muttered when he caught up alongside her. 'Even by my standards, that was particularly crass.'

'Yes, it was.'

She'd stopped at his car and he could read on her face the emotions he'd provoked. Why did he have to keep poking at her? Needling her, upsetting her. None of this was her fault. 'I repeat,' he said clearly, gazing at her lovely face. 'I'm really sorry.'

She was standing so close to him. So close that if he reached out his hand he could trace his fingers down the smooth curve of her cheek. Inside his trouser pocket his fingers twitched, desperate to do just that, uncaring that they would be batted away before they got close.

'Apology accepted.'

He didn't deserve her kindness, but he clutched at it anyway, needing it more than he wanted to admit. 'So what happens now?'

'I guess,' Megan replied slowly, 'if the theory of your mother being framed is correct, I need to establish what motive Reg might have for killing the victim.'

At her words, Scott stilled. 'You think I'm right?' he croaked.

'All the evidence still points towards your mother, Scott,' she warned him sharply.

'I know,' he conceded. 'But that's not what I asked.'

'I'm willing to admit that, if I look at your mother and then at Reg Blake, it's not hard to deduce which of them is more capable of murder.'

'Okay, good.' He rested his hands on the roof of the car. For the first time since his mother had walked through his front door with a knife in her hand, he felt a glimmer of hope. 'So how are we going to work on Reg?'

'*We?*' She shook her head. 'I'm going back to the station to make some discreet enquiries. You said that man you're defending, Kevin Rogers, believes there's an officer at the station who's turning a blind eye to certain illegal establishments, in return for a percentage of the takings?'

'Yes.'

'Well, if there is such an officer, then it strikes me that Reg Blake would be the type of man to benefit from such a deal.'

'And if our victim happened to hear rumours about the deal and ask questions—'

'Not so fast, Scott. First I need to establish if such an officer exists.'

He nodded his head in agreement, but inside his mind was racing. The very fact that Megan was considering other angles, and not just taking the easy way out and charging his mother, made him want to fling his arms around her and kiss the sense out of her. Then again, he'd wanted to do that all bloody day.

Suddenly everything looked brighter. The hope he'd begun to feel earlier was blossoming into a real sense of belief. Megan was going to find the murderer. He was sure of it. And hadn't she just said she was going to make discreet enquiries regarding a bent officer in the station? Something she'd torn him off a strip for suggesting only a few days earlier. Was it a sign she was willing to understand his side of things a little more? Or just the despairing hope of an eternal optimist?

Chapter Twenty-Six

Megan was very much aware that she was doing exactly what she'd previously said she wouldn't do: ask for dirt on a fellow officer. This was different, she reasoned to herself. Before Scott had asked her to do this in his role as a defence lawyer, keen to get his client off a rape charge. Now he wasn't asking. She'd offered. And not to do him a favour, but because she was convinced that Scott was right. His mother hadn't murdered the call girl. It might be what the evidence was saying, but it wasn't what her instinct was telling her. And so, just like that, Megan found herself almost on the other side of the fence. Looking for a way to prove that Cathy Armstrong *hadn't* committed murder. It made her wonder, if she hadn't lain into Scott when he'd first asked for her help on the Rogers case, would they still be together now? One question she did know the answer to. Did she regret being quite so opinionated about defence lawyers? Answer: yes.

Her fellow officers were clearly uncomfortable about dishing out gossip on a colleague, but finally she got a name. Her most likely suspect was an inspector called John Foster. From all accounts he'd travelled around a bit, serving in forces all around the country, but for the last few years he'd been working in the vice unit, based out of their station. It didn't take much digging to find out which car he drove.

A short while later, Megan was sitting in her own car, watching his, ready to tail him. The colleague who'd tipped her off had just phoned to say that Foster was getting ready to leave the building. She scanned the doorway, eyes straining to look for a slightly overweight, grey-haired man, when her concentration was broken by the jarring serenade of Bach's Fugue ringing out from her phone. She looked at the caller ID and sighed.

'Scott.'

'You don't sound too happy to hear from me.'

'I'm in the middle of something here. Why don't I call you when I'm done?'

'Why don't I get in the middle of that something with you?'

'Because I'm about to follow a lead, Scott. I can't afford to wait …' She trailed off as a tall, dark-haired man walked towards her car. A man who drew her eye far more readily than a vice inspector with a paunch. Shaking her head, she unlocked the passenger door and huffed with frustration as he squeezed his large frame inside.

'We should take my car. It's far more comfortable,' he grumbled as he shifted his long legs into her nippy but quite compact Golf.

'You're not going anywhere with me.' She didn't bother to hide her irritation. 'And anyway, your car is about as discreet as a charging bull.'

'Where's Cagney? Or is it Lacey? I was never sure which was which. Who was the cute dark-haired detective? That's definitely you.'

Megan couldn't stop the corners of her mouth from twitching. 'Ann is typing up the notes from this morning.'

'Ahh. Have you found our man?'

She could try and deflect his question she thought, but past experience told her it was hard to stop Scott from getting what he wanted. He'd once wanted her. She bit on her lip and kept her eyes straight ahead. 'Yes,' she replied finally.

'Is that why you're here? Waiting for him to come out?'

She was about to shoot him a deadly look when her attention was caught by a movement behind the glass door of the station entrance. Bingo. 'Get out, Scott,' she told him, her eyes following the man as he walked to his car.

Scott narrowed his eyes. 'Foster.'

She snapped her head round to look at him. 'You know him?'

'Yeah. I've been up against him in court once. Smooth, know-it-all.'

That made her smile. 'I suppose it takes one to know one.'

He looked utterly insulted. 'You really think I'm like *him*?'

'Well, I don't actually know him, so I can't say. I was just going by your observations.'

A muscle twitched in his jaw. 'He's moving,' he remarked tersely, nodding over to the car that was backing out.

Megan turned on the engine. 'Go.'

He just sat there, putting on his seatbelt.

She hesitated a fraction of a second, torn. Foster was making his way out the car park. She didn't have time for a full-scale argument with Scott. She also didn't have time, or probably the strength, to forcefully manhandle him out of the car. With a deep sigh of resignation she turned on the engine and set off a discreet distance behind the man she was trailing.

As they moved through the slow traffic, she shot a quick look at Scott. It was long enough to tell her he was still bristling from her one-dimensional view of him. She should keep it that way. Keep him at arm's length. It was much safer all round. 'They aren't the only words I would use to describe you,' she found herself saying.

'I bet.' Stony faced, he stared ahead.

'There's also pain in the arse, which is exactly how I'm viewing you right now.' She looked over again, but he didn't return her glance. Instead, he continued his surveillance of the car ahead, his expression almost sombre. She decided she preferred the cocky look. The one where amusement danced in his eyes. 'But I'd add caring and compassionate, too,' she added quietly.

This time she'd caught his attention. He angled his head towards her. 'Better. Where did they come from?'

'From the way I've seen you act with your mother.'

He seemed to consider, then nodded his head. 'Thank you.'

The atmosphere in the car became mellower, friendlier. 'I've got quite a range of words to describe you, too, if you're interested.'

Megan's hands stilled on the wheel. She was in the middle of a murder investigation. Unless she found some fresh evidence pretty quickly, she might have to charge his mother with murder. Now was not the time for this sort of discussion. 'I'm not sure I am. Not at the moment.'

Scott pushed his head back against the seat and sighed. No, of course she wasn't interested. Hadn't she already told him that? Had he really thought the last few days would have changed her mind? Her kind words just now had been exactly that. Kind. Not a hint for him to try and pick up where she'd so forcefully left off. 'Please yourself,' he replied, pretending indifference. 'Though there were some pretty cool ones. Mainly beginning with S. Smart, strong, sexy, sassy.' He paused. 'Then of course there's stubborn, secretive ...'

'Secretive?'

'Well you haven't told me what you've found out since we last talked, so I have to include that.'

'Jesus, Scott.' She thumped on the steering wheel with her left hand. 'You try my patience, you really do.'

'Shall we add that to my list then? Smooth, know-it-all, caring, compassionate, trying. I like two out of the five, at least. Smooth is okay, but only when it's associated with debonair. I've got a feeling you mean smooth as in oily.'

'I'm going to add some more words you won't like if you don't bloody shut up,' Megan shot back sternly, though inside she was trying really hard not to laugh. She'd missed his sense of humour.

Before she could lapse into a litany of all the other things she'd missed about him, the car in front indicated right. Megan refocused her thoughts and followed it into the outside lane.

'He's heading towards Reg Blake,' Scott remarked quietly, watching.

'I think you're right.'

Around fifty yards further down the road, they sat in the car and watched as John Foster got out of his car and walked into an office block. Megan had interviewed Reg there only a few hours ago.

'I wonder what they're talking about.'

Scott turned to her. 'I'd like to wager Blake is telling Foster the cops were here, questioning him. He thinks he's got away with it, but the female detective looked like a smart cookie. They can't afford to underestimate her.'

Megan tried to ignore the flush of pleasure at his words, and failed. Just as she'd failed when he'd called her sexy, earlier. She could push him away, tell herself they were over, but she couldn't stop it mattering what he thought of her. Which reminded her. 'Scott, earlier you called me secretive. In a sense, you're right. I have been keeping something from you. Well, that's not quite true, because you already know this something, but what you don't know is that I know ...'

He was looking at her as if she'd sprouted horns. 'Since when did you start beating about the bush?'

Since she'd fallen for a man who churned her up so much she couldn't think straight. Letting out a slow breath, Megan rested her hands on the wheel. 'Why didn't you tell me about your father?'

There was a death-like silence. Scott sat rigidly, staring out of the window, his jaw clenched. 'What about him?' he finally asked, glancing back at her. His eyes were wary and there was a touch of defiance in the set of his shoulders, as if he was ready to spring into defensive mode at a moment's notice. Then he let out a humourless laugh. 'Oh, you mean the bit about how he did time for murder.' He turned away again, fixing his attention on the road ahead. 'I can't think why I didn't tell you about that. It's just the sort of thing you tell the woman you're trying to win over. Especially when she's a cop.'

Megan willed away the emotions that threatened to swamp her. She was on duty. Technically she was still surveying a superior officer, though she'd probably seen all she was going to see on that front. But she certainly wasn't free to give in and cry – for some crazy reason, she wanted to. 'It would have helped me to understand you more,' she told him. 'Explained what drives you to do what you do.'

'Yeah?' He took in a long, deep breath. 'Would that be before or after you started to wonder whether he really did murder his brother or not? Whether a cunning defence lawyer managed to get another murderer out of prison?'

He was so very bitter. She could understand that, but it didn't mean she was happy to have it directed at her. Even if she did deserve some it. 'That isn't fair, Scott.'

'No?'

'From what I read, your father was a man with a previously unblemished record. It was his brother who was the small-time criminal. If I'd been investigating the case, I would have asked a lot of questions. When it came down to motive, as you said earlier with your mum, it simply didn't work.'

'No, it didn't.' It never had, but the prosecution had made up a story about a bitter animosity between the brothers. Never mind that the battles had all been about his father trying to get his brother to go straight.

Megan put a hand on his arm and squeezed tightly. 'He was acquitted, Scott. I'm guessing, by the way the date of his appeal tied in with the dates you must have qualified, that you had a lot to do with it. If he'd had a decent defence lawyer in the first place, he wouldn't have lost all those years.'

'For a woman who doesn't know all the facts, you seem awfully certain he didn't do it.'

'Do you think he did?'

He let out a harsh laugh. 'Of course not. Christ, my father couldn't even get rid of a spider in the house without shoving a glass over it and easing it out the door. Murder? His own *brother*?' He shook his head. 'No way on God's earth.'

'Then he didn't do it.'

Slowly he absorbed her quiet words, alarmed at how much her simple belief meant to him. 'We weren't able to prove he didn't do it.' Even now that particular scar hadn't healed. 'Only to show that it was possible that others did.'

'But he died a free man, didn't he?' She looked at him questioningly. 'That must have been some consolation.'

'Yes.' It had been. It still was. It was just a crying shame that he'd only had six months to enjoy it before the cancer had robbed him of both his freedom and his life. He turned to Megan. 'How did you find out about him?'

'My father. He remembered the surname.'

'Great,' he muttered. Not that her father needed any more reasons to find him unsuitable for his daughter.

'What do you mean by that? He was trying to help me understand you.'

'He was trying to get you to see why I wasn't right for you,' he found himself replying, overcome by a sudden bone-deep weariness. Sadly he wasn't so tired that he didn't notice his slip back into self-pity.

'I didn't have you down as being paranoid.'

'Have you ever been on the other end of that death stare he gives to people he doesn't like?' Wow, his petulance rating was nearly off the scale now, but he was too tired to control his tongue.

'It's not people he doesn't *like,* you fool, it's people he doesn't *know*.'

Scott was alarmingly close to replying with *whatever*. That was when he knew he was running on empty. He'd had no sleep last night, not if you didn't count the occasional times he'd nodded off by his mother's bed at the hospital, only to awaken with a start every time his head dropped too low.

'I'm sorry,' he apologised quietly. 'I'm being churlish. I like your dad. He's a stand-up guy.'

'Yes, he is.' Megan kept scanning the doorway of Blake's premises but nothing was happening. 'What about your father? What was he like?'

'One of the best.' Even now, years since he'd died, Scott felt the sharp pain of grief. He hadn't spent that long with him. The first seven years of his life, and then another six months when he'd been freed. Between that he'd only seen him on occasional visits to the prison – infrequently in the beginning, as his mother had worried about the effect it would have on him. Towards the end, when he was studying law, determined to one day clear his father's name, he'd got to know him better.

'It can't have been easy, growing up with your father in prison.'

'No, it wasn't.' It was the classic understatement. 'Kids at school don't exactly take it easy on you when they know your father's doing time for murder and your mother's a raging alcoholic.'

He felt her small, slim hand reach over and gently stroke his face. A gesture of comfort, he reminded himself, nothing more. Still, he briefly shut his eyes and let himself feel.

Megan's fingers traced the smooth planes of his cheek, something she used to tell herself she didn't want to do. Now it took all of her willpower to pull her hand away. 'I won't pretend to understand fully, but I think I can sympathise with the name-calling at school. As I told you before, it wasn't always a bundle of fun having a police officer as a father.'

He opened his eyes and turned to look at her. 'No, I'm sure it wasn't, and, anyway, in the main I could put up with the insults. Sticks and stones, etc. It was the fact that people automatically thought the worst of me, that was harder to take.'

It was then that it all became blindingly clear to Megan. His smooth veneer. The outrageous, almost breathtaking, arrogance. It was a defence mechanism, carefully constructed to deal with the barbs thrown at him throughout his childhood. He'd had to become indifferent. Uncaring of what others thought of him. To show sensitivity would have been to reveal a weakness. Tears welled in her eyes and she had to look away before she made a fool of herself. Another reason to love him. As if she'd needed one.

Swallowing hard, she turned on the engine. 'You know, I think I'm at last beginning to understand you.'

He frowned. 'Oh. Is that a good thing?'

She pretended to consider. 'It depends on how you look at it. I think I've now got a handle on why you go around with that insolent swagger of yours.'

'You do?' He'd have asked *what swagger*, but he had a feeling he knew, and wasn't at all sure he liked where the conversation was heading. He didn't actually want her to understand him more, just to accept him as he was. To like him. To ache for him as much as he still ached for her. Damn it, he wanted her to love him, warts and all.

'Yes, I do. It comes from your childhood. You had to put on an act, like you really believed you were God's gift, in order to stop their comments from hurting you.'

'You think?' He shifted on the seat, uncomfortable with her perception. 'Or maybe I simply knew I *was* God's gift?'

Pulling out into the road, she let out a scream of frustration mixed with laughter. 'Okay then, Mr Perfect, there's nothing else going on here. I'm taking you back to the station so I can work on putting these facts together.'

'How about working on that with me, over a bite to eat, preferably somewhere that doesn't look like the inside of a police station?'

She shook her head at him. He was pleased to notice her face was no longer showing sympathy or irritation, but amusement. 'Were you listening at all when I told you I'm not allowed to discuss this case with anyone outside the team?'

'Yeah, but I'm not just anyone, am I?'

Her lips twitched upwards. 'You're not on the team, Scott.'

'Okay then, how about this. You interview me, as a person of interest in the case. I gave you Foster, didn't I? Who knows what other information I may have? Probably worth paying me another visit.' He waited while she parked and then undid his seatbelt.

'It could work, as long as I bring Ann.'

His grabbed on to the door handle and flung it open. Then, shutting it behind him, he bent to peer in through the passenger window. 'If you must.'

The resignation in his voice made her smile.

Chapter Twenty-Seven

Scott carefully set out the table for a business meeting and not, as he would have liked, a romantic dinner for two. Which of course was bloody impossible anyway, because she was going to bring her fellow detective along, who hated him on sight because of what she'd been told by Megan. Unless she hated all defence lawyers, of course. Or simply hated men. Yes, he'd go with that one, though he had a feeling the first was closer to the truth.

Nudging open the fridge door, he took out a couple of pizzas. She'd told him they wouldn't need food. It was, after all, an interview. But he couldn't think on an empty stomach, so he shoved the pizza in the oven anyway. Maybe filling his stomach would help ease the tension that was currently tying it up in knots. How he wished this was just him and Megan, putting their minds together on the same side for a change. If it had been, she might have started to realise he wasn't quite the devil lawyer she sometimes thought him to be. As they picked through the case together, she might even have started to look at him with respect. Then, with them both gazing blissfully into each other's eyes, he would have leant over and kissed her. She'd have melted – hey, this was his fantasy, so yes, of course she'd dissolve at his touch. Not just that, she'd then rise on to her tiptoes and kiss him back. Hungrily. As if she'd really missed him and couldn't get enough of him. Her hands would begin to wander all over his body, under his shirt, opening his fly. And then ...

And then what, Armstrong? You wake up, that's what. As far as Megan was concerned, they were through. Even if he chose to ignore that small problem, he couldn't ignore the complications of the current situation. Trying to get back into bed with the detective working on a murder case in which your mother was the chief suspect? Not the smartest of moves. Not least because there was a huge chance she would misread his motives. So, for the time being at least, he'd have to ignore the fact that every time he looked at her, his chest tightened. Along with other parts of his anatomy.

A few miles away, Megan was making tracks to leave the house. As she put Sally to bed, she'd managed to gloss over her daughter's questions about where she was going, but her parents weren't proving quite so easy.

'Let me get this straight. You're going over to the house of the man you used to go out with, to talk to him about a murder case in which his mother has the starring role?' Her mother was looking at her as if she'd grown another head.

And yes, when the situation was put like that, Megan could see it didn't sound like the greatest of ideas. She was only going along with it because Scott had asked her when she wasn't thinking straight. Which was, admittedly, most of the time when he was around. 'I'm going with Ann,' she replied a tad defensively. 'We're going to interview Scott. Squeeze him for information, just as we would any source close to a case.'

'Be careful,' her father chimed in. 'I don't need to tell you how bad this could look if it isn't handled carefully.'

'I know,' she acknowledged quietly. It would look like she was willing to let her infatuation with Scott Armstrong muddle her thinking. Perhaps even that she let him persuade her to drop any murder charges. Oh God, what was she doing?

By the time she arrived at Scott's house, having picked up Ann on the way, Megan was battling with all forms of guilt. Not helped by the fact that Ann was uncommonly quiet.

'You think this is a bad idea, don't you?' she asked as she pulled up outside.

'I'm worried you're trying to prove Scott's mother didn't do it, rather than simply solving the case.'

It wasn't a point Megan found she could easily argue. 'Look, if you'd rather not come in, I understand.'

'What, and leave you alone with him?' She snorted, undoing her seat belt. 'No way.'

Megan smiled. 'What are you worried about? That he'll tie me up and beat me until I agree to let his mother off, or try to seduce me in order to persuade me to let his mother off?'

'From the look of him, a combination of both. First he'll tie you up. Then he'll seduce.'

It wasn't hard to see what Ann meant when Scott answered the door. He must have caught some sleep because his previously haggard look had diminished, but in its place was a cragginess that gave his handsome features a slightly dangerous, but incredibly sexy edge.

'Detectives.' Scott held out his hand to shake theirs, all business.

'Scott, thanks for agreeing to see us,' Megan replied, equally formally.

'You know me. Always happy to help out our fine police force in any way I can.'

She glanced at him sharply, saw the twinkle of humour in his eyes, and itched to smack the knowing grin off his face.

'Please, go through to the sitting room. Can I get either of you a drink?' He was playing the gallant host to perfection.

'Coffee, thanks. White with one sugar.' Ann nodded briefly over at him before walking discreetly through to the other room.

'I'm not sure what the heck I'm doing here,' Megan hissed at him under her breath. How she hated the fact that he looked all calm and composed and she felt like a bag of nerves.

'Helping me,' he replied simply.

'Yes, I know, but ...'

He gazed at her, his eyes softening. 'I've put you in a really awkward position, haven't I?' Standing only inches in front of her, close enough that her senses were surrounded by the fresh male smell of him, he tenderly tipped up her chin. 'I know you're going out on a limb for me, Megan,' he whispered huskily. 'I can't tell you how much that means to me. How much I appreciate it. I'll behave, I promise.'

Her heart did a slow flip inside her chest. Earlier she'd asked him to trust her. Now, she guessed, it was time to trust him. 'Okay.' Then she eyed the oven. 'Please don't tell me you've made pizza. This isn't a social call.'

'Hey, a man's got to eat. And I thought if I laid out the table with wine glasses and candles, you might run a mile.'

'Scott, you can't say that, not even in jest.' She rubbed at her face. 'I can see the headlines now. *Detective in charge of murder investigation is caught being wined and dined by son of chief murder suspect.*'

He pulled a face and went to grab the pizza out of the oven. 'When asked to comment, Detective Taylor replied, *but he only made me pizza.*'

She looked towards the plate he was piling high with hot slices of pepperoni pizza and had to laugh. 'As long as you visit me in prison when I'm convicted of perverting the cause of justice.'

'It won't come to that. I know a great defence lawyer.'

Their eyes met and held. Amusement danced in his, but it soon faded, replaced with something deeper, more intense. If she'd been asked in that instant to say what she saw in them, she would have said longing. Then Ann came back into the kitchen to check on them, and the moment was broken. She was left wondering if it was just her vivid imagination, or her own feelings, reflected.

As Ann fired off question after question, Scott found his eyes wandering more and more frequently to Megan. It wasn't that he wasn't concentrating. He was. It was just that he hadn't had his fill of looking at her yet.

'So, what is your summary of the situation regarding Blake and Foster?' Ann asked, pen poised on her note pad, her glare clearly stating that if he didn't stop gawping at Megan, she'd come over and make him stop.

Scott reminded himself why they were here and forced his mind on to the question. 'From what I've gathered from the Rogers case I've been working on, Reg Blake runs a series of girls from a terrace of houses where he lives. Basically Reg is their pimp. They pay him to find them the business and keep them out of trouble. It's not strictly a brothel, but as near as damn it, considering several girls are working out of each house, and they all live next to each other. Keen not to incur the wrath of the law, Reg has worked out a deal with a local vice cop,' he looked over at Megan. 'I'm not sure of his name.'

'John Foster,' Megan interjected, her eyes silently thanking him for not dropping her in it.

He should have looked immediately back at Ann. Instead he found himself staring at Megan as she trailed her tongue across her lips, something she often did when she was concentrating. It never failed to unhinge him.

Swinging his eyes away, he cleared his throat. 'Okay then. Well, in return for Foster turning a blind eye, our Reg gives him a percentage of the weekly takings.'

'All that is very interesting,' Megan interrupted, her face a mask of cool detachment and professional poise. Something he was longing to ruffle. 'But most of what you say is rumour and speculation. Is there any evidence to back it up?'

He resisted rolling his eyes, but only just. Megan and her damn evidence. 'It's taken some digging, but we can prove a money trail from Reg Blake to the cop we now know is Foster.'

She looked slightly taken aback, and he took some pleasure in knowing he'd surprised her. The only pleasure he'd get out of the evening, he thought glumly to himself as he picked up another slice of now cold pizza.

'Do you have a theory as to why the prostitute was murdered?'

Scott shifted his eyes back to Ann. Ann with the all-seeing eyes and uncompromising stare. 'As a matter of fact, I do have a theory, yes. I would hazard a guess that the victim was fed up with having to give Reg such a chunk of her takings. When the other girls told her Reg skimmed off so much because he was paying off a copper, she saw a chance for blackmail. Facing up to the slimy pimp, she told him she knew about the dirty officer and promised to keep her mouth shut in return for keeping all her earnings.' He sat back and looked over to Megan. 'Seem plausible?'

'Yes, it could work.'

Encouraged, he continued. 'Reg, terrified he's going to lose his deal with the copper, panics and threatens her. Tells her to shut up or he'll harm her. It gets nasty. In a blaze of anger, Reg grabs at a kitchen knife, lashes out and kills her. Possibly it was an accident, and he only wanted to scare her, but who knows? Left with a dead call girl and a bloody knife, Reg decides to do the only honourable thing he can think of: he frames my mother for the murder. Drugs her, which was why she was so spaced out when she was first brought in, then drags her to the murder scene. Once there he wipes the knife clean, shoves it in her hand and then smears some of the blood on to her shoes and clothing for good measure. Hey presto. When she comes round, she takes one dazed look at the murdered body and, running on pure instinct, goes to the only person she can think of to help. Me.' A fact he would never forget for as long as he lived. 'What do you think? Any obvious flaws?'

'You mean aside from the fact that there isn't a shred of evidence that backs up any of it?' Ann regarded him with a rather scathing look, obviously of the opinion that what she'd just heard was a work of total fiction and not a possible, thought-through version of events.

Scott controlled his temper and looked coolly back at her. 'Yes, aside from that.'

Megan suddenly rose to her feet and began to pace the room, her slim, toned body a bundle of coiled energy. How he'd loved watching that body move beneath his, the vital energy suddenly released when he'd brought her to a shuddering—

'It's worth considering,' she replied at last, a cold but timely blast of reality on his salacious thoughts. 'We'll need to interview the girls again. All of them.'

'Interviewing them won't be any use if all they know is rumour.'

Sitting down once more, she eyed him speculatively. 'What are you suggesting?'

'Get one or two of them on your side. Ask them to wear a wire and then go and have a full and frank conversation with Reg about where the majority of the money they earn is actually going. You never know, it could be fruitful.'

'You really think a group of working girls are going to cooperate with the police?' Megan gave a disbelieving laugh. 'Think again.'

'They might not want to cooperate with the police, but I don't see why they wouldn't help me.' He shrugged at her shrewd look. 'I doubt they really believe my mother is capable of murder. I suspect, if anything, they probably feel sorry for her. Especially knowing she had to put up with Reg. They might want to help.'

'It's possible.'

'Then again, if they don't want to do it for my mother, they might want to do it for me. I can be quite persuasive when I want to be.'

Behind her, Megan was certain she heard Ann snort with laughter, then cough to try and cover it up.

'Well, what do you think?'

He was watching her, waiting for a reply. Suddenly

Megan became conscious of the warmth of the room. Of how breathtakingly attractive he was. And of how much she missed being held by him. Quickly she stood up. 'We'll discuss it and let you know.'

Ann eased off the sofa. 'Thank you for your time,' she told him formally. 'Mind if I use your loo before we go?'

Scott pointed her down the hallway. The instant she was out of view, he walked over to Megan and placed his large, muscular frame directly in front of her. He filled her senses, the warmth from his body, his fresh, citrus smell. It brought back memories of the time they'd showered together. And that really wasn't a good thing for her to be thinking about right now. Not when she was looking straight at the tanned column of his neck.

She moved her eyes up, away from the hypnotic sight of his Adam's apple and into his even more hypnotic eyes. Electricity sparked between them. Those silver pools darkened and burned into hers, the intensity of his gaze sending her highly sensitised body into meltdown.

He cleared his throat. 'Megan.'

Just her name, said in a husky murmur. Involuntarily she swayed towards him, her head tilting up towards his. His mouth descended, those clever, sensual lips gently touching hers, nibbling, probing. A soft moan escaped her and he took that as an invitation to dive deeper. Suddenly his strong arms were pulling her tighter towards him, his mouth was plundering hers and the kiss was taking on a life of its own. No longer gentle, testing. Now it was hot, fierce. In the back of her mind she was trying to remember why this wasn't a good idea, but her body wasn't interested.

The door to the bathroom slammed and Megan jumped out of Scott's arms, her heart racing.

His lips tugged in a reluctant smile. 'Not a good idea, I guess.' His voice sounded thick and throaty.

She could only just manage to shake her head. 'No.'

'Ready Megan?' Ann was back in the room, and giving her a pointed look. They all walked towards the front door, but as they neared it Scott tugged her gently back and whispered in her ear, 'You and me. We're not over, Megan. Not by a long way.'

His words were still ringing in her ears, and the feel of his breath still warm on her neck, when she and Ann reached the car.

'Well, what did you think of his theory?' she asked brightly as they set off. She knew she sounded false, trying too hard to be casual, but prayed Ann wouldn't notice.

'I think it's in Scott's best interests to put forward any scenario that takes the heat off his mother.'

Yes, that's what any normal police detective would think, Megan conceded. One who wasn't as hopelessly involved in the case as she was. 'Do you really still think Cathy Armstrong murdered the call girl in a fit of jealousy?'

Ann studied her, then let out a resigned sigh. 'No, I guess I don't. I agree she's an unlikely murderer.'

Neither of them spoke again for a long while and Megan began to find the quiet between them awkward. She sensed there were things Ann wanted to say but that she was keeping quiet. Showing Megan a kindness and respect that, after the display she'd just put on in Scott's living room, Megan knew she didn't deserve. 'Ann, I'm sorry about what I think you saw back there.'

'You mean the part when you found you had something in your eye and Scott had to get really, really close to you in order to try and fish it out? Using his tongue, and going via your tonsils, which I have to admit was an interesting technique.'

Laughter burst out of her. 'I knew that was why you'd slammed the door.'

'Good job I did, or I'd still be stuck there, cowering in the hallway, trying not to watch while—'

'I think we can stop there.' She glanced at Ann and smiled, but then remembered the circumstances. 'I know it was unprofessional. I shouldn't have let it happen and I'm really sorry you had to see it.'

'The only thing I saw,' Ann replied quietly, 'was two people who clearly care a lot for each other, sharing a passionate embrace. I've tried hard to hate the man,' she added with a rueful smile, 'but that's hard to do when I can see how crazy he is over you.'

Though something warm unfurled in her chest, Megan knew Ann wasn't seeing the whole picture. Sure the heat was still there between them, but there was so much gunning against them, too. The way their jobs clashed, his inability to commit. Oh, and the small fact that she might still end up having to charge his mother with murder.

Chapter Twenty-Eight

Megan's beef with Scott had often been that he was too charming, too sure of himself. Both traits were out in full force as she watched him chat to the call girls the following morning. Though they'd answered the door angry at being disturbed so early – just after nine o'clock, a full three hours after Megan herself had woken up – following a few minutes of banter with Mr Charm, they were like bees swarming round a flipping honey pot, Megan thought with disgust.

The wink he gave her as he walked away said it all.

'You enjoyed that, didn't you?' she asked testily.

'I can't help it if women find me attractive.' He shrugged and then made a great show of sighing deeply. 'It's a hard cross to bear sometimes, but, hey, if I bring a bit of sunshine into their lives ...'

'Jesus, cut the crap will you please? I've only just had breakfast.'

'We got what we needed, didn't we?' he pointed out calmly. 'They've agreed to go and talk to Reg, while wearing a wire. Now all we have to do is follow them, wait and listen.'

There he went again. 'There is no *we* in this, Scott. At least not as in you and me.'

'Hey, come on. Give me a break. I got them to wear the device, didn't I? The least you can do is let me hear what it picks up.' His voice was seductively persuasive, but just short of whining.

'The least I could do was not let you anywhere near this ruddy investigation,' she mumbled in reply, narrowing her eyes at him. 'That would have been my most sensible course of action.'

'Ah, but then you wouldn't be quite so far down the line of catching the real killer, would you,' he goaded.

Reluctantly she let him into the car. 'Look, I'll take you back to the station. There you can pick up your car and go about your business.'

Once more he eased his long legs into the passenger side. 'Okay, but you know I'm only going to follow you, don't you? So really, you might as well keep me in the car with you. At least then you'll know what I'm up to.'

She kicked him out at the station, even though she knew full well he would probably do exactly as he threatened.

And he did.

An hour later she was parked up near Reg's office, watching out for the two girls. Scott was in his own car, right behind her. At least he had been, when she'd last looked in her mirror.

There was a tap on her window. 'Any suggestions of what we could do while we wait?'

The glint of mischief was back in his eyes. There was no doubting what he was thinking. 'You can go and make yourself useful and find me a coffee,' she told him firmly.

'What am I now, a gopher?'

'White, no sugar, preferably a latte.'

She smirked at his retreating back. Smirked even more at the look on his face as he returned five minutes later, a paper cup in each hand, only be told he'd missed all the excitement.

'I don't bloody believe it,' he complained, thrusting the cup at her through the window. 'What happened? What did he say?'

His frustration was almost comical. 'Let's just say we now have evidence that he is paying off a vice cop.'

'And?'

She raised an eyebrow. 'You're sure there is an *and*?'

'Has to be. You wouldn't have such a smirk on your face if there hadn't been.'

'Smart arse.' She took a slow, measured sip of coffee, deliberately baiting him. She should leave it at that. Should tell him that the contents of the taped conversation were police business, not his. Then again, if it had been her mother who had a potential murder charge hanging over her head ... '*And* Reg told them the last girl who started to ask questions about that arrangement ended up dead. They'd better butt out, now.'

'Bingo.' He felt the relief drain through his body. When he straightened up, his legs had definitely lost some of their steadiness. Slowly he walked round to the passenger side and slipped into the seat.

'It isn't enough, Scott.' Megan was studying him, her eyes serious. 'It's a pretty strong indication that it wasn't your mum, but you know better than I that in a court of law—'

'I know.' He ran a hand through his hair. 'But it's looking a hell of a lot better than it was this time yesterday.'

'I also think it could look even better if we'—she looked at him hard—'that's we as in the police. Anyway, if we keep tabs on Reg, we might find what we're looking for. He's scared shitless that the cops have been asking so many questions. I'd like to bet that his next move will be to speak to the one man he thinks can fix it for him. Foster.'

'And if you happened to be there, listening in ...'

'Exactly.'

Scott looked at her. This stubborn, strong, sexy little detective who had snuck under his skin all those months ago. And stayed there. She'd put her job on the line for him these last few days. He knew that. There was no way she should be letting him anywhere near the case, and yet she had. She'd listened to his ideas, even shared, to some extent, what she'd learnt. Enough to reassure him that things were moving in the right direction. Now she was calmly telling him she'd found a way to end it. 'Megan, I ...' He stopped short, stumped, too overwhelmed to continue.

'Yes?'

'You don't know what it's meant to me to—you know—to work with you on this.' He closed his eyes, willing the words to come. 'I just wanted to say, well, obviously, thank you, but really that isn't enough.' He swore softly.

The look she gave him was half quizzical, half teasing. 'Scott Armstrong, are you actually stumbling over your words? What happened to Mr Smooth?'

He laughed, appreciating the release of tension. 'It's kind of hard to play that part when the woman you're trying to impress knows every damned thing about you.'

'Impress?'

'Yes, you know I still am. Trying, at least. God, Megan ...'

She put a hand over his lips. 'No, please. Now isn't the right time.' She started up the car. 'I need to get back to the station, update the team and sort out how we're going to catch our two suspects red-handed.'

She appeared so detached, he thought as he climbed out of her car and walked towards his own. It left him wondering if there was ever going to be a *right* time in Megan's book. He was falling more and more in love with her and yet she was pulling further and further away. As he watched her drive away, his heart felt like a lead brick in his chest.

The plan, to keep a trace on Blake, might have been a simple one, but Megan had to jump through all sorts of hoops in order to arrange for a surveillance team to bug his phone. She figured there was a chance he'd talk to Foster over the phone, though she doubted either Blake or Foster would be that stupid. But at least they might be able to glean some further information. Like details of a meeting that she and the team could then secretly witness, while the two men dropped themselves in it. Then, hey presto, they'd make the arrests and this whole saga would be over. What could possibly go wrong?

She grimaced to herself. Of course there was always the fact that Blake and Foster wouldn't talk on the phone at all. Or that when the two of them did get together, despite the best listening devices in the force, they wouldn't actually be able to hear what they were saying. Or if they could hear the conversation, it wouldn't actually relate to the killing at all. So, actually, there was a fair amount of room for disappointment and failure. Much like her love life.

God, when Scott had told her he was trying to impress her ... her heart tightened painfully at the memory of his words and the blazing sincerity in his eyes. If only she could believe him. If only she hadn't been so badly let down before by a similar, dazzling charmer. Then she might have been brave enough to risk giving Scott another chance. As it was, she, Megan the invincible, was too damn afraid to go down that route again.

The phone on her desk sprang into life. She knew exactly who it would be.

'Heard anything yet?'

Megan looked at her watch. 'I'll give you the same answer I gave you five minutes ago. If I hear anything, I'll let you know. Meanwhile, get off this line and go and do something useful.'

'Like finalising the case to get Kevin Rogers acquitted you mean? I think when you finally get Blake and Foster in your interrogation room, that case might get settled before it even reaches court.'

She had to concede he might have a point. 'I don't care what you do. Just stop annoying me.'

He chuckled. 'I guess annoying is okay. It's a reaction, at least, even if a bit negative. I'll have to work on making your reaction towards me more positive, once we've caught the bad guys.'

'There is no *we*, Scott,' she warned him for the umpteenth time, sounding more and more like a broken record. 'You have to leave this to us.'

'I read you, Detective, loud and clear. However, I don't believe there's any rule to prevent me from taking a drive past the station in a while. It could be that, by sheer coincidence, I'll then find my way to the same venue as you. Once I'm there, I might even park and rest for a while.'

Megan knew she'd already overstepped the boundary of what was right and wrong regarding Scott's involvement in this case, and that was putting it politely. Actually she'd leapfrogged over it so far she almost couldn't find her way back. She also realised that to stop him from witnessing, at a safe distance, what would hopefully be the final act in the drama would be pretty mean. That was supposing she could stop him, which she doubted. 'Fine. As long as resting in your car is all you'll be doing. Now get off the phone. Don't call me. I'll call you.'

'I bet you say that to all the guys,' she heard him drawl before she put the phone down on him.

It was several agonising hours later when she received the call from the surveillance team. They had details of a rendezvous between the two suspects, thirty minutes from now, in an old warehouse that Blake used to own.

Megan quickly put in calls to Ann and the two armed officers who were going to back her up, and dashed to her car. The warehouse was a good twenty minutes' drive from the station. The very last thing she wanted, after all this, was to miss the damn meeting because of traffic.

Weaving her way through rush hour, she was very much aware of the sleek black sports car on her tail. A tall, dark-haired man at the wheel.

Trying to keep up with Megan, Scott found himself driving like a maniac. Controlled maniac, he liked to think. His car was, after all, designed to take corners at sixty miles an hour. It was the other road users who weren't too happy about it. He doubted the police would be either, if they caught him.

It was worth the risk, though. He wanted to see the two men go down for this one. Reg Blake for being an evil bastard to his mother, shoving her on drugs, framing her for murder. A true gentleman. Then there was Foster, the cop turned dirty. He wanted to watch him nailed as a warning to all other cops who thought they were above the law. Able to twist the facts to suit their purpose. He hadn't been able to prove that's what had happened in his father's case. At least getting Foster would be some small consolation.

He followed Megan to a run-down, disused warehouse on the outskirts of a trading estate. Once there he parked a discreet distance away and cut his engine. In the gloomy light he could just about make out Megan's car ahead of him, tucked in the car park of an empty office building, right opposite the warehouse. Scott hazarded a guess that nobody used any of the buildings in this part of the estate. Many were boarded up and all were badly in need of repair.

He hit number one on his speed dial. 'What's happening?'

'If you stopped bloody calling me every five minutes I'd be able to find out,' she shot back.

He loved it when she was slightly pissed with him. Hell, he just loved it when she was taking any sort of notice of him. 'Okay. Just tell me if you've seen them yet.'

'No. It's all clear. I'm about to tape a listening device to the outside of the warehouse so we'll be able to hear any conversation when they turn up. If they turn up.'

'Why wouldn't they?'

'God, I don't know, there could be any number of reasons. They found the bug, they suspected we might be listening in so they were speaking in code—'

'Have confidence in yourself. I have.'

There was a moment's pause. 'Thank you,' she replied softly. 'Now get off the phone so I can do my job.'

He obeyed, watching as she moved out of her car and efficiently wired up the warehouse.

Time seemed to stand still. He sat, waiting, drumming his fingers on the steering wheel as dusk turned slowly into evening. It was probably only ten minutes since they'd arrived, fifteen at a push, but finally he heard the sound of an engine. He pressed speed dial again.

'I hear a car.'

'Yes. Foster, I think.'

He swore. 'Where's your back up?'

'I told them where to meet me. They'll be here soon. I thought you had confidence in me?'

Despite the tension of the moment, he smiled. 'I do.'

'Then get off the damned phone.'

Five minutes later, and Scott was still tapping impatiently on his wheel. He hated waiting. Hated not being in control. All he could do was watch and hope.

Just then a second car turned up. The man climbing out had to be Reg, the snivelling bastard. God, how Scott hoped he was about to get what was due to him. Reg Blake was one man he wouldn't be defending in court. Foster, already inside the building as far as Scott could tell, was another. In a flash Scott recalled one of his conversations with Megan; his dogged insistence that everyone was entitled to a defence. Objectively, that was still true, and he stood by what he'd said. But right now it was hard for him to look at these two villains and believe it. He could only think that scum like Reg deserved to be sent straight to jail. Perhaps, he conceded, that was how Megan felt every time she worked hard to bring in the bad guys.

His attention was caught by movement from Megan's car. She was getting out. What the hell? Where was her backup? Screwing up his eyes he scanned the area, but he couldn't see any other cars. Without thinking, he leapt out of his own and went to follow her.

Chapter Twenty-Nine

Megan looked round with a start.

'Scott, Jesus, you scared the living daylights out of me,' she hissed, her heart racing like the clappers. 'What are you doing out of your car?'

'What are you doing out of yours?' he countered, crouching down by her side near the entrance to the warehouse.

'It's getting heated in there. I heard Foster threaten Blake. I think he's got a knife.' She drew out her badge and started towards the door.

That was when she felt a hand on her arm, dragging her back. 'What the hell are you doing?' he growled under his breath.

She tried to shrug off his hand. 'I can't just stand by and let one man kill another, no matter how appealing it might sound.'

'You're not going in there,' he ground out, pushing her away and standing in front of her.

'Of course I am.' She shoved back at him. 'It's my job, Scott. Get out of my way.'

'Wait for backup,' he told her tersely.

'It'll be here in one minute. But someone in there could be dead in ten seconds if I don't go in there now.' She risked a peek through the window. Sure enough, Foster was waving a knife.

'Well I'm going to make bloody certain that someone isn't you,' he replied through gritted teeth.

Briefly she shut her eyes. She didn't have time for this. 'Of course it won't be me.' She wanted to yell at him, but couldn't. 'I know what I'm doing. Now budge.'

Stubbornly he remained in her way. 'Let me go first.' She'd never seen him look so serious. So intense. 'Please.'

'I'm the police officer. You're a civilian. If you come in at all, which I'm telling you not to, though when have you ever listened to orders? It's behind me.'

Her annoyance must have finally got through to him – he relented and moved out of her way. 'I know you know what you're doing,' he whispered as she moved past. 'You're brave and smart and tough, but I just can't …' Momentarily he shut his eyes. 'I can't stand by and watch you walk into danger by yourself. Please don't ask me to.'

Her heart squeezed, but there was no time for her to reply.

As she moved into the small hallway, he was right behind her.

They could hear the voices of Foster and Blake coming from round the corner, in what at one time was probably a small reception area. The glow of the moon through the window highlighted the two men, facing up to each other.

'When I told you to sort it, I didn't bloody mean kill her, you stupid fool. I meant make sure she didn't talk,' Foster was saying, his voice cold.

'She'd followed us. She knew everything, for Christ's sake. How else could I shut her up?'

'And what about you, huh?' Foster waved a knife at the other man. 'How am I going to shut you up?'

'You don't need to.' Reg's voice was pleading. 'You know I won't talk. I haven't talked for years. Why would I start now?'

'You might not have talked, but people are finding out. I can't afford to let that happen.' Foster's tone was low and menacing. 'I can't have my name linked with any of this.'

'It won't be. I promise.'

Megan sensed the moment Foster was about to pounce. She shot out from behind the doorway and into the middle of the room. 'It's over, Foster. Drop the knife.'

Suddenly Foster wasn't glaring at Blake any more. 'Well, if it isn't Detective Taylor.'

With a twisted grin on his face, he walked menacingly towards her, the knife still clutched in his hand.

She felt a moment of fear, but squashed it. She knew how to disarm a man with a knife. She was trained for this. Ready. Unconsciously she shifted so she was balanced on the balls of her feet, her eyes steady on the knife.

Megan braced as Foster raised his hand aloft. The blade glinted in the moonlight. Scott appeared out of nowhere and charged forwards.

Megan watched in horror as everything unravelled in front of her in slow motion. About to knee Foster in the groin and grab the knife, she found Scott in her way. She was powerless to do anything as the knife Foster was holding came flashing down. On Scott.

Who crumpled to the ground.

Instinct took over. With Foster's attention momentarily drawn to Scott, Megan aimed her knee and thrust hard into the bastard's most sensitive parts. He let out a loud squeal and, before he knew what was going on, she'd kicked the knife out of his hand and cuffed his wrists.

Blake made to scarper, but the armed response team were already at the door, blocking his path.

It was over.

With her heart in her mouth, Megan rushed over to where Scott lay. Gently she turned him on to his back so she could see where he was hurt.

There was blood on the floor. Far too much blood. Her stomach recoiled at the sight and she had to work hard not to give in to the urge to heave, or thump at the ground, break down and sob. Oh God, no, don't let him die. She loved him, damn it. She loved him.

'Stay with me,' she whispered, her voice thick with fear. Lovingly she pushed back the dark, silky strands of hair from his forehead.

Just then his beautiful eyes blinked open, thankfully alert

but filled with pain. Her heart, which had momentarily stopped, began to beat again. 'Where were you stabbed?'

'Shoulder,' he grunted.

A huge red stain bloomed against the blue of his shirt. 'Stupid bloody fool,' she muttered under her breath.

'Hey, I heard that.' He groaned as he tried to sit up.

Immediately she pushed him, none too gently, back towards the floor. 'Stay where you are.'

'You want me flat on my back, eh?' He grinned weakly and slumped on to the concrete.

Her eyes filled. How could he make a joke? He'd nearly died for God's sake. She wasn't able to joke back. All she wanted to do was cling to him. She'd nearly lost him, for good, forever. Losing him to another woman, as she'd lost Luke, was one thing. Something she'd tried to protect herself against by breaking off with Scott first. But losing him forever ... eyes blinded by tears, she let the paramedics take over as she stumbled away, into the cool, dark evening.

Scott didn't remember much about the journey to hospital. He was fairly certain he remembered Megan calling him all kinds of fool, but after that it was pretty much blank until he woke up in a hospital bed with a drip in his arm.

'You'll live.'

He turned his head to find Megan sitting next to his bed. What more could a man ask for when he came round from surgery? He studied her more closely: beneath the sexy features she was looking too damn tired for his liking. 'What time is it?'

She looked down at her watch. 'Just after midnight.'

'*Midnight*?' He pushed himself up but then winced as a pain shot through his shoulder. 'Where on earth did the time go?'

'You pretty much slept it.'

'And you?'

'In between checking up on you and trying to explain to my superiors what on earth you were doing at the scene, I've been arresting Reg Blake on suspicion of murder.'

'And Foster?'

'I've turned him over to the vice team. He's in their hands, but I don't think he'll get off lightly.'

'What a day.' He lay back down against the pillows, his eyes still on hers. 'God, to think you actually do this for a living.' She flinched – he frowned. 'What was that for?'

'What?'

'You flinched.'

'I didn't.'

He sighed. 'Megan, give the injured man a break here. You flinched when I said you do this for a living. I saw you. Tell me why.' Then he froze. 'God, they haven't disciplined you because of me, have they?'

To his immense relief she shook her head. 'No.'

'What then?'

'What I do for a living is …' she paused and sighed. 'Is hard for most men to understand.'

He regarded her steadily. 'Not for me.'

He watched with interest as she dropped her eyes and fussed about with his sheets, straightening them out, even though they were so flat they might have been ironed by a steamroller. 'Yes, well, we don't know that for certain. You don't really know me.'

'I know all I need to know about you, Megan. I also know for certain that what you do for a living doesn't bother me.'

'What about that business back at the warehouse? You know, the moment where you didn't want me to go in first, even though I was the one with the badge?'

He gave her an ironic smile. 'Okay. Point made. I'm sorry. I told you, it wasn't that I doubted you could take care of yourself. It was just my innate, He-Man instinct coming out, I guess. You know. Man protects his woman.'

She glared back at him, though he wasn't certain how cross she actually was as her eyes were much softer than her expression. 'It was a stupid thing to do.'

Scott sighed and sunk further back against the pillow. Yeah. He'd heard that before. Why did he have to fall for woman who wasn't impressed by machismo? 'Can I help it if I'm a natural born hero?'

'I mean it, Scott. Throwing yourself at a man wielding a knife was a dumb move. One that could have got you killed. Besides which, I had it covered. I was about to take him down when you got in my way.'

He wasn't sure what hurt most, the stab wound to his shoulder or the one Megan had just delivered to his ego. 'Well, right now my shoulder hurts like buggery, so yeah, it probably was a dumb move.'

Megan studied him for a few moments and then did something he'd given up all hope of seeing. She smiled. 'It might not have been the wisest move, but it was kind of sweet.'

'Sweet?' He lurched forward: a huge mistake. One he regretted as soon as the pain seared down his arm. Once more he slammed back against the pillow. 'I get myself cut to shreds trying to save your life and you call it *sweet*? What does it take to really impress you?'

Slowly Megan moved towards the bed and took hold of his hand. 'You didn't need to throw yourself in front of a knife to try and impress me, Scott. I was impressed a long time before that.'

'You were?'

'Yes. Your patience with my daughter impressed me. As did the loving, protective way you've handled your mum. A lot of men, ambitious men like you, might have washed their hands of an embarrassing mother a long time ago.'

He let her words slowly soothe his ruffled ego. 'Does my mum know about Reg?'

Megan shook her head. 'The hospital say she's asleep at the moment. I thought maybe it was something you'd like to tell her yourself, tomorrow.'

He nodded. Telling his mother that she wasn't a suspect any more was something he'd take great pleasure in doing. The part when he had to say that actually it was the man she'd been living with who'd killed the girl and then tried to frame her. No, that part he wasn't looking forward to at all.

Megan was watching him thoughtfully. 'I'll come along, too. If it helps.'

He grimaced. 'Thanks, but no. It's probably something I need to do by myself.' Then, realising he'd sounded harsh, he reached for her hand and raised it slowly to his lips. 'Besides, you've done more than enough already,' he added softly.

Fleetingly, she raised her eyes to his and he noticed her surprise and her uncertainty. God, there was so much he wanted to say to her. How could she ignore this heat that was between them still? Surely she could feel it now, just as he could.

Jerkily she stood to her feet. 'Right then. I'd better get home. Remind my family that I still exist.'

'Why are you running off scared, Megan?' he asked quietly, watching as she studiously avoided any further eye contact with him. 'You face bad guys with knives without batting an eye, yet you won't look at me.'

'I'm tired, Scott.' It was an evasion. He knew it, she knew it. 'I just want to go home.'

He desperately wanted to push her. To find out what was really going on in that active mind of hers. But she did look dead on her feet. There was a time and place for the type of conversation he wanted to have and this wasn't it. 'Okay. I'll say goodnight then. Thanks for getting the bad guys.'

Finally she glanced at him for longer than a nanosecond. 'No problem. Thanks for diving in front of the knife.'

'Even though you had it covered.'

'Yes. Despite that.'

After she'd left a wave of tiredness came over him once again and he closed his eyes. It was a mistake. All he saw was Foster clutching a knife and striding towards Megan with cold intent in his eyes. He'd lied when he'd said he didn't have an issue with what she did for a living. It scared the hell out of him. Not enough to stop him from loving her, though. Not enough to stop him from doing whatever it took to make sure she realised that.

Megan let herself quietly into the house. Apparently not quietly enough. Her parents pounced on her as soon as she'd closed the door.

'Oh, my darling.' Her mother hugged her. 'How are you? Let me see for myself.' She stood back and gave her a thorough once over.

'As I told you on the phone, I'm fine. Quit worrying.'

'My daughter gets a knife waved at her and you tell me not to worry?'

'I tell you not to worry because I'm good at defending myself. If anyone was going down, it was him.'

'I heard it was actually Scott who went down,' her father interrupted, his eyes gently probing.

'Yeah, well, the dumb fool decided to play hero.'

'What happened?'

She shrugged off her coat, walked into the living room and sat down, gratefully accepting the glass of wine her mother handed to her. After the day she'd had, she figured she deserved it.

'Despite me telling him otherwise, he insisted on coming into the warehouse with me. When I moved in on them, Foster started coming towards me. Scott took one look at the knife and dived between us. Nearly got himself killed, the idiot. And there was no need for it because I was a heartbeat away from disarming Foster by kneeing him in the groin. I damn near caught Scott's groin instead.'

Her father nodded, a small smile playing round his lips.

'What's so funny?' she huffed. 'The thought of me crushing Scott's testicles?'

He shook his head. 'No, sorry, that wouldn't have been funny at all.'

'What then?' The wine was slipping down nicely, but as fast as it was doing its job of relaxing her weary muscles, her father's humour was undoing it.

'Well, I admit to finding it slightly amusing to see you so riled at the thought of Scott diving to protect you. He's a man, Megan. The decent ones are programmed to protect the people they love.'

'He doesn't love me.'

'No?'

Megan drank back the rest of the wine. She'd have swigged back another one, if she could have been bothered to get it.

'Well?'

She looked back at him. 'To be honest, I don't know how he feels. He does still want us to be together.'

'And you?'

'I want what I can't have,' she replied tiredly, getting to her feet.

'What's that, Megan?'

This time it was her mother asking the question. Megan shook her head. She was too tired for this conversation. 'It doesn't matter. I'm going to bed.'

It was only when she'd showered and lay in bed, staring up at the ceiling, that Megan admitted to herself what she really wanted. She wanted Scott Armstrong back in her life. Not for a few weeks, or a few months, as he was no doubt planning – but forever.

Chapter Thirty

Scott pulled into a space in the hospital car park and turned off the engine. With a sigh of relief he eased back his shoulders and made a mental note to himself: driving with a knife wound, not a particularly clever idea. It wasn't that he hadn't been in control of the vehicle; it was an automatic, so he hadn't needed his left arm much. That hadn't stopped it hurting like a bugger every time he'd moved it, though. No doubt that was why they'd given him a sling and a strict warning not to do anything that required use of his arm. Like driving, probably. But he was damned if he was going to start hailing taxis when he had over fifty thousand pounds of powerful motor vehicle sitting on his drive. That being said, the way his shoulder was throbbing now as he got out of the car might actually put him off doing this again. At least until it was time to drive home. Threading his arm back through the sling he acknowledged that yes, it did actually feel a heck of a lot better when it was supported, and went in search of his mother.

It was with a great deal of trepidation that he turned the corner into her ward. Last time he'd seen her ... well, he wasn't going to dwell on that. Not when the woman sitting up in the bed before him looked so much more like his mother than she had done in years.

'Hey.' He bent down and kissed her on the cheek. 'You look ...' He struggled for words.

'Better?' she asked, smiling.

He shook his head. 'No, better than better, if you get my meaning.' Pulling up a chair, he sat down next to her and searched her eyes. For the first time in recent memory, they were clear and bright. 'Frankly, you look like my mother again.'

Her eyes welled up. 'I think I'm starting to feel like her again, too.' She squeezed his hand.

As she was looking so much stronger, Scott took a deep breath and came straight out with it. 'They've arrested Reg for the murder of the girl, Mum.'

He watched as a string of emotions flooded across her face. Shock, confusion, disgust. The final one was anger. 'My God.' She shut her eyes for a moment. 'To think I was living with that man.'

Scott wasn't going to let her slip down that road. 'You weren't in your right mind,' he told her sharply. 'You haven't been for years. That's why you've been behaving as you did. You have an illness, Mum. Now you're getting treatment for it. Things will change. You'll start to feel like you want to live again.'

'Yes,' she acknowledged softly. 'I know you're right. I already feel better. Whatever they've given me, it's starting to work. This time I want to get better. I want to stop drinking. Before—'

'You did it for me.' He looked down at their clasped hands and then back up at her face. 'They've recommended another stint in a clinic. One you haven't been to. I think it would be a good idea.'

To his relief, she nodded. 'Yes, they mentioned it. I think it would be good, too.'

'Then you come home.' He studied her face, the beauty that was still there beneath the tired and worn features. 'It's your home too, Mum. Bought with Dad's compensation money. He'd want you to live there.'

'I want to live there. It's just these last few years ...' She sighed and sank back against the bed. 'I haven't wanted to stay for long because I was too ashamed of the woman I saw in the mirror. I didn't want to be an embarrassment to you.'

'God.' He put both hands round hers and held them – and squeezed his eyes shut in an effort to stop them filling. 'You weren't,' he told her, only just managing to croak out the words. 'You aren't. I just wanted to find a way to help. It hurt that I couldn't.'

'I know and I'm so sorry.' She wiped a tear away from her eyes and smiled. 'My darling boy. One day a pretty young woman is going to see you for the good catch you are. Once she does, she'll never let you go.' Her eyes narrowed and she fixed him with a long look. 'Perhaps that young lady police officer. She looks smart enough.'

The mischievous look in her eyes set him off and he found himself laughing. Something he hadn't done with his mother for longer than he cared to remember. 'You must be feeling better if you're starting to meddle.'

She chuckled. 'Yes. I think I'm going to enjoy watching my son finally fall in love.'

Scott thought of the way Megan had practically run away from him last night. 'I only hope I enjoy it, too.'

Megan spent the day putting together the case details on Reg Blake, ready to hand over to the crown prosecution team. She also found out some very interesting information on Scott's father, from John Foster. She'd noticed earlier that he'd worked in homicide at the time of Donald Armstrong's arrest. Not only that, he'd worked out of the same station where Armstrong senior had been charged. Now that Foster had been caught red-handed, he seemed prepared to grass on anything and everything. Including what had happened on the day that Scott's uncle had been killed. Megan had listened with a strange mixture of delight and horror. Delight because she would finally be able to tell Scott exactly what had happened that night. Horror that men, who should have been on the right side of the law, had conspired to sentence an innocent man to a lifetime in prison rather than risk their own careers. It was beyond shameful. It reminded her of what her father had told her only a few days ago. Not everything was black and white. And the shades of grey weren't always obvious at first glance.

On the drive home, Megan realised that if she'd met Scott now, she would have been far less antagonistic over what he did for a living. Not that it would have made much difference in the long run.

Her phone rang as she let herself into the house. 'Scott?'

'Missed me?'

Her heart leapt at his voice and as she looked at the clock on the wall, she couldn't resist a wry smile. 'It's been less than twenty-four hours since I last saw you.'

'That is a fact, but it doesn't answer my question.'

'How are you?' she asked, deliberately changing the subject.

'I'll take your lack of an answer as a yes.'

'Believe whatever you want.' She almost laughed. He'd always put his own spin on her replies anyway, twisting them to suit his own needs. *I don't want to go out for a drink with you. Great, then we'll have dinner.* 'Now tell me how your shoulder is.'

'I thought I'd pop round this evening. Give you a chance to see for yourself.'

Her heart stilled, though she should have expected he'd want to see her. In fact he was probably so grateful for her help in clearing his mum that he'd be bombarding her with affection. For a while. Something her fragile heart really wasn't up to receiving. Safer not to see him, then. But she had information about his father. Information she knew Scott needed to hear. 'Okay. If you can wait until Sally's in bed. Come around eight?'

'I was hoping to see Sally.'

'No.' Her reply was sharper than she'd intended. 'Look, I think it's best that you don't see her.'

There was a brief silence on the other end. 'Because of the picture she drew.'

It was said in a flat, heavy voice that clearly telegraphed his hurt feelings. 'I'm sorry,' she answered, this time more gently, 'but I don't want her getting the wrong idea about us.'

'And what, exactly, would be the right idea?' he replied tersely. Before she had a chance to formulate some sort of reply, which for the life of her she didn't know quite what, he cut in. 'Forget it. I'll see you at eight.'

Scott was still quietly fuming when he pulled up outside her house as scheduled. He had half a mind to loudly rev the engine on the drive and then stomp into the house, shouting at the top of his voice, so Sally knew exactly who had just arrived. To say he felt aggrieved was an understatement. Not the best frame of mind in which to talk to Megan about their future.

She greeted him warily. He didn't know whether that was because she sensed his annoyance, or whether she was worried he was going to talk about issues that made her uncomfortable. Like what was going on between them. Like the fact that he knew damn well she still wanted him as much as he wanted her.

'Would you like a drink?'

What he wouldn't have given for a stiff measure of whiskey. 'A coffee would be great, thanks.' Whiskey, painkillers and fast cars. Not a combination to be recommended.

He followed her into the kitchen where she set about making two mugs of coffee with quick, tidy movements. He loved to watch her when she wasn't looking. Loved the way she moved with such lithe grace. Then she turned and caught him staring.

'How are you getting on with the sling?' She looked pointedly at the object in question, which was currently dangling out of his jacket pocket.

'Fine.'

'I'm not a doctor, but isn't it more effective if you actually put your arm in it?'

'Funny girl.' Refusing to smile, he pulled the sling out of his pocket and shoved it round his neck.

'Here, let me.'

Carefully, she eased his arm into the sling and straightened out the material, her arms looping round his neck as she smoothed it down. At that moment he made the mistake of breathing in. His senses got a double dose of Megan heaven. She smelt as fresh as a daisy and as sexy as a siren. What a combination. As his good arm automatically reached for her, itching to pull her towards him, she spun out of his grasp and went to pick up the drinks. He took some satisfaction from noticing that her hands weren't totally steady.

'We can take these into the sitting room. Mum and Dad have gone upstairs.'

Frustrated, aching in parts of his body that went far beyond his shoulder, Scott followed behind her, unable to stop staring at her cute buttocks as they moved beneath the tight material of her trousers. God, he loved everything about this woman.

She waited for him to sit down and then deliberately chose a seat as far away from him as possible, which made him want to yell with frustration. But before he could do or say anything, she shocked him to the core with her opening words. 'I found out some interesting information about your father today.'

'Oh?' He was aware of his whole body tensing as he reached on to the coffee table for his mug.

'John Foster was there on the night your father was arrested.'

'Christ.' Coffee spilled from the mug on to his hand. Shoving it back on to the table, he wiped his hand on his trousers. Then he braced himself and looked up. 'What did he have to say?'

'He was there as part of the back-up team. The police

had a tip-off that your uncle was about to set up a deal.' She hesitated. 'He was involved in counterfeit money. I don't know if you knew?'

'Yeah. Dad told me.' Thrusting the hand that was still smarting from the spilt coffee into his pocket, he tried to marshal his scattered thoughts. While he desperately wanted to hear the police's view of what had happened that night, to see if it matched his father's interpretation, he desperately *didn't* want to discuss more of his family's shady past with Megan. A round of conversation about his fraudster uncle and jailbird father wasn't going to create the right atmosphere for what he had in mind. That went more along the line of spilling out his feelings and persuading her to give them another chance. He just hadn't worked out the mechanics of how he was going to do it yet.

'Well,' Megan continued, clearly set on telling him what she'd found out, whether he wanted to hear it or not, 'It seems the police were watching your uncle from a next door room, waiting for the deal to go down. Then your father burst in. He spoke angrily with your uncle, demanding he stop what he was about to do and come with him. A fight started between the two of them. Then the man your uncle had been about to do business with arrived. In the chaos, one of the police officers fired a warning shot. At least that's what was supposed to have happened.'

'The officer accidentally shot my uncle,' he filled in slowly. It was what his father had always believed.

'Yes. Terrified that he might go down for it, or at the very least it might ruin his career, the three policemen there that night concocted a different story. That your father shot his brother. They figured your father was involved in dodgy dealings anyway, so he deserved a stint in prison.'

'He wasn't,' he said sharply. It was vital she understood that.

'I know.'

256

Scott tried to picture the events of that night. The confusion on his poor father's face as he'd not only had to come to terms with the loss of his brother, but also the fact that he was being charged with his murder. The image left him shaken. 'What happened to the officer who fired the gun?'

She gave a small shake of her head. 'He died from a heart attack several years ago.'

His body suddenly felt chilled and he reached for his coffee, needing the heat. 'Is this all going to be put on record?' His voice was shaking and he couldn't stop it. 'It's too late for Dad but damn it, it's only right that he should have his name officially cleared. Even if it has to be posthumously. I want every bugger that ever besmirched his character to realise they were wrong.'

'I'll make sure it is, Scott. We can get the press to print something. It'll make quite a story.'

He glanced over at the slim body curled up on the sofa opposite. 'Thanks.' Then he laughed. 'Jesus, what a totally inadequate word. I mean it though. Really. If Dad were here now, he'd be giving you the strongest hug you'd ever known.' Slowly he put down his cup and walked towards her. 'Will you accept one from his son, instead?'

Megan swallowed as Scott's arm reached out towards her. Refusing would be rude, so she stood and allowed his good arm to circle around her. Accepting it wasn't a hardship. Far from it. For a brief moment she rested her head on his chest and allowed herself to feel. It felt too good. Too right. Too utterly perfect. She took a step backwards.

Scott let out a deep sigh. 'There you go again, pulling away from me when I know damn well you want this as much as I do.' His eyes searched out hers, locked and held them. 'Go on, Megan,' he demanded roughly. 'Tell me you don't want me to touch you. Tell me you don't want me to make love to you.'

Feeling like a cornered animal, she backed further away

from him. 'You know I can't tell you that,' she whispered. 'But it's irrelevant, Scott. We're over.'

He shook his head. 'No. It can't be over, not when all this heat still exists between us.'

She'd known he wouldn't let go without a fight. His ego wouldn't let him. But she had to be strong. 'Heat soon turns cold, Scott. Surely your vast experience with women has shown you that. All I'm doing is saving us both the bother of having to go through that angst when it does.'

'So cynical.' He took a step back himself and thrust his free hand into his pocket. 'Why do you assume what is between us won't last? It isn't all about heat, Megan. Not on my side. I've fallen in love with you.'

His quietly spoken words knocked her totally off her stride and for a heart-stopping moment she felt a rush of sheer pleasure. Then she remembered how good Scott was with words; how he could use them to his advantage to suit his needs. 'You say that now, but what will you be saying a month from now? Two months? Words are meaningless. That's one useful thing I learnt from my sorry time with Luke. Words slip easily from the tongues of men like you and him. How long would you want me, Scott? How long before you found yourself wanting someone else instead?'

Scott swore, loudly and angrily. 'Christ, Megan.' He walked over to the mantelpiece and put one hand on either side, gripping it until his knuckles turned white. 'I've told you before that I won't be compared to any other men you've known.' Pushing himself away from the fire, he went to stand before her, his eyes blazing. 'I love you, damn it,' he told her fiercely, uncaring of who might overhear. Desperate for her to understand. 'Don't you trust me enough to believe me? Whatever happened to a man being innocent until proven guilty?'

'Megan, is there a problem?'

Her father stood in the doorway, hands on his hips and a worried look on his face.

Scott let out a deep breath. Bloody fantastic. That was absolutely what he needed right now. Her father, coming to protect his daughter from the angry boyfriend. 'I was just leaving,' he replied through gritted teeth. With his heart shattering in his chest, he ignored Megan and strode out of the house.

Megan turned to her father and burst into tears.

Chapter Thirty-One

'Mummy.'

Megan glanced over to her daughter, currently playing with the breakfast cereal in her bowl, swirling it around with her spoon. In her experience, when Sally was distracted like that, she was on the verge of asking a difficult question.

'Don't you like Scott any more?'

And yes, there it was, right on cue. 'Why do you say that, darling?' She'd been around lawyers enough to know the best way to answer a hard question was with another question.

'I heard you shouting at each other last night.'

Another one for the increasingly long list of why it was impossible for her to have a relationship while she lived with her daughter and parents. They heard and saw everything. 'Sorry, did we wake you?'

She shook her head. 'I wasn't asleep. I heard Scott's car and I thought he might come up and say hello, but he didn't.'

Sally looked so crestfallen, Megan knew it wasn't fair to leave it at that. 'Oh, honey, that was my fault. He wanted to, but I said you'd be asleep.'

'Why were you fighting?'

Lord, why did she have such an inquisitive daughter? 'We weren't really fighting. It was just a difference of opinion.'

'Different how? What did he mean by innocent until … something guilty.'

The questions were tumbling from her daughter's lips and Megan didn't have a clue how to answer them.

'The word you're looking for, my darling granddaughter, is *proven*.'

Megan looked up to see her mother enter the kitchen. Inwardly, she thanked God. Hopefully she could help her out here.

'What Scott was trying to say was that your mother was accusing him of something even though she didn't have any evidence, any proof, that he would actually do that.'

Megan caught her pointed look and abruptly changed her mind. Her mother wasn't going to help the situation at all. In fact, if she wasn't careful …

'That's not very nice.' Sally was now looking scathingly at her.

'No, it's not, is it.'

Exactly as she'd feared. The man was relentless when it came to getting women on his side. 'Now, wait a minute.' They both arched an eyebrow, almost in unison. 'Neither of you knows the full story, so I don't think you're in a position to judge.'

'So what are the facts, Megan dear?' Her mother poured herself a cup of tea and sat down at the table across from her. 'Is it correct that Scott told you he loved you last night?'

'My God.' She shook her head in disbelief. 'Did you hear *everything*?'

'Well, not everything, but towards the end, when voices were raised, we couldn't really help but hear.' She sipped her drink. 'So, did he or did he not say he'd fallen in love with you?'

Megan looked from her mother to Sally. Both were staring at her expectantly. 'Yes, he did.' And even though he hadn't meant it with a capital *L*, Megan's heart still flipped as she recalled his quietly spoken words. And his louder follow up.

A gleam of triumph snuck into her mother's eyes. 'To which you replied how, exactly?'

She groaned and glanced warningly over at Sally. 'Mum, come on, give me a break here.'

'I think it's important for us both to understand what's happening. After all, in some ways it affects us all. So when Scott told you he'd fallen in love with you …'

'I told him they were nice words but I'd been told them

261

before and I knew they were meaningless,' she finished quickly.

'Why did Scott say words he didn't mean?' Sally asked, clearly puzzled.

Right now Megan knew exactly how it must feel like to be in the dock. 'It's not that he *didn't* mean them. He probably thought he did, but—'

'You thought you knew better?' her mother interrupted. 'Even though these are Scott's feelings, you thought you knew how he felt better than he did?'

Megan stared at her mother. 'Heck, Mum, did you ever consider a career in law?'

They all laughed, releasing some of the subtle tension that had built up. They loved her, she knew that, but right now they weren't on her side. Then again, they hadn't been let down before, not like she had.

Her father chose that moment to come in search of his breakfast, and Megan let out a sigh of relief. Finally, an ally. Someone who understood the importance of self-protection.

'We were just finding out from Megan what happened last night,' her mother explained as she ferreted around for the cereal bowls.

'Even though you apparently heard it all anyway,' Megan murmured to nobody in particular. Deciding to keep her head down, she focused on eating her breakfast. Maybe if she was lucky her mother would leave this alone now.

'We'd just got round to the interesting question of why she assumed Scott didn't mean it when he told her he loved her.'

Then again, maybe not. She sighed in exasperation. 'That's not exactly what I said.'

'Isn't it?' Having found the bowls, her mother turned to give her a quizzical look. 'I'm sure it was how he heard it.'

Her father took one look at the two of them facing up to each other and calmly went to sit next to his granddaughter, who was watching the conversation unfold with increasing confusion. He patted her on the hand. 'Sally, you know your Mum loved your father very much, but that he left her? Left you both.'

Sally nodded.

'Well, now she's worried every man she falls in love with will do the same thing. That they will leave her. That, I think, is why she's scared to believe what Scott says.'

'But that's silly,' Sally replied. 'Just because one of the girls at school stopped being my friend, it didn't mean that all the others would stop, too. They didn't.'

Her father chuckled. 'She's smart, your daughter,' he replied, glancing over to Megan before tucking into his breakfast.

Watching her family go through their morning rituals, Megan felt the first twinges of doubt. She'd been so sure she was doing the right thing by pushing Scott away. Her heart couldn't take another hammering. Once in a lifetime was enough for anyone. And now there was Sally to consider, too. She was old enough to know what was going on. To be heartbroken, too, when Scott left them both, as he would surely do. Wouldn't he? *But that was what you thought before he confessed his feelings for you*, a voice in her head was shouting. *Before he told you he loved you.*

She turned to stare out of the window, gripping the sides of the worktop. Shit. Had she just made the most God-awful mistake? Could he really and truly love her? With a capital L? And was she brave enough to take the chance that he might?

Scott looked around the room that would be his mother's home for the next few months and said a silent prayer of thanks that they'd chosen to go private. The place had more than a hint of a luxury hotel about it, and was much more welcoming than some of the more functional places he'd viewed. It was going to be tough enough for her to get through the programme. At least here she would have some dignity while she did it.

So far, he'd liked all the counsellors and nursing staff he'd come across. Along with the professionalism and dedication that he expected, they seemed warm and compassionate. In fact he'd had a strong sense that this wasn't just a job to them. It was a vocation.

'Do you think you'll be okay here?' he asked as they sat in her room.

'Scott, for the hundredth time, yes. Stop fussing. You're making me feel like the child here, not the parent.'

He acknowledged her gentle rebuke with a sheepish grin. 'Sorry.'

She reached over and kissed him gently on the cheek. 'You know you've spent far too much time with me these last few days. Bringing me here. Staying the night. Clucking over me like a mother hen.' She smiled, softening her words. 'Anyone would think you were trying to escape from something. Or someone.'

'I just want to make sure you're comfortable,' he protested, evading her eyes. She was definitely getting more like her old self every day. When she hadn't been riddled with alcohol, she'd always had an uncanny knack of being able to see through people. Him especially.

'You just want to take a few days to recover from your latest argument with the cute detective, more like.'

He shook his head but had to laugh. It served him right for confiding in his mother. Then again, he'd been so hurt he'd had to talk to *someone*. 'Yeah, okay, there is a bit of that in there, too.'

'She's a clever lady. She'll work it out in the end.'

'Work what out?'

'That you're meant to be together.'

He sighed. 'Perhaps. At the moment she's convinced herself that I'm just playing with her. That in a few months' time I'll have had enough and want to move on.'

'And will you?'

'Jesus, Mum, of course not.' He stretched his legs out in front of him and moved his shoulder so it was more fully supported by the sling. 'I'll be the first to admit I've done a lot of playing in my time, but with Megan ...' He shook his head. 'Megan is very different. She's got to me so much that I can't think straight. All I want is to be with her.' He paused and looked his mother in the eye. 'I'm in love with her.'

'And have you told her that?'

He recalled their angry conversation a few nights ago. The way she'd effectively taken his words and shoved them right back in his face. 'Yeah, I told her.'

'And?'

'She wasn't interested.'

'Is that really the case? Or was she just not convinced you meant what you said.'

Scott shifted forward so he could rest his head in his hands. 'How the hell should I know? I did mean it. Either she didn't care, or chose not to believe me. What am I supposed to do now? Keep telling her I love her till I'm blue in the face? Browbeat her into falling for me?'

His mother smiled. 'I doubt that will be necessary. Maybe she just needs more than words, Scott.'

If he closed his eyes, he could picture Megan's face as she told him she'd heard words like *I love you* before. There had been anger, yes, but also pain. He looked over to his mother. 'What do you suggest?'

'If you're really serious about her, then show her that you mean what you say. Ask her to marry you. Nothing says I love you more than that. Of course she's been badly let down before, so she might feel it's too early to accept, but at least by asking her you're showing your intent. Declaring that you want to spend the rest of your life with her.'

Scott stared at his mother open mouthed. Marriage? A chill ran through him. Now that was a scary step. An enormously scary step. Then again, wasn't that what he'd been moving towards, in his mind? After all, he couldn't actually imagine *not* spending his life with Megan. Or with Sally. The word marriage might sound terrifying, but the implications didn't.

'Well?'

He got up and, crouching down to her level, kissed her resoundingly on the cheek. 'God, I've missed you, Mum.'

She chuckled. 'Is that a yes, you'll ask her?'

'It's a bloody hell, why didn't I think of that.'

'Because you're a man, honey.'

As he made to leave, she walked with him to the door. 'Remember to give me a call. Let me know how you got on.'

He kissed the top of her head. 'I will. Who knows, if all goes well I could be bringing your future daughter-in-law to see you next weekend.'

'I hope so, Scott. I really hope so.'

He walked back to his car with a skip in his step. Suddenly the pain in his shoulder didn't ache as much. He was going to ask Megan to marry him. Prove to her that he was serious. She had to have feelings for him, didn't she? This couldn't all be on his side. An image popped unwillingly into his head. One of the look of horror on Megan's face when she'd first glimpsed Sally's picture of the three of them on the beach. He thrust it out of his mind. That look could have been for any number of reasons. It didn't automatically mean the thought of him as a husband and father was thoroughly repugnant to her. Of course it didn't. Megan wasn't one to be put off by his dodgy family background. She was made of better stuff than that. And she'd learn to accept what he did for a living, wouldn't she?

When he finally climbed into his car, his mood was decidedly more pensive.

Megan tried Scott's mobile phone number several times but it was switched off. There was no answer at his home. Where on earth was he? Was he screening his calls so he didn't have to talk to her? Had she hurt him that badly? Or was he now acting true to type: he'd got what he'd wanted off her, hadn't he? He'd wriggled his way on to his mother's case and made sure Megan had seen his point of view on it all.

With a curse of annoyance she turned off her computer. Thinking like that wasn't helpful. The case was over, but he'd still come to see her last night. And told her he loved her. At the memory, her heart did a little dance. It was time she stopped being so insecure.

On the off chance Scott was working and had turned off his phone, Megan decided to drive by his chambers on her way home. After all, she told herself, it was only a couple of days since he'd been injured, trying to protect her. She had a right to be concerned for his welfare. To make sure he was okay and not lying in a crumpled heap of pain somewhere, unable to reach the phone.

'Looking for Scott?'

Her head swung towards the voice. Great. Of all the people for her to bump into, it had to be Nancy. 'Yes, as a matter of fact, I was.' She returned the woman's inquisitive stare with one of her own.

'He's not here. I've just been to drop off some papers.'

'Oh.' It was on the tip of her tongue to ask if she knew where he was, but she stopped herself. She wasn't going to give Nancy the satisfaction of knowing she was that interested. 'Never mind, I'll catch him some other time.'

As she turned to walk away, Nancy's voice halted her. 'He's a hard man to pin down in many ways, our Scott. You've been dating him, haven't you?'

Calmly she stopped and looked back. 'Yes.' No point in saying she wasn't dating him any longer.

A slight smile came to the older woman's face. 'Well, watch your step, Megan. Don't let all that gorgeous charm fool you. He's not a keeper.'

'I know.' Megan bit her lip. Nancy was only fishing. Trying to bait her. To dig a barb into her soft, vulnerable underbelly. She couldn't let her see she'd struck home. 'I don't want to keep him. Just to play with him for a while.'

Nancy shook her head. 'You don't have to pretend. Not with me. You see, I've been in your shoes. I know what it's like to want something the other person is incapable of giving you.'

Megan watched a flicker of pain run across Nancy's face and realised she wasn't telling her this to be cruel. She was trying to be kind, to warn her. 'You loved him, didn't you?' she whispered.

Nancy's lips tilted in a sad smile. 'Foolish, I know. He was young, dynamic and beautiful. I was older and totally besotted. I should have known better.' She shrugged her shoulders. 'I wish you luck, Megan.'

With that she turned and headed back down the corridor. As Megan watched the slim figure of the retreating solicitor she finally saw her for what she was. A glamorous lady in her forties, still pining away for a man she could never have. She felt her heart tighten as she wondered if that would be her in fifteen years' time, too.

Chapter Thirty-Two

Unbeknownst to Megan, while she was looking for Scott, he was knocking on the door of her home.

His heart sank when it was opened by her father. 'Good afternoon. I wonder, is Megan home yet? I was hoping to have a word.' He cringed at his wooden formality: he'd only just stopped himself from adding Sir.

'I'm afraid she's still at work.'

The reply was polite but not unfriendly. If only the man would smile warmly at him for once. 'Do you mind if I wait?' He'd plucked up the courage to come all the way here. He wasn't about to leave without achieving what he'd come for. At least not without a fight.

Stanley briefly nodded and opened the door wider to let him in. Scott was led into the living room where he was motioned to sit down, Stanley sitting in the armchair opposite. As Scott shifted uncomfortably on the couch, he noticed her father stretch out his legs, his pose relaxed. Why wouldn't it be? He was the one in the driving seat, Scott was the one in the hot seat. Again. Megan's father had that uncanny ability of making him feel like a boy instead of a man. But now he thought about it, he realised the problem was actually all on his side. Megan did more than simply love her father. She worshipped him. Scott knew if he was to have any hope with her, he needed to win her father's respect. And that went a long way towards explaining why his gut churned every time he spoke with him.

Scott cleared his throat. 'About last night. I'm sorry if we disturbed you.'

'You didn't. We were awake.'

Okay. Scott drew in a deep breath and said what he knew the other man had been thinking last night. He would have been, if it had been his daughter facing an angry male. 'I wouldn't have hurt her.'

'I know.'

Well, that was something, at least. 'Good,' he replied, automatically standing up. 'Then you should know this, too. I want to marry your daughter.' Before Stanley could say anything, Scott rushed on. 'The way I see it, I'm not a bad prospect. I own my own house and earn a decent living, even if it is doing something Megan can't quite understand. That doesn't matter to me. In fact I can see where she's coming from. I can see how, when she works on a case, it gets personal. Having worked with her on this last one, I sure as hell don't want to defend the accused parties. So I'm happy for us to agree to disagree. If she wants, we can even argue about it every day. As long as it's for the rest of our lives, because I'm not prepared to settle for anything less. Then there's Sally.' He looked Stanley in the eye, his face earnest. 'I can't promise I'll be a great father. I've not had any experience with children so it will be a huge learning curve for me. But I can promise I'll always be there for her. That I'll treat her as if she were my own. She won't want for anything. Neither of them will.'

Stanley held up his hand. 'Whoa, stop there, son. You're not addressing a jury here. Just the father.'

Scott paused and took stock. Without being aware of it, he'd started pacing up and down the living room, just as he did in court when he was summing up his case. In Scott's mind, that's what he'd felt he was doing: presenting his case. No wonder Stanley was mocking him. He'd gone into flaming barrister mode. 'Sorry,' he said tightly, feeling the heat of a flush creep over his face.

'Look Scott, all I want to know is the important part. Do you love her?'

Feeling more than a little ridiculous, Scott slumped back down on to the sofa and let out a laugh. 'That's the easiest question I've ever had to answer. Yes, of course I do. With all my heart. Sally too. In fact I think I fell in love with her first, though it was a pretty close-run thing. Perhaps falling in love with Sally just felt easier because she didn't insist on keeping me at arm's length all of the time.'

Stanley chuckled. 'Megan has never been the shy, pliable type. Strong-willed and stubborn as a mule more like. At least you know what you're letting yourself in for.'

'I've fallen in love with stubborn and strong-willed.'

At last her father laughed. A real warm, rich, belly laugh. 'Then all it leaves me to say is good luck. For what it's worth, I think you'll suit Megan very well. You don't take any nonsense and you've proven already that you'll protect her even when she doesn't want protecting. Most of all, you love her. I can see that. A man's got to be in love if he's prepared to put up with a girl's family.'

Slowly, Scott started to relax. Her father had as good as given his blessing. It felt like he'd leapt one giant hurdle. Only two more to go. 'Speaking of family, is Sally in? I'd like to see her.'

The look Stanley gave him was full of understanding. 'She's out in the garden with her grandma. I'm sure she'll be pleased to see you.'

Feeling a lot better than he had when he'd first arrived, Scott opened the back door and stepped out into the garden. He immediately spotted the mini whirlwind that was Sally, dressed in pink and running rings round her grandmother. As soon as she saw him, she stopped, but didn't immediately rush towards him as he'd been expecting – as he'd been hoping. Burying his concern, he walked towards her.

'Hey pumpkin, how are you doing?'

'Okay.' She hung back and eyed him suspiciously. 'Why haven't you been over very much? Have you and Mum had a row? She said you hadn't but I think you must have.'

He heard Dot chuckle as she came up behind her

granddaughter. 'Hello, Scott.' She, at least, greeted him warmly, kissing him on both cheeks before ruffling her granddaughter's hair. 'I think I'll go inside and leave you to your inquisition.' Then she grinned. 'Good luck.'

He was left alone with Sally and an uncomfortable feeling that he might need every ounce of that good luck. Her beguiling blue eyes were letting him know she was waiting for an answer to her question, and she'd continue to wait until he provided one she was happy with. 'We haven't had a row, exactly,' he replied cautiously as he drew her towards the garden bench. 'But I do need to persuade her that I love her.'

Sally didn't bat an eyelid. Taking a seat next to him on the bench she simply nodded, as if his declaration of love was old news. 'She thinks you don't mean what you say. That you'll leave her, like my dad did.'

Ouch. 'Do you think I'll do that, too?' he asked in a voice that sounded distinctly scratchy and raw, like his emotions.

She stared into his eyes, assessing him with the simple candour of a six-year-old child. He found himself holding his breath, as time appeared to stand still. 'No,' she finally replied. 'I think you keep your promises.'

Instantly his shoulders sagged with relief and the breath rushed out of his lungs. 'Good. Good.' God, he felt emotionally exhausted. And he hadn't even tackled Megan yet.

'Are you going to marry Mum?' Sally wasn't finished and she was still giving him that careful, watchful look.

Blinking, he stared back at her and suddenly found himself laughing. The delightful innocence of a child's question. He'd give anything right now for a handbook on how to deal with them. 'I'm afraid I can't answer that. It's something I need to discuss with your mother. I would like to see a lot more of her though. And of you. Would that be okay?'

'Does that mean we could go to the beach again?'

'If you both wanted to, yes.'

272

Finally she smiled. A big, beaming smile that went straight to his heart. 'I'd like that.'

He felt those damn tears begin to prick again. He was floored by the depth of emotion the simple words of this pretty, pint-sized version of her mother stirred in him. 'Of course, first I have to convince your mum that's a good idea. How do you think I should do that?'

Sally cocked her head to one side. 'Ask her, I guess. Course if you were asking her to marry you, you'd have to go down on one knee and give her a big sparkly ring.'

Ring. Bugger. Scott's heart sunk. He really hadn't planned this at all. The confidence that had been slowly building since the conversation with Megan's father was now rapidly receding. What had he been thinking? Wait, that was the trouble, he *hadn't* been thinking. As soon as his mother had suggested he propose, that was all he'd had in his mind. He'd dashed straight over, convinced this was the answer. All Megan needed was to hear the four words *will you marry me* and she'd dance with joy and then leap into his arms, weeping with happiness. But this was Megan Taylor he was talking about. Stubborn, wilful, hard-headed. She'd need more than a few stumbling words from him to be persuaded to marry him. The least he could have done was give himself a few advantages. Romantic meal, candlelight, music. Damn.

The moment she caught sight of Scott's car on the driveway, Megan's heart picked up its pace, pounding so hard inside her chest it almost rattled her ribs. Wherever he'd been, whatever he'd been doing, he was back – which didn't mean she was going to rush over to him with arms outstretched. She might desperately want to, but she couldn't. Partly because she was spitting mad at him for disappearing without a trace. If he'd bothered to let her know where he was, he might have received an apology for the way she'd spoken to him the other night. But he hadn't. He'd left her dangling, which brought her to the second reason why she hung back. If he did truly love her, as he'd claimed, why hadn't he called?

It was with these conflicting thoughts in her mind that Megan strode out into the garden to find him. Wouldn't you know, he was deep in serious conversation with her daughter. Heaven only knew what that was all about.

'Ah, the elusive Scott Armstrong.' She'd meant the words as a joke, but they'd come out as harsh and cutting. Clearly she was more upset with him than she'd thought.

Scott turned to Sally. 'What do you think, Sally? Beneath her unfriendly greeting, is your mum secretly pleased to see me, or not?'

Sally, her traitorous daughter, giggled. She looked at her, and then back at Scott. 'She's pleased. She's always happy when she sees you, even if she doesn't show it. Her eyes go all sparkly and gooey when she talks about you.'

'Sally, that's quite enough, thank you.' Megan could feel herself blushing furiously. Since when had her daughter noticed things like that? And she'd like to bet that she *didn't* go gooey-eyed. She'd never gone gooey-eyed. It wasn't her. At least it hadn't been. Scott had her in such a tangle she was no longer sure what *her* was any more.

Sally turned to whisper something to Scott, who laughed and replied in the same hushed tone. Sniggering like the schoolgirl she was, Sally then wriggled off the bench and darted towards her. Oblivious to the fact that she'd just dropped her mother right in it, she proceeded to wrap her arms around Megan's mortified body and squeeze tightly.

'I'll deal with you in a minute,' Megan warned her daughter as Sally skipped inside the house. Then she turned her attention to Scott, who was sitting back casually on the bench, his jean-clad legs stretched out in front of him, his eyes lit up with amusement. 'What's going on?'

He shrugged his delectable shoulders. 'I don't know. You tell me. You seem to be the one with the attitude.'

'Attitude?' She stared at him wide-eyed. 'How do you expect me to react when you tell me you love me—no, wait, you didn't tell me, did you? You angrily shouted that you'd fallen in love with me and then disappeared off without a trace.'

'I didn't disappear. I went to settle Mum into a new clinic.'

His calm, softly spoken reply sucked all the heat out of her anger. She was left with only a terrifying uncertainty over why he'd come round. 'Oh, sorry.' Swallowing hard she gingerly perched on the edge of the garden table. 'How is she?'

'Good, thank you. I really think this time it's going to work out.'

She managed a smile. 'I'm pleased. For both of you.'

He inclined his head slightly in acknowledgement. 'So, feeling a heck of a lot more positive about life than I have done in a long while, I came round to talk to you, only to find myself greeted with all the warmth of a polar ice cap.'

Once more she flushed. 'I'm not sure how you expected to be greeted. If I remember correctly, the last time we spoke, we argued.'

'I remember that, too.' He regarded her steadily, his grey eyes darkening. 'I also remember telling you that I'd fallen in love with you, but you dismissed it. Apparently it was the sort of thing somebody like me would say. It didn't mean anything.'

Megan winced. When he put it like that, so bluntly, in the cold light of day, it made her sound very harsh. 'I'm sorry,' she whispered. 'I didn't mean it to come out like that.' She caught herself chewing at the flesh by her nail and thrust her hand away. 'Why didn't you phone me? Let me know where you were these last few days.'

'Ah, so you did try to contact me then?'

'Yes, I did,' she replied stiffly. 'To apologise.'

'Is that why you're cross with me now? Because I didn't tell you where I was? Because you don't like apologising?' He smiled, his eyes glinting. 'Or because you missed me?'

The last point was too close to the truth for her to answer honestly. 'I'm cross because I'd worked myself up to apologise for my rudeness the other night, but your phone was turned off, so I couldn't. After the third attempt to get hold of you, I started to wonder why I was apologising. If you couldn't be bothered to put your phone on or let me know where you were, then maybe this was all just a huge game, after all.'

Swearing softly, he sprang to his feet. 'How many times do I have to tell you? This is no bloody game, Megan. Can't you see how desperately in love with you I am? I came here today all psyched up to ask you to marry me.' Her heart literally stopped beating and she gaped at him in open-mouthed astonishment. He seemed not to notice. 'I was so keen to ask you,' he continued, practically shouting the words at her. 'I forgot all about the trimmings. You know, the important things, like the ring, the flowers. The things you'd have thought a man like me would have taken care of.'

During his outburst he'd moved towards her. Right now he was standing so close he was almost touching. His jaw was clenched, his eyes on fire, his face stripped of so much of its usual guard that she could quite clearly read what he was he was thinking. The wonder of it made her dizzy. There was love. Passionate, hot and powerful. But there was also something else. Uncertainty. Vulnerability.

As she struggled to say anything in reply, he reached out to take her hands.

'Now I'm actually here, facing you,' he continued, his voice turning husky, 'all trace of my original confidence seems to have vanished. I'm left wondering whether you would ever want to spend your life tangled up with a man you clearly have so little faith in.'

Oh my God, was he really telling her he wanted to *marry* her? Gripping tightly on to his hands, Megan asked shakily. 'Is this a proposal?'

He raised his eyes to the sky then back to hers. 'Yes and no.'

'That's an odd answer.'

'I know.' Suddenly the shoulders he'd been holding so rigidly straight started to droop. 'I'm sorry, this isn't at all how I played this out in my mind.' Still clasping her hands he brought them to his lips and slowly kissed each of her knuckles. 'Megan Taylor, I love you. I love your smart, sassy mouth as well as your gorgeous sexy body. I also love your daughter. I want to marry you. Both of you.' He bent his head so that his forehead rested against hers. 'I know it won't be sweetness and rose petals all the way—'

'I hate roses,' she whispered softly.

'Good. That's one less flower I have to buy.' He gave her a slight smile, but there was a tension still around his eyes. 'So what do you say? Will you marry a defence lawyer, even though you'll probably spend every evening arguing with him?'

With her brain too stunned to think, he spoke into the silence. 'That was the proposal, by the way.'

Inside her chest, her heart swelled and a weight seemed to lift off her shoulders. But the spectre of the past was still there, lodged in the back of her mind, niggling away like a flashing warning sign. 'I ...' Her voice trailed. With all her heart she wanted to say yes, but the word simply wouldn't come out.

'Is that a no?' His face, so close to hers, was as tight as his voice.

Tears streamed down her face. 'It's definitely not a no,' she managed. How could this man, who never took no for an answer, really think she would refuse him?

There was a slight relaxing in his expression. 'Too soon?'

'Yes.' Relief that he understood made her almost giddy. 'I need to be sure that you're sure.'

'I'm more than sure, Megan,' he told her unflinchingly. 'I'm absolutely bloody certain.'

He looked it, too, she thought, and her heart was now so

swollen it was threatening to burst. 'Then you won't mind asking me again in six months? It's not that I don't love you.' The moment her words were out, his beautiful face lit up with the most incredible grin and she marvelled that he hadn't known. 'Yes, you idiot, of course I love you,' she told him softly, rubbing her nose against his. 'Not only do I love you, I trust you. And I respect you. Totally.'

He had the look of a man who'd hoped for a ripple of applause but received a standing ovation. Tenderly she kissed him. 'Oh Scott. What you did for your father, what you continue to do for your mother.' She shook her head. 'You're incredible. And while we're on the subject of things I should have told you earlier, I should say that I don't even hate what you do any more. I understand what you do and why you do it. We might still argue from time to time—'

'I'm counting on it,' he murmured, nuzzling her neck, sending tremors through her body as his lips caressed her throat.

'Yes, well, I'm sure we will.' How did he expect her to have this serious conversation when he was doing *that*? 'But as long as we agree that when we shut the door to the bedroom—'

'It'll only ever be you and me,' he finished softly, moving to place a tender kiss on her lips.

Slowly she pulled away and eyed him thoughtfully. 'What were you colluding with Sally about?'

'Ahh.' He kissed her again. Thoroughly, deeply this time, savouring her. 'I explained that I was here to persuade you to go out with me again. She wished me good luck.'

Megan arched her brow at him. 'Did she now?'

'I told her thanks, but I was pretty sure it wasn't necessary. Sooner or later a smart woman like her mum was going to realise what a good catch I was.'

She started to protest, but he silenced her with another drugging kiss. Just when she was starting to forget that she was in the garden, in full view of her family, he suddenly drew back.

'About the good catch bit. You do know I'm kidding, right?'

Laughing she threaded her hand through his silky dark hair. 'Not only do I know you're joking. I also know that for me, you are, actually, the perfect catch.'

About the Author

Kathryn Freeman was born in Wallingford, England but has spent most of her life living in a village near Windsor. After studying pharmacy in Brighton she began her working life as a retail pharmacist. She quickly realised that trying to decipher doctor's handwriting wasn't for her and left to join the pharmaceutical industry where she spent twenty happy years working in medical communications. However her life-long love of reading romance often led her to wonder if she could write about it, too. If only she had the time.

In 2011, backed by her family, she left the world of pharmaceutical science to begin life as a self-employed writer, juggling the two disciplines of medical writing and romance. Some days a racing heart is a medical condition, others it's the reaction to a hunky hero …

With two teenage boys and a husband who asks every Valentine's Day whether he has to bother buying a card again this year (yes, he does) the romance in her life is all in her head. Then again, her husband's unstinting support of her career change goes to prove that love isn't always about hearts and flowers – and heroes can come in many disguises.

Follow Kathryn on:
Twitter @KathrynFreeman1
Facebook: https://www.facebook.com/kathrynfreeman

More Choc Lit

From Kathryn Freeman

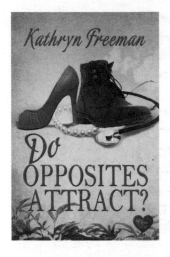

Do Opposites Attract?

There's no such thing as a class divide – until you're on separate sides

Brianna Worthington has beauty, privilege and a very healthy trust fund. The only hardship she's ever witnessed has been on the television. Yet when she's invited to see how her mother's charity, Medic SOS, is dealing with the aftermath of a tornado in South America, even Brianna is surprised when she accepts.

Mitch McBride, Chief Medical Officer, doesn't need the patron's daughter disrupting his work. He's from the wrong side of the tracks and has led life on the edge, but he's not about to risk losing his job for a pretty face.

Poles apart, dynamite together, but can Brianna and Mitch ever bridge the gap separating them?

Visit www.choc-lit.com for more details including the first two chapters and reviews, or simply scan barcode using your mobile phone QR reader.

Introducing Choc Lit

We're an independent publisher creating
a delicious selection of fiction.
Where heroes are like chocolate – irresistible!
Quality stories with a romance at the heart.

See our selection here:
www.choc-lit.com

We'd love to hear how you enjoyed *Too Charming*.
Please leave a review where you purchased the novel
or visit: **www.choc-lit.com** and give your feedback.

Choc Lit novels are selected by genuine readers like yourself.
We only publish stories our Choc Lit Tasting Panel want to
see in print. Our reviews and awards speak for themselves.

Could you be a Star Selector and join our Tasting Panel?
Would you like to play a role in choosing which novels we
decide to publish? Do you enjoy reading romance novels?
Then you could be perfect for our Choc Lit Tasting Panel.

Visit here for more details…
www.choc-lit.com/join-the-choc-lit-tasting-panel

Keep in touch:
Sign up for our monthly newsletter Choc Lit Spread for
all the latest news and offers: www.spread.choc-lit.com.
Follow us on Twitter: @ChocLituk and Facebook: Choc Lit.

Or simply scan barcode using your mobile phone QR reader:

Choc Lit
Spread

Twitter

Facebook